Sparks

E. J. Wenstrom

Praise for E. J. Wenstrom
Rone Award Winner

"The finale delivers on everything the series has been building up to. It is dramatic, oddly sad, and gloriously beautiful."

— *READERS LANE*

"In the Third Realm, perils await, but anything is possible—and readers who venture there will find a rewarding escape into a very creative and fully imagined world."

— *Literary Hill, Hill Rag*

"From beginning to end, a thoroughly enjoyable story that any lover of fantasy stories will be able to lose themselves in."

— *In D'Tale Magazine*

"The Third Realm War is going full throttle and this is the finale that the series has been building toward... Even the heroes are not infallible which kept me guessing the outcome. "

— *Amazon reviewer*

"**Wenstrom's storytelling is superb, and she creates a writing style of her own to give the story a grand scale, ripe with emotion and magical adventure.**"

— *Amazon reviewer*

Join E. J. Wenstrom's Monstrosity

Stay in touch with the weekly newsletter

JOIN E. J.'s MONSTROSITY newsletter for sci-fi and fantasy, publishing and other news highlights weekly, plus download the Third Realm War prequel novella.

Subscribe now at EJWenstrom.com

To Christopher

Contents

CHAPTER ONE

HAVEN IS NOT WHAT it used to be.

Ever since Rona returned from the dead and destroyed the half-angel Koreh, ever since Koreh destroyed the city of Ir-Nearch, the full weight of the Third Realm War has settled upon us. Ever since, the realm of Terath has been lit ablaze.

Our once-little village of Haven is still recovering from the terrors of her undead ash soldiers and the damage they wrought on the people of our sister city. And yet hope beats at us, as adamant as a war drum.

In all of Haven's years of providing refuge to those who flee from the tyranny of the city-states, in all its years of preparation to fight for the Gods in the third and final realm war that was foretold in the Texts, the city has never lived up to its name more fully. The remaining people of Ir-Nearch took shelter here after Koreh's attack, and ever since, others have fled to us at an increasing pace.

They find their way to us from out in the Wasteland, somehow seeking out a village they do not know to look for. They bring with them tales of survival, of escape from terrible dictators as bad as my old home of Epoh and worse. They have continued to find us even through the layers of protective charms the Firsts have wrought around Haven's borders—the only way to stave off the rebels fighting their way free of the Underworld to take down the Gods once and for all. They wait at the edge of what appears to be nothing but more Wasteland until one of our guards lets them pass through.

Each of them reaches us ready, answering a call they cannot explain, something driving them out into the Wasteland to us. And it isn't only humans. First

Creatures are coming to us, too. Angels and sprites line the village's borders, standing guard. When they're off duty, they cluster along the shore.

It is good. It is necessary if we are going to win this war against the rebel First Creatures and the men they continue to recruit.

Yet with every day that passes, every new person who arrives over the bluff to Haven, my shoulders tighten and knot, waiting for the day when we run out of space in this tiny village, for the day the wrong person is welcomed in and destroys us all, for the day the war finds us again.

The realms have woken up. The Third Realm War is here in earnest, and something in the realm of Terath is calling to people, summoning them to join us in the fight for the Gods.

"That is one fine looking sword."

The words snap me from my thoughts. I look up to see Xamson across the fire. He is tall and strong, his dark skin glistening in the sun as he stands just outside the metalworking tent. One eyebrow is cocked, and a grin parts his lips—he is feeling playful.

I try to smile back. But even play has felt strained for us these days.

"When an army is eternally multiplying, so must its weaponry," I say.

"The metalworker could use some touching up, though," Xamson continues, walking around the fire and stepping to my side. He traces gently over a burn that runs up my forearm.

"There has been too much else to do to worry about such a small thing."

I have retreated to the metalworking tent to keep out of the bustle of the village. Since I was ousted as Haven's leader, I have not known what to do with myself, and the work has become a welcome refuge. The crackle of the fire, the heavy clangs of the hammers, the sting of tired muscles, they take me out of my head. And I need that, because my head is the worst place for me to be these days.

Since my rule over Haven was dismantled, I have become a churning meld of shame and worry and fear. I spent so many years preparing these people for this moment when the Third Realm War would come to our door. Now that it is here, I have been pushed out. I fear what might lurk in the days ahead for us. I fear I will not be enough to stop it.

At first, others tried to help with the weaponry repairs, or at least divide the work into shifts. With so many more joining all the time, there is much to do. But I preferred the isolation—I deserved the isolation—and I turned them away. I stay by myself at the fire's edge as much as I can.

Xamson continues to run a hand down my arm and wraps his hand around mine. His calming presence forces my mind still, and I relax into his pull.

"You do not take care of yourself," he says.

"It's fine."

"It isn't, Jordan. You have to stop trying to shoulder everything on your own." He leans over to look into my eyes. His expression flickers to serious, and I brace for the fight we have already had countless times over. But then with a forced twitch the playfulness comes back. He pulls me in and murmurs into my neck. "Lucky for you, I know just what you need. Let me take care of you."

Xamson's other hand traces over my side, an invitation—but all I can feel is the tightness of the tent drawing in on me.

"Careful. The fire." I step away.

I love Xamson. I do. But when the people of Ir-Nearch fled to Haven, and Xamson with them, he moved into my hut, and ever since, it feels like there has been less air to breathe.

He sighs. "Please tell me you are at least stopping soon and coming to the Sonsadh festival. Some are already donning their headpieces. The whole point of having it was because we need a break from all these troubles. And that means you as much as any of us."

Sonsadh—the annual celebration of Gloros, Goddess of Passions. My shoulders tighten and I turn toward the fire.

"I still don't think we should be doing this," I say.

There is too much to do. Weapons to craft. Soldiers to train. Battle plans to make. But they don't listen to me anymore.

Xamson's brows twitch into a confused frown. "This is what we are fighting for in the end, isn't it? The Gods? Freedom? Life? Rona is right, we cannot let this war take everything from us—if it does, the rebels win. And some of Gloros' sprites are among us now. What of them?"

Why celebrate a Goddess who has fallen silent?

The Gods' presence has been absent for so long now, I am no longer sure They are there at all. But then, most do not feel Their absence like I can. Perhaps others do not understand the way They have pulled away from Terath since the war began. No good will come of dredging it back to the surface now. So I take a breath to unclench my stomach and say nothing.

Xamson runs a hand over his shaved head, and I feel his eyes on my back as I return to my work.

"Just, please, come for a little bit," he says. He is already turning away, already giving up.

"Alright," I say. I do not know if I am lying to him or not.

I keep my focus on the fire in front of me as I stick the sword back into it, trying to avoid seeing his disappointment in me. He huffs out an exhale, then leaves.

I cannot find a way to tell Xamson that it is more than just Haven that isn't what it used to be. I am not what I used to be, either. I am no longer these people's leader. And I can no longer connect them to the Gods. And I hardly know what I am without these things.

All of Haven is gathering, starting from the center of the village and overflowing down to the shore, where the light of the stars glitter over the ocean waves. A bonfire roars at the center. A Sonsadh tradition symbolizing Gloros' undying passion for Her creation, it must remain lit all through the night. Somewhere from within the celebration, drums pound a rhythm over a flood of chatter and laughter.

Xamson is not hard to find among the crowd, towering inches over the others. He stands with a few of his fellow soldiers from Ir-Nearch, and he has had enough to drink to broaden his beautiful smile and loosen his posture. A crown of braided straw sits lopsided on his head.

I stop and watch him a moment. Something about his smile makes him feel far away. But I like seeing him like this. The war has stolen this from all of us. Then he glances over and catches me. His smile widens even more, and I feel it reflected at the corner of my own mouth. Something giddy sparks in my chest, promising to rekindle if only I will allow it.

Xamson gestures for me to come to him, and we wade through the crowd toward each other.

"You came," he says.

His fingers trace over my skin and caress around my shoulder. As our arms brush against each other, he starts swaying, pulling me along beside him in rhythm with the drums.

"You are drunk already," I observe.

He smiles again. "So catch up." He offers me the cup in his other hand.

I look down into the dark liquor within and consider. Even with protective charms shielding the village and angels watching over its perimeter, we are still at war. Then I remember I am not a soldier, not anymore, not under Helda's army. What the hell. I toss back the cup and the liquid burns sweetly as I gulp it down.

I hand the empty cup back to Xamson. He laughs and squeezes my arm, still swaying.

More is pushed into my hand, and then more, and more still, and I drink all of it. The world around me dims to a distant haze. The loss of command of this camp, the sense of failure, the constant, suffocating fear of another imminent battle, they all fade. Only Xamson remains in focus. We laugh and flirt with one another like we haven't done in weeks.

Sometime in the night it starts to rain—the weather seems to turn more suddenly these days than it used to. But we are too drunk to care about the wet or the thunder, and the festival carries on. We lose ourselves in each other. For the first time in a long time, I taste a hint of happiness. It is tainted by the ever-present fear of something horrible looming on the horizon, but the alcohol dulls it enough, for now.

Chapter Two

I wake up by the shore on damp sand, Xamson's body pressed against me. We are layered in blankets to protect us from the chill of the Wasteland night. My neck is stiff and my head throbs.

Xamson's arm wraps over me from behind and his slow breaths release in warm puffs against my back, and I cannot will myself to rise. I cannot remember the last time we slept like this, wrapped around each other. It was probably on my last trek to Ir-Nearch, back before it was destroyed by Koreh and her ash soldiers.

So I lay here and I try to understand when it stopped feeling like this, and why I cannot fix us.

I love him, I remind myself.

"Festival is over." Someone kicks my leg.

I moan and open my eyes.

It is so early the air is still crisp from the night. The sunrise glares over Rona's shoulder and beyond the bluff that guards Haven's edge. She hovers over me, her dark hair loose and tangled around her.

I spring to my feet. Sand sticks to my skin, and my head lurches with the aftereffects of the liquor. Rona glances me over, takes a sharp breath in, and whips around, turning her back to me. Only then do I realize I am bare. I scramble and find my robe on the ground near Xamson's feet. I grab for it and hasten to tie it around me, even though it is wet and sticky from last night's storm, and matted in grime.

Gods. Gloros may not have shown herself to us last night, but it looks like Xamson and I did our part to revel in Her passions. I wish I could remember it—it has been so long.

"Okay," I call to Rona. She cautiously turns back. Dark blotches under her eyes hint at a long night. Knowing Rona, hers was not spent reveling, but guarding over the revelers.

"Back to the old routine again," she prompts.

I stretch, trying to work myself free of the stiffness from the night before. "Right behind you."

I drop to the ground and begin the pushups that start the daily drills I have done since I was a child. It seems pointless now, when it has become so clear I am not the leader chosen by the Gods that my mother believed me to be when she started all of my training. But even with my head swaying and my balance shaky from last night's drinks, this is still a cornerstone to start each day I cannot shake.

Rona rolls her eyes, then heads off toward the village. When I am done, I follow after her, picking my way through the sleeping, passed out bodies strewn across the sand. At the village center, the flames that roared so high last night in Gloros' honor are nothing but charred logs. The rain must have been too much for it. Did it make it through the night before dying out? I am not sure if it even matters anymore, the way the Gods have fallen silent.

The boaters have been up for a while—or maybe they did not sleep at all. The fruits of their labor—enough fish to feed the growing village for the day—is laid out in their nets over the rocks. I drop myself next to the others already at work to prepare the day's food, pick up a gutting knife, and get to work. After last night, it feels good to fall back into familiar routine.

Soon a hulking figure drops into the sand next to me. Adem. He stood guard with some of the Firsts last night while the rest of us made fools of ourselves in Gloros' name.

"No trouble last night?" I ask.

Adem shrugs with a low rumbling growl. "More darkwolves. Some other creatures. Nothing that wanted a fight," he says.

The howls of the darkwolves wind through the huts in the dark, a nightly reminder that even with the magical shields our First Creature allies have placed around us here, there is much in the realm these days that hunts us.

I hardly think any of them could have been a match for Adem. Even in Haven, many still fear his bulk and his silence, the blankness of his eyes, all the little ways his presence reminds he is not quite human. But being a chthonus makes him powerful too, and indestructible. Especially as he learns to harness the incredible power that made him. With Calipher grudgingly teaching him magic alongside Rona, he is becoming almost as powerful as any First.

One would never guess that under those hunched, hulking shoulders and his worn, old robe, Adem is carrying the cursed necklace that started all of this destruction. Or at least, no one has managed to guess it yet.

We tried other ways. We tried to destroy it. But nothing we did could leave a scratch on it, even with the magic of the Firsts. Even Calipher, who created the necklace himself back in the Beginning, could not work against it. Its power seems to have grown with each use, with each possessor, and it seems to have taken on a life of its own.

When we could not destroy it, we tried to protect it. But the necklace's pull was too strong for a human, and they all were all swayed by its pull. Adem, on the other hand, had carried it for ages without being tempted by its whispers, within the small box his maker had bound him to guard. So he took it back again, the very thing he had tried so hard to escape for so many ages, willingly this time. The Firsts did their best to layer protection charms over it, and over Adem too, to obscure the necklace's lure from the rest of us.

Perhaps it works so well because Haven's people do all they can to avoid Adem.

Murmurs still float that the Third Realm War is Adem's fault, that he has brought this onto us. But he always means well. How could he have known an angel, of all creatures, had set out to take advantage of him? The Third Realm War was foretold. It was coming for us no matter what Adem did. The ones who mutter behind his back as he lopes through Haven do not understand how lucky we are to have him on our side in this war.

But people fear what they do not understand. It is why I talked him into helping with these tedious daily chores in addition to everything else he does. How much can they fear something that helps to prepare their breakfast each day? We cannot afford to fear each other in these times; there is too much else to fear out in the realm. Darkwolves and other creatures of the realms are becoming more and more common by the day.

Has another helmuth already opened to replace the one Rona destroyed, I wonder? Were there already others letting the Underworld break free? Whatever the rebels are up to, the Wasteland is more dangerous than ever these days. A day is bound to come when the protections we have cast around ourselves will not be enough.

But despite it all, what is needed from us as the Gods' army in this war is the same. Once the people are all awake, we come together for morning prayers. We eat, and then Helda leads the soldiers in drills. Some things never change. These are the rhythms of life that keep us ready, keep us anchored. Their force keeps us moving forward, day to day, in spite of the looming fear.

Next to me, Adem jumps to his feet, breaking my reflections.

"Adem?" I twist my neck to look up at him.

A muscle near his ear twitches, and he drops the fish he was working onto the sand.

"Something is not right," he grumbles.

"What is it?" I ask.

He growls in response, then turns and trudges toward the village, shoulders hunched.

"Adem!" I call, but it is no use. He is already racing away up the bluff and toward the Wasteland. I leave my work behind and chase after him.

Perhaps new allies have arrived to join our ranks.

Perhaps a new rebel threat has come to end us once and for all, like Koreh did to Ir-Nearch.

Haven has woken up in the time since we started our work. As I dodge through the groggy flow of people and Firsts trudging through the village center, trying to keep one eye on Adem racing toward the Wasteland ahead of me, I almost run right into Xamson.

"Hey there," he says, a lazy smile breaking over his face. "You left so early this morning."

He reaches for me, and my skin tingles as I remember a flash of us together last night.

But Adem is disappearing over the bluff, leaving only a cloud of the sand he kicked up in his haste. Panic and an impending sense of doom forces my mind blank.

All I can say is, "Fall in!" I do not speak it to Xamson alone. I shout it, breaking the morning calm. "Fall in! Fall in!"

The command registers, and groggy soldiers shift into alert action. They grab shields and blades and helmets, and race to join me as I cross through the village. Instinct kicks in and they forget I have been ousted as their leader. I am grateful—who knows what waits for us over the bluff. It could be anything. Hangovers or not, we must meet this threat. This was exactly why I did not want to lose myself in revelry last night. I should have listened to the knotted dread in my gut.

Xamson's smile disappears as he catches a shield another soldier tosses his way and draws his sword.

As I race up the bluff, a cluster of half-armed soldiers are in step with me, Xamson at one side and Rona at my other. The protective shield of charms around the village blurs the Wasteland beyond. We push through it, and I brace myself for an attack—for another army of ash soldiers to fight off, maybe, for bolts of magic to come at me from rebel Firsts, for creatures worse than I can imagine.

But when I can see, I order an abrupt halt, and almost run right into Adem's broad back as I skid to a stop.

There is nothing here.

My heartbeat rises, pounding against my ribs and rushing in my ears. Adem is taking quick, heaving breaths—it cannot be from the run, he does not tire.

Rona pushes her way past me. Her eyes are sharp and dark like a storm as she glares at Adem, then me. She clutches her twin blades in her fists.

"What is this?" she demands.

"Adem—" I start. But I hardly know what to say. There is no attack, no army. Nothing waits out here in the Wasteland at all. I already hear the murmurs of the soldiers behind us, confused and unsure.

But then—a single figure stands out in the distance, watching us. A spindly man, clothed in a dark royal blue robe with a long beard and a twisted staff. A wide-brimmed hat hides his face in shadow, but even from here, the crinkled texture of his hands and the grizzled whiteness of his beard indicate old age.

Something about this isn't right. I move around Rona and step to Adem's side. The hairs on his neck raise, and his lips pull back to bare teeth in an animal grimace.

"Adem? Who is that?"

Did he know this man was out here? All the way from our perch at the shore? He could not possibly have felt an aura from as far as the sea—could he? Even when my abilities had been strong, I would've had to have been much closer to sense a First's presence, let alone a man.

Adem shakes his head. He keeps looking around, like he expects there to be more.

A stiffness creeps up my neck. What danger a solitary old man could be to an army of trained soldiers and Firsts, I do not know. But if I have learned anything since the start of the Third Realm War, it is that there are many things that are real and threatening and terrible that I never could have imagined.

I glance back toward Haven on instinct, checking if the protective shield still keeps the village safe. The mirage of continued Wasteland holds strong. It is only then that I realize: This man is standing here waiting because he expected us. Despite all the magical protections we have cast around Haven, he knew exactly where to find us and exactly how to draw us out.

Fear burns through my veins, and I understand what has Adem so riled. Our eyes meet, and I nod.

"Ready," I order to the soldiers behind us.

A unified shuffle of sound echoes as blades are drawn, arrows poised, spears lifted. Shields go up. My blood hums with a heated hunger. It feels good to lead an army again, to do something to fight back against the darkness pervading our realm.

But Rona cuts me off.

"Wait," she says. "What is this?"

"Something is not right," Adem repeats. He leans forward and glares over her head toward the man. Rona holds her ground, placing one fist, blade still gripped tight, over his chest to brace him.

"But what is it?" she says. "Why did you bring us out here?"

He looks down, and for a moment everything stops while their eyes lock and they hold silent conference, tense and humming with an energy I cannot understand. Something has been different between them ever since Ir-Nearch—a bond, a challenge, a charge.

Adem growls in response. His jaw clenches as he grinds his teeth.

"I did not have a choice. He made me."

Chapter Three

"WHAT DO YOU MEAN he made you?" Lines of concern and caution deepen around Rona's eyes, flickering with busy thoughts. "That man, out there on the horizon? How?"

A shiver shoots down my spine.

The tense morning sun presses down on us, already sizzling with intensity.

Adem shrugs. "He called me. I had no choice but to follow."

I shake my head. "From the shore? No way. I know your hearing is better than ours but..."

"No," he says. "With magic. He summoned me."

Summoned?

As I struggle to understand, my eyes drift to Rona. She frowns back me, her dark eyes flashing like a storm on the sea.

"What are we doing out here?" she demands again.

I look past Rona to the strange man. He stands still as a stone in the middle of the Wasteland, as if awaiting his audience. There is only one way to find out.

I venture out toward him a few more steps. "What do you want from us?" I call out.

The man's head cocks to the side. His lips curl into a sly smile. "You have something of mine."

"What could we possibly have of yours?" Rona calls. "Our village was built from nothing. Our people are free. Everything we have here we made for ourselves. Who are you?"

The man takes his time, soaking in our outrage like it is the sweetest of flavors. Finally, he calls back, "You may call me the Forger."

I cannot help it—I laugh. A loud, cutting laugh that makes both Rona and Adem turn and look at me.

"The Forger?" I call back. "You mean like in the Texts?"

When I was a child, the Texts were the only stories I knew, my only escape from the tyranny of Epoh. I engulfed myself in its stories and marveled at the mysteries of the Gods. One of the strangest and most fascinating tales the Texts held was the story of the Forger. A man so righteous and favored by the Gods that he came to wield the magical forces of the realms as well as any First Creature. He created his new life of his own—or the closest thing mankind has ever come to it. Chthonuses. He was the first, and the greatest maker of chthonuses to ever be. That is why they started calling him the Forger. To create life, it was said, was a power the Gods would only gift to the most righteous and loyal of Their Chosen. Yet the Forger built an entire army of his own creations.

The way my mother used to go on, she made me believe I was meant for such greatness, too. I was too young, back then, to understand the illness that had been creeping into her mind. The way she rambled about my Chosen-ness, how could I not have such power bestowed upon me? It seems like a cruel joke now, when my gifts have been stripped away, along with any blessing the Gods may have ever given me. But back then the Forger felt like he was part of me. A predecessor who had already lived my own destiny. My future.

After Adem saved me from Epoh, brought me to Haven, and left me behind, I knew what Adem was, and the tales of the Forger were all I could think about. I was dazzled by his power, and he became my hero. The idea of a man who held the power to make something like Adem from nothing—I was in awe.

But for someone to show up and proclaim themselves as the Forger, well, it's preposterous. The Forger of my childhood imagination was nothing like the grim old man standing before us now.

This man must hold some kind of power, certainly, to have summoned Adem to the Wasteland. But whatever this man is, he does not appear to be here to join the Gods' army in the coming war. I cannot reconcile the idea of the Forger I have held in my mind since I was a child with the distant figure in front of us now.

"Not like the Forger from the Texts," the man says. "I am the Forger. The one and only."

I stutter, the last of my laughter falling dead on my tongue. It cannot be possible. The tale of the Forger is from many ages ago, before the Second Realm War even took place. And I stopped believing in the literal truth of the Text's stories years ago.

But then, being impossible has hardly stopped other terrible things from reaching us lately.

Behind me and at my sides comes the metallic shuffle of armor as the soldiers shift and brace themselves.

What was it the Forger said when he first spoke? You have something of mine.

My stomach knots as I start to understand—if Adem really was summoned here against his will, then this man is not only claiming to be the most powerful being in the realm—he is also Adem's maker. And if that is true, he can do much more than simply call Adem to him through Haven's protective charms.

A heated anxiety hums over my skin. The Forger? This cannot be right. The Forger was so much more than his power. He was righteous. Chosen. The most Chosen. This man before me in the Wasteland clearly has ill intents.

Whatever this man may be, he is not going to intimidate us into submission. Next to me, the morning sun glints off Rona's blades. She has stepped out so she partially blocks Adem from the Forger's path. Behind her, Adem's broad muscles twitch and tense, his bulk alive with rage.

"We will never hand him over," I call to the Forger. "He does not belong to anyone anymore."

Handing Adem over is out of the question. He has never harmed anyone, not willingly. And he is far too powerful to be left in the wrong hands, especially if this man wields as much magic as the Texts' legends imply. Adem saved me, and I will stand by him until the day I die.

But the Forger—if that is who he really is—only smirks. "Oh, that you can keep for now. I did not come all this way for another mud doll."

As his words sink in, my expression slowly melts into a frown. I turn and eye Rona. She grimaces back at me, and I see confusion churning behind her eyes.

"Today I have come to settle a different score," he says. "An unfortunate consequence of your latest victory, if that is what you are calling it."

Rona does not wait for me to consider. She steps out in front and speaks for us all, as Haven's leader.

"Whatever it is you want from us, we do not yield to attacks and threats."

But even as she speaks, the Forger steps closer. Goosebumps raise up my neck and I hold my sword tighter. We may not know yet if this man is what he claims to be, but he shows no concern for the threat of our army's swords.

"I was afraid you would choose to be difficult," the Forger says.

He shakes his head and bares his teeth in a terrible smile. He stretches his arms wide. "Anatus!" he calls out, as if to the sky. His expression darkens as he sets loose his command, and it makes the hairs at the back of my neck stand on end.

Sword at the ready, I prepare for the worst.

Chapter Four

The Forger's spell echoes off the sky, a declaration. Behind me a shuffle rises as the soldiers brace for whatever will come next. My muscles tense so sharply they ache. But in the pause that follows, nothing happens.

I scoff, relief huffing out of me in a sharp breath.

But then a rumble like thunder breaks the tension, quivering from the earth below our feet. The ground splits and crumbles around us in a ring, and Adem, Rona, Xamson, and all the soldiers who answered my call stumble back into each other. From the crumbling depths emerge grasping hands and arms, then heads, then shoulders, until full bodies have sprung from the Wasteland's packed, dried earth.

Behind us, the soldiers lose order to a scramble of exclamations.

I call them to order. "Hold formation! Shields!" We tighten our circle into a defensive ring as the creatures shake free and surround us with an animal ferocity.

Then they halt, as if waiting for something.

Each is different from the next, monstrous beings trying their best to emulate humanity and falling short. Their skin is dull and dusty, their eyes dark and flat, their forms hulking and disfigured. They stare ahead blankly, as if empty on the inside.

There is something monstrous about these creatures.

And something terribly familiar.

Something like Adem.

I look back to the Forger, and though Adem was crafted with more care, his inner workings clearly much more complex, he wears the same blank eyes, the same hulking posture.

Chthonuses. All of them.

And all of them made by the Forger.

I look them over again, and this time I am filled not with horror, but with empathy. Their faces slump like melted clay. Some are missing eyes, even limbs, and there are other malformations. There must be something terribly wrong with this man to create such beings without care, to prolong them in this state when, as powerful as he appears, surely he could fix them.

Righteous? He certainly is not now, if he ever was.

Powerful? Absolutely. Far too much.

And now he has us surrounded.

The chthonuses stand in stiff formation, creating a ring around us, awaiting further command.

My focus tightens and adrenaline courses into my veins. I have slid into a fighting stance on instinct, my years of training kicking in.

If these chthonuses are anything like Adem, they have a lot of advantages over us in a fight. Starting with, no matter what we do to them, they cannot die. Will they simply exhaust us until we can fight no more, and then end us one by one?

What have I led these soldiers to? Guilt and fear for what might come next sears through my gut like iron hot off a fire, reminding me of all the failures that came before this one.

But it is too late now. We must do what we can. We cannot go down without a fight. I shout the command, and the soldiers shuffle into formation to take on the chthonuses from all sides, weapons drawn.

All except for Adem. Adem does nothing.

He just stands there, arms at his sides and his expression blank. As if he is waiting.

"Adem?" I urge.

He grunts. His eyes roll toward me, but he doesn't turn his head. He stands frozen except for twitching muscles, his face even more drained of emotion than normal, as if he were pinned down by some invisible force.

The searing burn of panic pierces through me again. Is he?

I look to the other chthonuses. They stand in just the same way—stiff, shoulders back, arms at their side.

Dread wrenches through me, a twisting flame. Is it not enough that the Forger has tricked us to coming out to him, and that he has us surrounded? Will he try and make Adem turn against us, too? I cannot bear the thought of fighting Adem, of what that would do to him.

I turn to the Forger. "What do you want from us?" The words fly out of me like biting embers.

He studies me, lips pursed.

"Koreh," he says slowly. "Where did she go?"

Koreh.

The name echoes behind me in whispers as it travels from soldier to soldier. One by one they look to Rona. She is the one whose mysterious burst of power destroyed the demigod.

For a moment Rona remains still, the veins of her forearms standing out as tension gathers through her muscles. Finally, she steps forward.

"Koreh is gone," she declares. The words sit in the air as she pauses, giving them time to sink in. "And you should go, too. Take your chthonuses and leave, or we will make your exit as permanent as hers."

Does Rona have it in her to summon a wave of power that strong again? She only had the ability to siphon power from the First Creatures because Kythiel's desperation to reach her after we banished him from the realm blew a hole through Rona's psyche. It has been weeks now since the battle with Koreh, and though Rona still can take some power from the Firsts who have joined us, the hole has begun to heal. With it, her abilities are waning. Even when her powers were fresh, the way the magic burst from her, we were sure it would destroy her along with Koreh and the helmuth. It almost did.

So her threat to the Forger must be a bluff, but it is a convincing one. Her shoulders are set and her eyes are sharp. The only thing hinting at fear is her hand, which quivers ever so slightly, clasped around her blade. When she catches me looking, she clenches it even tighter, turning her knuckles white.

The Forger looks down to the ground, a malevolent smile twitching in the wrinkles at the side of his mouth. For a moment I am afraid he will command the chthonuses surrounding us to attack.

"Oh," he sighs. "That is unfortunate. That is very bad."

Then he starts to approach, and I can finally feel his power. My ability to sense auras is a whisper of what it once was, but this man's power is so vast it does not matter. It is a heavy, volatile energy that churns like a twister storm. This old man, the Forger, hides something even more menacing than he appears.

"And where is the necklace Koreh wore?" he says.

Oh no.

I cannot help but look to Adem.

He seemed like the only safe choice to guard the necklace while we figured out how to get rid of it. How could we have known he would end up being the most dangerous?

My mind crackles with a swell of thoughts.

If the Forger is really Adem's maker, that means he was responsible for Adem guarding it in the first place for all those years.

But Koreh claimed the necklace was hers.

And Calipher is the one who made it, for his human love, Nia, in the Beginning.

So how did the Forger get tied up in all this?

I shake the confusion away for later—right now all that matters is that the Forger has lured us out into the Wasteland where we are vulnerable, and we were foolish enough to bring the object he wants most along with us.

It is tucked within the folds of Adem's cloak even now. Just where the Forger left it when he ordered Adem to protect it within its charmed little box. One command from the Forger, and Adem would have no choice but to hand it over. My breath catches in my throat, and I hope with every particle of my being that the Forger's claim to Adem cannot overpower the protective charms we have cast around him and the necklace. Gods only know what he would do with it. Judging by the damage Koreh wrought with it, it could be disastrous.

But at least for now, it does not seem to occur to the Forger that after all this time, after all that happened, the necklace might be right where he left it.

Is he toying with us, or are the spells holding? He knew Haven was hiding behind its charms in the Wasteland. Will the magic of Adem's being be enough to camouflage it?

Adem looks back at me, and the corner of his eye twitches. The tension mounts between us, all of us unsure of what to do, what the Forger is playing at, until finally Rona bursts forward, snapping me out of my spiral of panic.

"You mean the necklace Azazel stole from us?" she snarls. "Even if we had it, why would we give it to you?"

Then she turns and blasts a sharp glare my way. What is wrong with you?

She's right—if the Forger did not know about the necklace already, my glance to Adem could have given us away. And if he suspects, there seems to be nothing we could do to stop him from simply ordering Adem to hand it over. All that power would be in the wrong hands. Again.

The Forger continues to tread closer, his tall, withered figure bobbing in and out of my vision through the chthonuses he has surrounded us with. Each step he takes feels like a threat. Is his power still what it was in the days the Texts speak of? Something tells me I do not wish to find out by being on the receiving end of his curses.

Rona glares at him, unflinching. My sword is at the ready, though I do not know what use it would be against his magic.

The Forger smiles.

"I mean the necklace I commanded my chthonus to guard, which he failed to do, and then stole as his own," he corrects. "That necklace is not yours, girl, and it is not Azazel's. It is no longer Koreh's either, no matter what she claims."

The Forger stops his approach and folds his hands in front of him, a menacing glint in his eye.

"And as to the why, well, let us see what we can think of to motivate you," he says.

A burning rage bursts in my chest—I am done with this vile man and his vague threats.

"Enough!" I bound forward, swinging my blade, and launch it into the chest of the chthonus blocking us from the Forger. "Leave now. Take your chthonuses with you."

The Forger does not relent. In fact he steps forward, a smile twitching at the corner of his mouth as he looks me over.

My chest heaves, my heartbeat throbbing against my ribs.

"This one thinks he is something quite special, doesn't he?" the Forger declares.

"No," I retort, "Only someone who will not stand by and let you intimidate us."

"Oh no, but you do. I see the Gods' residue all over you. They Chose you didn't They?" he says. Then the smile spreads like a dagger across his mouth. "How did that work out for you?"

"I—no—but—" He catches me off guard, striking at my most vulnerable spot.

"They turned against me, too. We are not so different, you know," he says.

"Impossible." I spit his words back at him. Unable to find any more words, I try to force through his chthonuses to attack him again, but they stand firm and hold me back.

"I see the rage and hunger in you, too." His voice winds and creaks around me. "Oh, you can hardly stand it, can you? Why fight it so hard, when setting it free would make you so powerful?"

My chest tightens, and my words come out rushed and thin. "I don't know what you're talking about."

The Forger grins. "I am not so sure of that. But you will."

He mutters under his breath and then pushes his hands toward me, thrusting something unseen my way. Every muscle in my being tenses in anticipation of the attack, and behind me, Xamson screams, "No!"

A breeze brushes over my face, and with it, a shuddering dread. But nothing else comes.

Xamson rushes to attack the Forger, but the Forger twitches his fingers, and Adem lurches forward, pulling Xamson back. He grabs Xamson by the neck and squeezes tight with both hands. Xamson stabs the air with a gasp.

The entire world tunnels down to only this, the air is sucked away.

Xamson.

My heart churns with alarm and darkness crowds the edges of my vision. A scream builds inside me, but I cannot let it out. The whole army is watching, and Xamson needs me.

The Forger cackles.

I have not felt this helpless since I was a child, in Epoh, watching the Silencers bully innocent citizens in the streets. I thought I was past it, that I would never feel this way again, but suddenly the old wounds are raw.

It takes all my will to choke it back.

"Adem," I say, fighting back the quiver in my voice. "Let him go."

Adem grunts but does not so much as turn his head. Xamson's face begins to flush.

"Adem, you are more than this," I beg, trying to fight the quiver in my voice. "You have to let him go, you have to. It's Xamson."

"It will let go when I tell it to," the Forger says. His tone is too calm. Callous. Amused.

The gravity of the situation, the new depths of danger we have stumbled into, hits me with a twist of dread.

"Come, there is no need for this. Hand over the necklace and I will be done with you, for now."

The Forger twitches his fingers again, and Adem growls. Then his arm lifts Xamson off the ground. Xamson flails and twitches, punctuated with terrible, gut-wrenching gasps.

I want to scream. I want to tear Xamson away, I want to slice the Forger in two. But none of these things happen. I am paralyzed in a burning panic, watching Xamson's struggle. It is getting worse, his flails turning to twitches.

And Adem—my hero, my friend—he has always been so strong, so powerful, that I cannot understand why he is unable to break free of this now, and something in me keeps waiting for it to happen. I know it is unfair, that this is not how the bind of the chthonus works, but I stand and I wait and I hope for it anyway, unable to think of anything else to do. If anyone could do it, it would be Adem.

Beyond myself, I become aware of sparks flying past my head toward the Forger—Firsts in our army trying to counter the Forger's hold.

It does nothing.

Xamson's stuttering gasps fill my ears, fill my mind, and my thoughts choke on the panic.

Do something.

But my body will not listen to my mind's command.

Finally Rona shoves past me and thrusts her blades down, cutting straight through Adem's arms.

Xamson drops to the ground gagging and coughing.

Adem's arms fall to the sand, fingers twitching.

I look to Adem. Despite the stumps where his arms were cut from his torso, his shoulders slump in relief.

"Xamson—"

But before I can drop to his side to see if he is all right, Rona pounces at me.

"What is wrong with you? I am your commander. When I shout an order at you, you follow it," she snaps.

She was shouting? I could not hear anything beyond my own panic, like the entire world had flattened into nothing.

She scowls and shoves me. I stumble back.

"Get your head on straight," she barks. She points to Adem. "He is not human. He cannot feel pain. How could you put him over Xamson? Or any human in our ranks?"

How can she say such things about Adem? And right in front of him. We all have felt how the air tightens when she and Adem are near each other, the way they seem to gravitate to each other, even if they are determined to ignore it.

But she is right. As my heart calms, I know I should have thought of it. Would have, if I were not so adamant in thinking of Adem as the human he deserves to be.

I push it aside. For now, all that matters is Xamson. He is still gagging and coughing, slumped over on hands and knees.

I kneel next him and place my hands on the sides of his face. "Are you okay?"

But before he can respond, Rona's voice rings over us. "Attack!" she cries.

Blasts of magic burst overhead from behind us—Firsts making their attacks on the Forger.

The soldiers around us charge forward. I stand, lifting Xamson with me, just in time to see the Forger mutter a command, spin with a swoosh of his cloak, and apparate on the spot.

The chthonuses he left behind burst into movement, attacking from all sides.

Chapter Five

We're surrounded.

The chthonuses may be poorly formed, but even crippled by their poor construction, they are still chthonus, and will have the same relentless bond that requires them to fulfill their maker's commands. From the base, primal way they stare and snarl, the emptiness behind their eyes, it looks like that command was to destroy us.

They edge in. Xamson is still doubled over and gagging. Rona, Adem, and I edge around him, give him what time we can to recover. Through the choked breaths, he manages to get up and draw his sword.

Adrenaline hums through me. My always-busy thoughts fall quiet. The world beyond the battle flattens and slows.

The chthonuses are upon us in a burst, and it is all I can do to stay alive. They thrash and snarl through our swinging blades without a thought for the risk. I charge the one closest to me and stab through its core, then pull back again, attacking on the instincts of my training. It stumbles back, looks down to the gash through his stomach. The wound is already closing itself, just as Adem's do. It releases a guttural growl, and then charges at me again.

My stomach drops out like I've been shoved off a cliff—my training was for fighting men, not monsters. How are we supposed to defeat an enemy we cannot wound?

The chthonus is not a skilled fighter, but it comes at me with relentless force. It attacks again, and again, its fists like sledgehammers, and fending it off is not enough. It is impossible to break free from its untiring assaults.

Finally I check the instincts I have honed with years of training. Ducking instead of blocking its blow, I lean low and slash my sword through its legs at the knee. It teeters and falls back.

In the pause my mind swells, overwhelmed. They may be able to fight forever, but no matter my will, no matter my training, I can't. Rona can't, Xamson can't. Our soldiers can't.

Something grabs hold of my ankle and tugs me off balance—another chthonus, this one crawling on the ground, his legs disproportionally small and dragging limp behind him. It snarls at me, thrashing its head side to side before biting into my calf. Its teeth are sharp, and its clenched jaw sets deep to my flesh with a piercing throb. On instinct I swing my sword down and cut off the head, but as the body falls away, the teeth only sink in deeper, gnashing into muscle and nerve.

But I can't give in to the pain, not now. The first chthonus's torso has already found its legs again, and is working to pull itself back together.

It is not enough.

I am not enough.

We will never get free from these monsters if they recover so quickly—we have to make it harder for them to heal themselves. I slice the chthonus's arm off, then the other, following suit with the legs. That should keep him busy a little longer. Then I stare down at the body and on a final thought, steel myself and cut off its head, too. No blood splatters. It just drops to the ground with a thunk and rolls, still snarling.

The other chthonus's teeth still clench into my calf. I brace myself and rip the head away, trying to ignore the pain as it tears at my skin and hot blood runs down to my ankle. I toss it as far as I can.

In the afterburn of the pain, my sight fades and the sounds of the battlefield flood my ears: gnashes and snarls, clashing blades and tearing flesh, cries and panting breaths. Sounds I know too well these days.

Already the thirsty Wasteland earth is soaking up pools of red. Already my chest is heaving from strain. Already I do not know how long can we keep this up.

I twist to see how the others are faring.

Rona's blades tear through another chthonus not far from me, a hard grunt bursting from her, a smudge of blood on her cheek.

Adem rips off another's arm with bare hands and tosses it away, his face twisted in a terrible grimace.

Nearby, Xamson's shield fends off another, and he reaches around with a clean swing that cuts through the chthonus's middle. It hinges to the side and tumbles over.

Despite all our skill—and there is plenty among our numbers—the chthonuses are closing in around us, forcing us tighter together.

Then a whoosh of shadow darts between the bodies in battle. I twist after it, but it is already gone. What was it? Where did it go?

I pay for my moment of distraction—a chthonus charges at me again and claws at my arm. Whatever I thought I saw, it is gone, and there is no time to worry about it now. I barely manage to fend off another swinging fist.

I slice my sword through the chthonus as hard as I can, cutting deep from its shoulder and down into its chest, and its arms flail for something to grasp. As I fight it off, I catch the shadow again from the corner of my eye, crossing the other side of the battlefield. I slice the chthonus into pieces and kick them away, and then I whip around to chase the shadow—there it is again, darting through the soldiers in the madness of the fight.

It flashes out of sight, then skitters back around and past me so close I could almost touch it. A whirl of chaos explodes through me like an irritating itch in my soul. Has the Forger brought something else with him?

The chthonus charges at me again. I swing my sword, and this time I cut clean through its side. Its abdomen teeters and lops to the ground; the lower body wanders forward blindly, drifting past me and deeper into the fight.

No sooner have I managed this than another is upon me, this one lacking features on its face except two hooded openings for eyes, yet still quick and unrelenting.

The shadow passes again, then materializes in front of me. I brace for its attack, but its blurred figure casts itself at the chthonus instead, and gnaws at its arm. I stumble back, a chaotic whirl of confusion and relief crackling through me.

The chthonus flails in irritation and lets me go. I stumble, unprepared, and my hesitation gives me the moment I need to understand what I am seeing.

The creature is small and dark, with large black eyes, sharp teeth and glinting claws—which it uses now to tear away the chthonus's arm. When it drops to the ground, the creature turns on the chthonus's throat until the faceless head falls off, too.

Then it turns to shadow again and transforms into the figure of a man—tall and lean, shadowed in waves of dark hair that frame piercing, ice-blue eyes. The itching sensation creeps under my skin and into my soul, a dissatisfied craving that wants more, more, more. Hunger, desire, and ambition stir in me.

The aura of a demon.

He calls to me over the sounds of battle, "I cannot stop them from healing themselves, but we can at least make it more difficult for them. Tear them apart, and I will spread their pieces as far across the Wasteland as I can."

Then he is shadow again, transforming into the small creature that is his natural demon form. He latches his sharp claws into the chthonus's head and darts away with it. In a breath he is back, taking its arm, its foot, its torso, all in different directions in a continuous blur of motion.

A demon? Here? Helping us?

There is no time to question—he is our best chance to get out of this alive. I turn my attention to the next chthonus and begin lopping it into pieces.

The demon and I quickly hit a rhythm, cutting the chthonuses apart and carrying them too far away for them to find themselves again. Piece by piece, our attackers' numbers thin out.

As a chthonus's head falls away under my blade, I meet eyes with Rona. The demon-shadow whooshes past to catch the head before it has even hit the ground, and carries it away. Rona's eyes flit to it, then back to me—she understands.

She turns and shouts into the battle and soon they are all doing it. Soldiers hack the chthonuses into pieces, and the Firsts dart through the fight in glimmers and bursts of light, working together with the shadow to whisk the pieces away. The rest of the Forger's army are soon torn apart and scattered through the Wasteland, where they cannot do us any more harm. All that is left among our worn-out soldiers are a few spare twitching limbs and chunks of torso.

We scurry about franticly, making sure no one was killed or lays dying, followed by a pause of solemn silence as we take in what has just happened, what it means for the war to come. Then the dizzying rush of relief and the adrenaline of victory take over. A few wild laughs let loose, followed by a din of whoops. We made it. We are safe. Against all the odds, we have won once more.

I am filled with the swell of victory like the warmth of a hearth in winter. Yet it troubles me, too. It makes no sense. As relentless as his chthonuses were, the Forger let us win. It is lucky for us that he did not set Adem upon us too—and why not, after he took care to display the power he wielded over Adem? Why didn't the Forger take part himself? Surely with his power he could obliterate us all. If the Texts are to be believed, what we saw today is only a mere sliver of his powers.

He was not here to kill us, he said—this time. Anxiety singes under my skin. What about next time?

Whatever this man is, he is no Chosen of the Gods. I cannot reconcile what I remember from the Texts with the monster we just encountered.

Was it all just a distraction to keep us busy while he made his exit? Was he testing us? These are questions that will have to wait until later.

Right now there are much more urgent things. There are wounded to tend to. And I have to set things right with Xamson—I failed him terribly.

I scan across the blood-stained battlefield until I find him, and start toward him. He looks up, registers me, and his eyes grow stormy. I can fix this—I have to fix this. I tense and quicken my pace.

But then a voice cuts in from behind me—a voice smooth as velvet, growling with such grace it could be a purr. It is the angel Calipher. "No. Not a chance. Not him."

I turn to find him face-to-face with the demon, glaring at each other with fists clenched and teeth bared in a grimace.

I take another glance at Xamson's back. As much as the need to speak with him burns in me, it must wait. First I must stop a second war from breaking out.

Chapter Six

Calipher is hunched forward in an attack stance, his glossy midnight wings spread wide, making him even larger than usual. The glare on his face is a stark contradiction to the gentle glow of his moon-pale skin and the soothing aura of peace he always projects.

Opposite him, the demon has pulled back into human form and glares right back at Calipher with his ice-blue eyes. He is not as large as the angel, but he is a little too tall for a human, his eyes a little too pale-bright.

Soldiers are beginning to gather to witness the impending clash that the building pressure in the air promises. But they keep their distance with an open circle around them. My post-battle relief snuffs out—with Calipher's declaration, the relief of victory is already giving way to distrust.

I step forward into the open space and approach the demon.

"You saved us." I make sure to say it loud so the watching soldiers can hear. I stretch out a hand to the demon. "Welcome to Haven. What should we call you?"

"Bastus," he replies. He clasps my hand in his, and a burst of chaos rushes through me like bees shaken loose from a hive.

I draw my hand back a bit too quickly, fighting the impulse to step away, out of his aura's reach. Then I turn to Calipher, who is still glowering at the demon. The angelic aura of peace that wafts off him wars with the demon's chaotic aura seeping into me from the other side.

"It's all right, Calipher. Bastus helped us fend off the chthonuses. I saw it myself," I say to him. "He's on our side."

"I do not care," Calipher says. "Not him."

"Me?" The demon retorts. His fists clench at his sides. "If I knew you were here I would have thought twice about remaining trapped in the Underworld."

Rona steps next to me and leans in. "What is this about?"

I shake my head. "Seems they have a history."

"Great," she sighs.

Somehow it does not surprise me that Calipher has made a few enemies over the ages.

"A demon? On the side of the Gods? Is it possible?" It is Avi, calling out as he approaches.

My teeth clench down on my tongue—I hadn't noticed he had joined us as we raced into the Wasteland. Always so eager to doubt, my adopted brother, and sow its seeds to the others around him. Just as he did when he conspired with Helda to oust me as Haven's leader. Rage kicks up in me like hot embers.

"Is it so crazy?" I reply. "Are the demons not among the Gods' First Creatures too? Why wouldn't demons want to fight for Shael, the same as angels fight for Theia, and sprites for Gloros?"

When I turn toward Avi, I realize I am not only speaking to him—even more soldiers have gathered, watching with guarded interest. As if the demon is on trial.

"Yes, Firsts—the first to turn against the Gods," Calipher retorts.

It's true—to tell it by the Texts, the demons were the first to rebel against the Gods and sow discontent, back in the Beginning when everything began to fall apart. Between this and the edgy buzz their auras give off, demons are typically considered more trouble than they're worth, even among followers of Shael.

Bastus folds his arms, frowning. "You are hardly one to talk about abuse of power," he snaps back.

Calipher's dark wings, marking his fall from Theia, tuck in behind him, but his expression remains resentful. He narrows his eyes.

More of the soldiers are gathering around us now, the spectacle of the First creatures, especially a demon, putting the soldiers at awe. Some of them brandish their blades as they eye him and murmur to each other. The restlessness of his aura is working against him.

Bastus stretches out his arms and turns to address them. "I mean no harm. I wish to join you in the fight against the rebels."

Some of the soldiers start to step away, eyeing him with guarded glares.

Calipher continues. "You say you came from the Underworld? I wonder what purpose a demon could possibly have had among the rebels of the lower realm. I think we can all guess."

The murmur of the soldiers intensifies in response to Calipher's stand, and the air hums with tension.

"What was I doing in the realm of Shael? The Underworld is my home," Bastus says, stepping forward to address not Calipher, but the soldiers. "It is not my fault the Gods also used it to lock away the rebels, and locked me and the rest of the demons in with them. Even now, with the barrier broken, crossing between the realms is anything but easy. I had to wait and use the Forger's crossing and break through on the tail of his spell."

The soldiers turn quiet.

Calipher shrugs. "So you say. How are we to know you did not come to spy on us for the rebels?"

Bastus snarls, a sound more befitting the strange small gremlin form he took in battle than the human one he holds now. "We both know that is not what I am, Calipher. Your quarrel with me has nothing to do with this war, or any of the rest of my kind at all."

Enough.

I step forward between them. "Calipher?" I turn to him and wait.

"I know this demon," he finally says. "And he is not to be trusted."

"Me?" Bastus steps toward Calipher until they are eye to eye. "Of the two of us, you think I am the one who cannot be trusted? Tell them, Calipher, why are you not in the Host? How was it you ended up trapped in Terath for so many ages? Which of us lost our way and was cut off from our God?"

Calipher glares back, his eyes hard, and then he steps away. "I made mistakes. There is no question. But I never meant to turn my back on Theia. I only wanted for Nia to be happy."

"As did I," Bastus said. "But I managed not to lose my way or steal magic from the Gods in the process." His expression turns darker—are his eyes actually changing to a burning red? "I managed to love her in a way that did not destroy her."

"Yes, and you could not win her over, either," Calipher mutters.

Heat flashes in Bastus' eyes.

"Are you telling me this is all about some ancient love triangle?" Rona steps forward, arms folded. They tower over her, but if they intimidate her, she does not let it show. "Calipher, do you have any real charges against this demon? Sounds to me like he has more to bring against you. Ones we have already chosen to overlook. We gave you a second chance. Can you give a reason why we would not do the same for him?"

Calipher's mouth drops open, but he can find nothing to fire back with.

"We are at war," Rona chides. "We are just out of battle, there are wounded still bleeding into the sand. No more dissension—go find someone to heal."

Calipher's wings slump. He grimaces at Bastus one last time, baring his teeth, then turns and storms away. Bastus glares after him a moment, tightens his fists, then turns off in the opposite direction.

One situation diffused, I scan the battlefield of writhing chthonus limbs and blood-drenched earth and find Xamson again on the other side of the battlefield. I run to him and place a hand on his shoulder.

"Are you okay?"

Xamson turns to me, not with his usual bright smile, but a glower.

"Am I—" He spits a hard laugh at me. "Gods."

Twisted dark streaks are blooming on his neck from where Adem's fingers dug into him. I want to throw my arms around him and kiss every one of them until they are gone. But the hard, unforgiving look in his eyes keeps me away.

He has never looked at me like this before.

I open my mouth to speak, but I have no idea what to say.

Then Adem rushes up, just on my heels.

"I'm sorry. I'm sorry. I'm sorry," Adem says over and over. "I wish..." He will not look Xamson in the eye, and instead fixates down, on the hands that betrayed them both, and shakes his head. Still, the sentiment is clear. We all wish for something these days. But there are too many things to wish for in the midst of this war to be worth speaking of.

Xamson's face slowly shifts into a hardened frown. He grips the sword in his hand and swings it, heaving it as far into Adem's shoulder as he can force it.

Adem does nothing, just stands there and lets the blow come. The moment Xamson pulls the sword free, Adem's chest begins knitting back together, just like the other chthonuses, as if nothing had happened at all. Nothing remains but the tear in his robe.

Xamson pulls his sword back and winds up for a second blow.

"Hey!" I cry, moving between them. Xamson's blade halts inches from my chest. His eyes widen, and I cannot tell if it is from relief that he stopped in time, or rage that I got in his way.

"It was not his fault," I say.

Xamson relaxes the sword down to his side, then lunges at me, glaring.

"Him? The Forger was right about one thing—it is a thing, not a person. I know you want to like it, that it was useful for you at a vulnerable time in your life. But after what just happened, it is nothing but a threat to us. What makes this one any different from the rest of them?" He shakes his head, gesturing out to the graveyard of twitching limbs. "We should slice it up and leave it here with the others."

He lunges again, as if he means to fight through me to carry out his threat, but when I hold my ground, he drops the sword and shoves me. I stumble back into Adem, who steadies me.

"Xamson, I tried, I—" I failed. My mind flashes back to the panic that paralyzed me while Xamson gagged and suffocated, dangling in the air. I have no words for the terrible knot in my stomach.

"We shouldn't have been out here at all. You and your Godsdamned heroics." He stabs his sword into the ground between us.

"Xamson—" I reach out, but I have no words.

Me and my heroics. It is an argument we have had before. In his better moods, he teases I must not be meant long for this realm. In his darker moods, like now, his accusations cut deep.

"Excuse me." A burst of anarchy cuts through me in a gust as Bastus joins us. "May I?"

He stretches out his hands and gestures to the bruises still growing darker on Xamson's neck.

Xamson runs his eyes over Bastus and swallows. "Yes."

His eyes are dilated wide, and with a pang, I wonder what Bastus' aura stirs up in him.

Bastus cuts between us, blocking me from Xamson, and cups his hands around Xamson's neck. They stand face to face, so close they could kiss, and a smoky cloud spills forth from Bastus' hands and around Xamson's neck.

I want to say something, anything to break their gaze, but as the dark cloud disperses, Rona beats me to it. "Come with me," she says. "All of you."

I turn to follow her.

"Wait," Bastus says. He points to my calf, still bloodied where the chthonus bit into me. Before I can speak, he has shot a dart of shadowed magic at it, and it heals.

Then he follows after Rona, and Xamson trails him. My leg prickles where it heals, leaving me wondering what he had to linger so close to Xamson for while healing him if he could do that all along.

Rona leads us farther into the Wasteland. As we approach, Calipher and the sprite Nissa turn to greet us.

Unlike angels, whose stature is larger than life, sprites are diminutive and nimble like children. Their skin is tinged with an earthy green, and their delicate wings are thin as petals, flushed with bright bursts color. As Nissa looks up to us, her large dark eyes sparkle even through her concern. As a creature of Gloros,

Goddess of passion, her aura magnifies emotions. The humming anxiety it ignites in me now tightens along my spine.

When we reach them, Rona stops and points to a blemished mark on the ground at their feet.

"You said you got here on the tail of the Forger's spell," she prompts, looking to Bastus. "How did he do it?"

The ground where the Forger stood is singed in rings of burnt sand and shards of glass, where it appears to have melted from the intensity of his spell. I do not know whether to be awed or afraid.

"There are remnants of the magic he used all over the place," Nissa adds, pointing in the air. I strain to see, but with my abilities faded, I can no longer spot the traces of magic like the Firsts can.

"It is as if the fabric of the very realm has been ripped," Calipher says. He shifts, fluttering his wings and blocking Bastus' view.

I glance to Bastus, bracing for another outburst between them. His jaw tenses, but he takes a deep breath and steps around to the other side, out of Calipher's reach.

"There was no spell," Bastus says. "All the spells to break through the Underworld and Terath require a new moon for passage. When word reached him about Koreh, he was not willing to wait. The Forger forced his way through with sheer magical force. It was...painful. But impressive."

Calipher frowns, his forehead creasing in concentration. "I have never heard of such a thing."

Bastus nods. "Even the Forger could not manage it before the barrier split, and he is the most powerful sorcerer I have ever witnessed. More powerful than some Firsts. Someone taught him well."

"An angel," Nissa says. "Judging by the spells he used."

"Can he come back again?" I ask.

Bastus nods. "He might need some time to rest and recover. If we are lucky. But he will be back. I do not think he broke through the realms again when he escaped. He is still in Terath."

The Forger of my childhood imagination was a man of fortitude and righteousness, but staring down at the burnished sand he has left behind, there is only destruction. The next wave of the Third Realm War is here in earnest now. I can feel it in the way the sun presses against the back of my neck. And that man—that monster—was a harbinger of it.

"How do we stop him?" I ask.

None of them answer.

Their silence is like flint that refuses to catch sparks.

I try again. "How do we break his bond to Adem?"

Bastus looks down to the ground. Nissa's wings twitch.

Rona steps back, scanning the soldiers and the few scattered chthonus limbs still nearby, already flailing and scrawling across the dried earth, trying to find their other pieces.

"Let's get out of here," she says, her eyes flitting to Adem. Is that a twinge of concern or fear in her voice? Both? I cannot quite tell.

The unanswered question hangs heavy in the air.

CHAPTER SEVEN

As we approach, the protective charms the First Creatures set to protect Haven work over me in waves of confusion, distraction, and the unshakable feeling that I am leading everyone the wrong way. Doubt pools with every step and my shoulders knot with tension. But I know to expect it and carry on.

We have grown stronger in these past weeks, but it has also made us a greater target. Perhaps part of me mourns for the small village and the simple life I lived here as a boy. Everything was so much easier in those days.

Adem found this village for us when we needed it, even at its quietest. Back then it was easy to believe fate had led us to Haven, that I was destined to lead this people through the Third Realm War and into a better age. I was so sure of it. I even did it well, for a time. But once Adem returned from his quest, once Rona was stolen back from the Underworld, once the barrier holding back the rebel Firsts in that realm was broken, it all turned to ash in my hands.

The Gods.

Haven.

Everything.

I used to think I was safe here, that we were tucked away in some special corner of Terath that the realm wars could not ruin. But that was foolish. If Adem could find this place, so could anyone else—anything else. Koreh found us. And now the Forger.

Perhaps there is no hiding anymore.

Perhaps there never was.

Ever since the war started, everything I believed in has been slipping away, as if my faith were built upon a crumbling cliff. I was raised better than this—by my mother, by my sister Miriam, by Lena, who took me in here in Haven after their deaths.

And all of Haven can see I have lost it. It reflects back to me in their eyes. It was no wonder they stood aside as Avi and Helda threw their coup. It is no wonder they cheered when Rona showed them a new strength—strength powerful enough to take down a demigod.

Now they treat her like she is the Chosen one. Like she is a demigod herself. She was not even supposed to be here.

I do not wish Rona anything ill. She was strong when we needed strength, when I was unable to keep the illusion any longer. She still is, even as she heals from the damage Kythiel did to her when he broke into her mind from beyond the realm...and as the powers she gained in her fight against him begin to fade along with the wounds. She knows what the people need in these times is not truth. It is hope, and she will give it to them at any cost.

But.

It was supposed to be me.

Whatever I tell myself about Rona, about my own failings, about all that has passed, this thought irritates from under my skin like of a grain of sand.

At any rate, Haven survived the Third Realm War so far. It is here, and it seems everyone can feel the shifts taking place, like a storm filling the air with pressure, its sparks threatening to set off an inferno.

We break through the magic's pull and the doubt falls away like a veil, exposing Haven and the sea just below.

It surprises me all over again, approaching from the outside, to see how much Haven has grown. The village has tripled in size. Angels, sprites, humans, all of them together, working and living side by side. It does not feel like the home I know until the salty breeze carries the sea to me.

As we make our way over the bluff and down into the village, people cheer in greeting. Children run to find their mothers and fathers among us, men and women to find lovers and friends, and the air swells with their exclamations. They slap me on the back and squeeze my arm, their eyes glistening and full.

Then Helda charges at me, brow furrowed and fists clenched.

"Helda," I say.

My back aches from the battle and my feet are tired. I do not have energy left to fight with her, too. But when it comes to a fight, Helda seems to never run out of energy. Or causes.

She tosses her gnarled dreadlocks from her face, her jaw tightening.

"Are you mad? Just what did you think you were doing?"

Helda's furious eyes drill into me.

"What?" I stutter. I expected cheers when we came back into the village. Not anger and accusations.

Helda leans in toward me. Her harsh accent cuts like glass.

"Exactly what," she huffs, "Do you think you were doing? Calling my soldiers out beyond the shield? Ordering my soldiers to attack, putting my soldiers' lives on the line?"

Her words kick up resentment in my chest. Years ago, I helped Helda build her city of Ir-Nearch. We were partners, leaders of two sister cities. We traded and protected each other. And when Ir-Nearch was overcome by Koreh and her ash soldiers, I fought side by side with them. Then we took in the survivors. Still she turned against me in a coup with Avi while I was tracking down Koreh, and still, even after she took my power from me, she continues to challenge my every move. How the tides turned against this relationship, I do not know.

"I tried to call for you, I called for whoever could join," I say. "But there was no time. Did you see Adem tearing through the village? Something was horribly wrong, we had to do something—"

"That's exactly it," Helda snarls. "You didn't have to do anything. We are layered in protections here. And yet without knowing what was happening—just that it was terribly wrong—you dragged my soldiers out there with you into vulnerable land."

Her soldiers.

My skin turns hot as my anger reaches a boiling point. She hates that her soldiers have a loyalty to me that she has not been able to inspire.

"And what of Adem?" I press. "Something was wrong, and even with all the Firsts' charms and the guards we line along the border at every hour, Adem was the only one to notice. What was I supposed to do, leave him to race off into the unknown all alone?"

A muscle twitches near Helda's eye. "Yes."

"Never," I bite back. "I could never do that. Not to Adem, not to any of the soldiers of Haven. I was trained to act with bravery, not for...for self-preservation."

"You call that bravery?" Helda spits. "I call it foolishness. You are right, he had no idea what he might be sensing. And yet still your impulse was to race right after him. That does not mean my soldiers need to follow. We are not all inhuman and deathless like that thing is, we cannot all be so thoughtless with our risks."

"I did not think—"

"That much is clear," Helda cuts in.

My chest puffs out in rage. "Does no one care that the Forger, the legend from the Texts, was at the very doorstep of our village? That he has allied with the Rebels? That he just attacked us?"

He is the villain here. Not me.

"Of course we care," Helda snaps. "While you were out fighting your little battle, the council arranged to meet at sunrise so we can put together a plan. Now get away from my soldiers."

My chest throbs with heated energy, as if holding lightning like a storm cloud. I dread addressing this all over again with the rest of the council tomorrow. Everything is a gridlock of drawn-out debate, when what is really needed is action.

"And what of Rona? Rona was out there with the rest of us."

The new leader they accepted in my stead after their little coup. She was at my side through all of this.

Helda glances to her. Their eyes meet, then Rona looks down to the sand. "I tried to call you back. But you were already racing off. We agreed one of us should go along."

For supervision.

Understanding hits me like a punch to the gut.

Helda gives me a final hard glare "This is not your army anymore. Fall in line. Or you can fall off the side of the realm for all I care."

Helda turns back to the tired troops, still collected and at attention following the battle. Muddied, some bloodied, and exhausted. It was a hard-earned fight.

Is that all who took up our charge and went with us? It seemed like a lot out there, but now, compared to the vastness of how the village has grown lately, it is only a small sliver of the army in full.

A stinging embarrassment licks through me in flames.

Even the soldiers do not listen to my commands anymore. Helda is right. This is no longer my army. Haven's people are still willing to follow me, but there is a divide with those from Ir-Nearch. I glance back at the soldiers who fought with me against the Forger—Xamson was the only soldier from Ir-Nearch who joined.

This split is not good for any of us. And I am at the root of it.

"It seems we must remind you fools whose command you are under, and whose you are not," Helda shouts. "So we will do what you should have been doing this whole time anyway—practice. I do not want to hear that you are tired from battle, because you should not have been in battle at all. You owe your real commander this morning's drills, and you will do them. In double."

From the edge of the formation, Xamson's eyes drift to me, full of...is it regret? Anger? I cannot quite tell. But I know what this feeling welling within me is, though I have felt it only rarely: shame.

"Wait," I say, running forward to them. My exhausted body is slow and stumbles as I force myself up and toward them.

Helda turns, her expression a sharp frown—she is not pleased to be interrupted by me yet again. But I cannot let this happen.

Especially not to Xamson.

"This isn't their fault. It's my fault." I can tell by the grumbles that rise many of the soldiers agree with me. Heated anger clouds my chest. "Let them go. I should be the one to do the drills."

Helda blinks back at me. "It is your fault," she says in her biting accent. "But you are not my soldier. Your penance means nothing to me. You are dismissed."

No, this is wrong. "But—"

"You are dismissed." Helda turns and calls a sharp order. The soldiers snap to attention and begin the drills, moving away in a brisk run toward the shore.

She then turns on me, calling orders, and the others fall in line, shields and helmets and all, starting toward the training area.

Xamson gives me a final, dismissive glance before he pulls his helmet over his head and follows.

Chapter Eight

For a while I stand there, where Helda yelled at me, too stunned to move. All I did was put my life on the line for Haven. All I did was jump into action before anyone else knew what was going on. And now the soldiers who were alert, brave, loyal enough to follow me are the ones paying the price.

When the tension tightening down my spine becomes too much, I head back to the shore to finish the work we abandoned when the Forger called to Adem, but the others finished preparing the fish for the day's food without us—one more way in which my actions were a burden to the village today. And it leaves me with nothing to do.

I look around to find a place to be, and catch Adem's figure up on the bluff, just short of the protective shields. He has always been hesitant to be among humans, no matter how long he has stayed here. I do not feel so good among them right now myself.

I turn and climb up the steep, sandy slope, and plop onto the ground at his side. Together we watch the soldiers in their penance to Helda—a small penance of my own. I feel as though I must bear witness as they suffer through the drills in their exhausted state. Bear witness and let the shame of causing their pain burn through me.

For a time, we sit in silence. This is something I love about Adem. He does not need to speak, and he does not need me to speak. With others, so often my words feel like a necessity, a salve that must be dispensed to keep the world around me running. Not here. Not ever.

But still, there are things that must be said between us after what happened.

They writhe, heavy and tangled in my chest, a mounting pressurized heat. The sun rises overhead and bakes into us as the soldiers do their drills under Helda's sharp commands.

Meanwhile, the Forger's chilling laugh haunts my mind, and I ache to understand Adem's past with him. But I already know Adem cannot remember that far back. Asking will only worsen his guilt.

Adem fidgets, practicing the magic Ca",ipher has been teaching him by rotating two small stones around him in mid-air. He is getting stronger. More controlled.

Eventually, when I am ready, I choke back the churning questions about the Forger and clear my throat.

"Xamson did not mean what he said. About you being a thing," I say. "He was upset."

Adem responds with a grunt. But I understand the thoughts he does not say—that whether Xamson meant it or not, Adem thinks he was right. That Helda was right. That even if he did not choose it, his connection to the Forger forced him into actions that put Haven in danger—again. That everything that happened today was his fault.

Through the palpable angst of his doubt, I feel Adem slipping away, like he always does, becoming the nothing he believes himself to be.

And I cannot bear for him to disappear. Not now. I need him.

"No," I say. I am surprised by the intensity of my voice. "Xamson knows you, he understands what you are. And what you are not. He knows how you are bound. He does not really blame you for what happened, I'm sure of it."

I reach over and squeeze his massive shoulder. He will not look at me. I press again. "You are different. You are good. We all know it, even Xamson. We have seen it."

"How is he?" Adem asks.

My mind flashes to Bastus' hands around Xamson's neck, the way Xamson looked up at the demon as he healed him—then the hardened anger that flashed over Xamson's face as he turned away from me for Helda's drills.

"He will get over it. Bastus healed his bruises easily enough." A lump tightens in my throat. "How are you?"

Adem shrugs. I know him well enough to understand that the guilt of what the Forger made him do today will stay with him and become part of the burden he carries always.

"You cannot help the magic that binds you," I press. "But we will fix it. As soon as we know how. The Brotherhood of Shael's Sworn—"

"The Brotherhood is not here," Adem says. "We do not know when they might return. Or if they will return at all."

The Brotherhood of Shael's Sworn hunted Adem through the ages, farther back than he can remember, chasing the necklace. Adem would have forfeited it if he could. But his maker—the Forger, I suppose—had bound him to the box it was locked within.

It was only weeks ago after we defeated Koreh that, together, we were able to finally stop one of them—Thane. From him we learned what the Brotherhood was and what it wanted and were able to explain why they could never win the box from Adem to destroy its magic.

When we told Thane all that had happened—the way Kythiel tricked Adem into stealing Rona back from the Underworld, the breach of the barrier between realms that set the rebels free, the necklace, the start of the Third Realm War—Thane promised he would return with the rest of them.

"Do not doubt. Thane said he would return with them, and he will."

He has to.

I wish I felt as certain of it as I sound. But Adem is right. It has been a long time. Weeks. No one will confess it out loud, but we all thought they would be here by now. My own faith in the Brotherhood has faltered and flickered, and sometimes in the quiet of night my mind wanders. I catch visions of my fears of what may have happened to Thane since he left Haven, everything that could have gone wrong between his departure and his promised return.

What the others of the Brotherhood might have to say about him returning without the magical artifact he was sent after, and the other strange news about Koreh and the war, I can only imagine. Who is to say, really, what might or might not come of it, or if the Brotherhood would decide the war is something they should be part of.

But I steel myself against doubt and choose to believe they will return as Thane promised. Because I have lost faith in too many things, and my spirit cannot afford to lose anything more in these dark times.

I say, "We will find a way to fix this. We will set you free. And then none of this will matter."

Adem shrugs. I place a hand on his shoulder.

Quiet settles between us again.

I feel more myself here with Adem than anywhere else these days. It is my one safe place left, where worries and failures and judgments are not constantly creeping in, where I am seen for more than my failings. It is the only place I can escape from the feeling that everything I touch burns to ash.

I have never felt smaller. The realm has never felt angrier, like it has been lit on fire.

The soldiers drill all through the day. Each wiped brow, each stumbled step flinches through me as if the pain were my own. My fault. Helda does not release them until after the sun dips down behind the sea.

Some of the soldiers bend over and gasp, others rip off their helmets and armor, some drop to the sand and lay out in it. Xamson is easy to pick out among them, the moon's silvery glow contrasting against the dark brilliance of his skin as it caresses his lean muscle, wet with sweat and dotted in grime. He peels off his soldier's shell and plunges into the waves.

At my side, Adem shifts and then hold his hand out toward me. "Here," he grumbles.

I reach out in response, then pull away when I realize what he is holding. It is the necklace. The brilliance of the large emerald glimmers in the light of sunset and calls to me.

I flinch away. "I cannot take that from you!"

Everything that has gone wrong today tangles up on itself into a knot in my throat. Adem carries the necklace for good reason—he is the only one who could bear its magic without it enticing him to use it.

After all, the necklace is one of the most powerful artifacts of magic within Terath—maybe the most powerful. Calipher created it for the woman he loved all the way back in the Beginning, when the gods separated the Firsts from our realm once and for all, starting the First Realm War. But Calipher's intent behind the necklace's charm went wrong, and it seduced anyone who took ownership of it. They succumbed to its lure and put it on—and once worn, the necklace caused others around the wearer to fall into a hypnotic, desperate, obsessive semblance of love. The kind of love that destroys lives, figuratively and literally.

I could not comprehend the power of such a curse until Koreh used it to turn our own people against us in Ir-Nearch and burned our proud sister city to ash. Now we all understand just what the necklace is capable of. Power such as this demolishes all it touches.

We tried to destroy it. We tried everything we could think of. Blades. Fire. Magic of all shades and curses. Even Calipher, the necklace's creator, could not make a dent in it. Every time we left it sitting for too long, someone in the village was lured to it.

After this morning's brush with the Forger, I know we need a new way to protect it. We were already luckier than we deserve today. It is a matter of time before he claims it from us.

But Adem's gesture is more than that, and we both know it. This is a forfeit. A goodbye.

And I will not let him give up and leave me, not after all we have been through. I need him here.

"You must take it," Adem says, pushing it toward me again.

"No," I lean away. "You must keep it."

"That was before. I am the worst one to have it now. I will carry it right to the Forger the moment he calls me."

"You cannot know that." My anger pushes me to my feet. "If that is true, why didn't he do it already? Today?"

"I don't know," Adem confesses.

"He did not because he cannot," I say. A nagging sense at the back of my mind questions if I really believe it, but I am too angry now to listen, even to myself. "You are letting him get in your head. Like the rest of them."

Adem stands, too, leaning down to try to meet my eyes. I cannot look to him. There is a long pause. The anger that has been building in me all day coiling through my muscles. But he does not try to argue further. Finally his large hand closes around the emerald, and he brings it to rest at his side.

"Later," he says. "All will be clearer in the morning."

"Right. Morning."

When we meet with the Council. They will never let him walk away, surely. Not when he is our only guardian for the necklace.

Today has been more than I was ready for, and my tomorrow is already overstuffed with more than I care to face. This, perhaps, is the true cost of war—bearing day after day of the unbearable, and coping with your own powerlessness in the face of it.

When I get back to my hut, Xamson is in bed. He starts at the sound as the door opens and shuts. I peel off my robe, and curl into bed next to him without a word.

For so long I was only able to see him on those occasions when I had cause to make the trek to Ir-Nearch for business between our two allied cities. And even then, I might stay in his bed through the night, but by morning I returned to my own to prepare for the day. Now we are constantly on top of each other. I cannot seem to make enough room for him within this small hut.

Many long moments later, Xamson rolls over and brushes hesitant fingers over the back of my hand.

"Are you okay?" he asks.

I turn and look at him. "I should be asking you that."

He shrugs. "Bastus healed me. I'm fine. Some sore muscles from Helda's drills, but fine."

"I'm sorry. That Helda took her anger toward me out on you and the others."

He purses his lips together. "Why did you do it?"

My mind goes blank. Why does this keep coming up? Anger kicks up like a reflex, but there is no attack in Xamson's tone, only curiosity. I swallow the rage back down.

"I—I had to. Adem needed me."

Xamson shifts. He pulls his hand away and tucks it under himself.

"What does that mean, Adem needed you?" he asks. "He is all but invincible."

His body is too close, crowding in. I shift to find more space toward the edge of the cot, but still he is pressed against me.

"What are you trying to say?" I ask.

"I don't know. I am trying to understand."

"What do you want from me? We are at war."

We are trapped in this cycle. Xamson fights to be closer-closer-closer, holding me tight like a flame under a cup. But the closer he tries to get, the more I fight for air. Not because I don't enjoy being held by him, but because I need to keep burning.

"Exactly," Xamson replies. "There is too much horror in the world right now to not lean on each other. Stop being such a good Godsdamned soldier, stop putting up this front, and just be here. With me. We are all going through this. I don't need a warrior. I don't need a leader. I don't need some Chosen one. I need you. Just you."

I cannot understand what he is asking me for. These things are all I have ever been. I break his gaze and stare down to our hands, pressed against each other between us. Why can't we just keep going like before? When he was in Ir-Nearch and I was here in Haven, he never asked so much of me.

I do not know what to say, so I just shake my head.

He tries again. "Tell me what weighs on you. You think you are so alone, that you carry such a unique burden because we all thought you were Chosen, but your burden is not so special. And that is good, Jordan. We are all feeling it. I know what you are going through. But you have to share. You cannot keep trying to carry it all alone."

The words sting. He is right. I am not those things anymore. Maybe I never truly was in the first place. I do not know which would be worse. Why does he insist in peeling away all that I am?

I pull back. "I don't know what is left of me without those things."

It is a whisper. A confession.

Xamson's hand tightens around mine.

"I love you," I say. "Isn't that enough?"

"I wish it were," he whispers back.

My mind clouds, like a haze of smoke has overcome it. "What are you saying?"

He breaks his gaze and looks down. "I don't know."

The quiet of the night falls over us, the hum of crickets swelling. His words empty me, and what is left behind is a hungry sort of fear.

He takes in a breath as if to say something more, but I lean in and stop him with a kiss.

No more talking. Not tonight. I cannot bear to go through the motions with him yet again. Just for tonight I want to pretend these problems are not there, that they never existed. I just want to block out all of these troubles and be.

So I kiss him again. He kisses me back, and pulls me into him.

Chapter Nine

I awaken with a lurch, bolting upright, with the sensation of eyes on me. The after-burn of an image is etched in my mind—a tall, wiry man with a knotted staff and a broad hat. The Forger. A shuddering dread fills me, just like when he thrust his curse at me.

I take a breath to calm my racing heart and squint into the glare of morning sun reaching in through the cracks of the thatched walls.

But there is no time to worry over strange dreams now. It is time for Council. After Rona's temper and Helda's stern chiding, this is likely to be as grim as any battle.

Xamson is still asleep, curled up with his back to me. I lean into him, wrap my arm around his bare waist, and kiss the back of his neck. In his sleep, his anger is not pulled around him like armor, and he reflexively shifts closer against me.

I resist the urge to squeeze him tight—it would wake him, along with the tension between us. Instead, I press my forehead against the nape of his neck, and silently swear to never hurt him again—to never let him be hurt again.

As I turn away, my old copy of the Texts, pushed aside against the wall in the corner, catches my eye. The same one my sister Miriam tucked into my pack along with food and water for our escape from Epoh all those years ago, when Adem led me here to Haven's safety. The same one I pored over day after day, when its tales of heroes and monsters and gods were my only way to reach beyond Epoh's walls. I had almost forgotten about it, shoved aside with my old things and hidden in stacks. I have not had much use for it these days.

But now, I reach for it. My fingers flip through its pages like coming home, right to the passage about the Forger:

There was in those times a boy who had many great gifts bestowed upon him. An angel noticed these gifts and took him in, and the boy learned their ways. Thus the boy took on powers that belonged only to the most righteous. He took the earth in his hands and shaped it to his will, and he took the Gods' power in his hands and created shadows of life. He repeated this skill to mastery. Then he walked away from this world, and cast it aside.

Is that all there is? I turn the page, but there is nothing more about the Forger. It is not even a page, this great story that so ensnared my imagination as a boy. Such dreams of greatness were sparked from these words, founded on so little. It says nothing about being Chosen. It does not even really say he was righteous. I forced that into the story myself, built him up to be more like myself each time I went over the story in my head. I shut the book, running my fingers over its faded cover, then toss it back in its corner.

I pull on my robe and leave for Council.

Outside, the tinge of dawn kisses the sky beyond the bluff.

I glance toward the cave down the shoreline, where the Council meets. A lean figure is already walking down the sand to it—Avi. I should make my way there too.

But first there is something I must do.

I turn and head up the bluff instead, looking for Adem. The more I mull on the Forger, the more questions I have for Adem. But I do not see him in his usual place at the bluff, and as I look around, I do not see him anywhere in the village, either.

My shoulders tense and pull in. I know he is not sleeping. So where is he?

He must be staying away to avoid any more conflict after yesterday. Or maybe he is punishing himself, doing that brooding thing he does when he is ashamed. But we need him at Council—even with his faded memories, he probably knows more about the Forger than anyone.

I scan over the sleeping village. Rona is making her way through the huts toward the cave, too.

I call to her. "Have you seen Adem?"

She hesitates, looking up and turning as she places my voice. Her expression flickers, then pulls back behind her usual stoic mask. "Not since the Wasteland yesterday."

Worry tightens down my back. With rushed steps, I run to Adem's usual perch, though I am not sure what I expect. There is no trace of him, but in his usual spot, the necklace is laid out in the sand, the chain piled up on itself in a tidy coil.

I stumble back, wishing I could turn away and make it untrue.

He is gone.

I shudder, and a rush of rage comes over me. Even after all Adem has done for us, the villagers have never welcomed him here. How could he help but see himself as a monster when that is all they reflect back to him—in sideways glances, in cold stares, in averted eyes.

And the Forger. Manipulating Adem like he is nothing but a toy. Using him to threaten us.

I should have stopped him. How, I do not know, but I still cannot shake the guilt.

And then, the necklace. He just left it here. In the sand.

The charms we have put in place to guard the necklace must be working, for it is lucky no one from the village has been called to it and scooped it up, seduced by its power.

I release a sharp exhale, trying to shake the panic from my chest. Adem is gone. The ungrateful people he watches over here night after night, they drove him away with their accusations and fear. The same people that turned their backs on me so readily.

Where did he go? How far could he have gotten? My heart pleads to chase after him into the Wasteland right now, just leave everything else behind until I find him.

But this is no time to lose myself. I need to be pragmatic right now. I need to think. I need to pick up the necklace before someone else stumbles across it and falls prey to its call.

I bend down and reach for it. As my trembling hand brushes against it, its magic shoots through my fingertips and into my core, a bolt of power and blinding desire splitting through me. I flinch away, then wrap my sleeve over my hand before trying again.

Who will carry it now that Adem is gone? Who can?

I look out to Haven and see more figures trekking down the shore toward the little cave at Haven's edge.

Right. Time for Council. Just the people who should be answering these questions. The ones who drove Adem away.

I race down the bluff, dart through the drowsy village and up the shore toward the cave, the necklace's power pulsing through the thin fabric of my robe.

I reach the cave gasping. Rona, Helda, Avi, and Calipher are already waiting inside. They turn to me.

"What is this?" Avi says. The concern in his voice cuts with a taunting edge. "Another battle to fight already?"

"It's Adem," I start between heaving breaths. I do not look to Avi, but Rona—she is the only one who might understand. I pause, trying to find the words. Calipher's aura edges into me, but instead of helping, the sense of peace it forces is distracting, a feeling too far from what I know to be true.

Rona's brow twitches into a frown.

Helda crosses her arms and sighs.

Why don't they understand? My heart pounds and my head still reels from the realization—he's gone, he's really gone.

"By the Gods, Jordan—" Rona starts. "Just tell us. What about Adem?"

"He is gone."

Her frown deepens, her jaw sets, but she does not respond.

Avi leans in to Helda and whispers to her. The side of Helda's mouth twitches, fighting back a grin.

"Adem. The Forger drove him away." I repeat. "He is gone."

I thrust the necklace out in front of me, its chain dropping down and dangling over the sides of my hand. Its emerald jewel glistens, rough and unpolished but still gleaming; its power quivers through the thin wrap of fabric and into my palm. The others pull away in response, and their cringe satisfies the hunger in me for their deference.

Rona's frown deepens, then fades, as if she has become lost in thought. She presses her lips together.

"Maybe it is for the best," she says.

"How can you say that?" I demand. How can she turn against him so easily, after everything? "I do not pretend to understand what is going on between you two, but do not pretend now that you do not care about him, on some level. Not now when he needs us."

Rona's cheeks flush bright, and I know I have gone too far by putting words to the strange tension between them. "How can you not say this is for the best?" she bites back. "After what we saw the Forger do to him yesterday? After what he did to Xamson?"

We stand eye to eye and toe to toe, shoulders heaving. Rona backs off first, her gaze dropping away.

"It isn't Adem's fault," she says. "I know that. If he could help it, Adem would hardly have it in him to harm a true enemy."

It surprises me that she is the one who gives in, and I am not prepared for it. When I say nothing, she goes on.

"But he cannot help it. And that makes him a weapon. A powerful one that could be used against us at any moment by someone like the Forger, one we do not know how to stop. What I might feel about him does not matter—he is a danger to everyone here, most of all to those of us who trust him."

She looks down, allowing her hair to drop over her face, and I am sure it is to hide her expression so it cannot betray her resolve.

"We are only lucky he cares about us enough to leave on his own, and before the Forger used him to destroy us all in our sleep. Gods alone know why he hasn't already."

She uses truths as ruthlessly as her blades, and they cut even deeper. I have no arguments against her point, though deep in my core I feel them to be wrong.

"We need to get him back," I say. I hear the petulance in my voice but I cannot help it. I feel as much the insolent, lost child as I sound.

"You have got to be kidding me," Helda mutters.

Rona ignores her and puts a hand on my shoulder. "We will. But we have to do it right. We must be sure he is no longer under the Forger's power. We have to destroy him like we destroyed Koreh. Then."

I bite my lip to keep myself from continuing to fire at her—my words will not be enough for me, not on this one. I need to think. I need a plan I can bring to Rona and the rest of the council that will get Adem back as quickly as possible.

"Why are we so sure he didn't go right to the Forger?" Avi cuts in.

I whip around on him, fists quivering. "What exactly are you implying?"

"The Forger is his maker, right? Why wouldn't he go to him? Where else would there be for him to go?"

Rage sizzles under my skin and my jaw clenches. But before I can put it to use, Calipher jolts to attention, shifting his gaze past me.

"What is he doing here?" he snaps.

I whip around with the others to find Nissa at the cave's mouth, and Bastus alongside her. Bastus' ice-blue eyes are already answering Calipher's anger with a chilling glare

"We agreed when we started this Council," Nissa says. "A representative for every population among us. We have a demon now, so he should be represented."

"I chose myself as my representative," Bastus says, flashing a hard grin Calipher's way.

Their auras butt up against each other in a battle between chaos and still-ness. Nissa's own spritely aura amplifies the tension, until she stretches out her hand and suppresses it with a wave of calm.

"What if more demons come? What then, they must all accept Bastus as their representative because he got here first?" Calipher snarls.

Nissa opens her mouth to speak, but Bastus cuts her off. "We will hold a vote to see which represents us."

"A population of one does not merit equal representation," Calipher rants.

Rona speaks over their squabble. "With Adem gone, Bastus is the only one of us with prior experience with the Forger. He stays."

We are losing focus.

"Speaking of the Forger, when will we head out to destroy him? What are we waiting for?"

Everyone turns to me and stares.

"We have to get Adem back!" I repeat.

Rona shifts, looking away. "Adem doesn't need us to worry about him. Remember what he is. What he needs is for us to protect ourselves, so he is not forced to do anything he could never forgive himself for. Do not put him in that position by hunting him down, Jordan."

It isn't the truth of what she says that breaks me, but the careless way she tosses it, as if this holds no consequence. A primal burst of feeling pulses over me, and I do not want to think anymore. I want to slam and hit and shove.

I settle for shouting. "So you suggest we do nothing?"

"What is there to do?" Avi mutters. "He made his choice. Let him."

"Have you even stopped to ask why you want to take action so badly?" Calipher's wings ruffle. "This is war. Bad things happen. We cannot go around playing the hero every time. Sometimes, you have to let things go."

My emotions bubble and boil with simmering rage. "Things happen? Adem is no thing. He is a person, he is one of us. We do not leave him stranded with some crazed sorcerer from the Underworld."

"But...he isn't a person," Avi scoffs.

The others shift away from him, but no one speaks up. A stupid grin lingers on his lips.

"What did you say?" I snap, striding across our circle to get right in his face. I want to shove him. I want to knock him to the ground and kick him until he curls into a ball and whimpers.

More than any of the others, Avi's continued little betrayals burn through me. When he and Helda tried to overthrow me as Haven's leader, Helda was simply following her nature, like a scorpion who stings. But Avi—we grew up as brothers. And he grew up with Adem as much as I did. Though they were not close like Adem and I, he grew up under his guarding eyes, too.

"Stop, Jordan. It is for the best. For now." Rona folds her arms and looks to the ground. "Adem is going to have to wait."

Her words are stiff, but forceful. "Right now, we have too many other things we are responsible for. We have to train the new soldiers who keep finding us, we have to make room for them in Haven, and the Firsts, too—there are more of them every day, in case you had not noticed, and we do not need them wandering around chatting. We need their help protecting this place and preparing for the next battle. An army. We have to be ready for when the Brotherhood returns. We have to be ready for that Godsdamned Forger, or anything else from the Underworld that might come back here again for another attack. That is what we need, Jordan. Not a chthonus."

Her lip is quivering. Is she going to cry? I am so angry I choose not to care.

I straighten, letting the anger settle over me like armor.

"What if he is not as invincible as you think he is?" I press. "You all saw what the Forger did. How powerful he is. And he is from the Underworld—am I the only one who remembers that Adem was vulnerable in the Underworld? Adem is strong and he may seem invincible, but he can die."

"Is it really—" Calipher starts to respond, then cuts himself off and glances at me.

A tension ripples over me as every muscle in my body tightens. "Go ahead. Say it, Calipher. Say it."

Calipher sighs. "Would it be fair to call it dying? Death is when a soul passes on to the next realm. Adem has no soul."

The helpless anger bursts inside me like an explosion. "I cannot believe you. All of you. After all we have been through together."

"Jordan..." Rona reaches out. As if she could console me after that.

"No. If you refuse to do something about this, I will do it on my own." I turn to storm away.

"And what exactly do you intend to do?" Rona shouts after me.

"I do not know yet," I snap, my heart pounding with rage. "But I have to do something."

Then I turn and storm away.

"What about the Forger?" Rona calls after me. "What about us?"

I do not bother to answer. They made their choice when they ousted me as their leader. They can deal with the other problems on their own. I will look out for the only one left who has not turned against me in some way.

If the rest of them don't care about Adem, getting him back is up to me.

Chapter Ten

I SLAM THE DOOR of my hut behind me, craving the quiet to clear my head. I shut my eyes tight and lean against it, exhaling slowly.

"What has you so angry?"

Xamson sits on the cot, tense and pulled in. From his posture it is clear we are still at odds after our fight yesterday. All the same, he seems concerned, eyes lingering on my face.

Where to even start. My rage combusts in crackling sparks under my skin.

"The Council."

"What about them?" he prompts. He is used to my brevity in anger now.

"They—" I cut myself off, realizing it will only make our fight worse. But then, how much more strained can things get between us? "Adem is gone. They refuse to do anything about it."

Xamson slumps, somehow losing some of his majestic height. "I should have known. You do not become so upset over other things. That chthonus is a problem that never goes away."

"It's not his fault," I lash back.

"Fault? You think this is about fault?" Xamson says, his voice erupting to a volume that makes the straw thatching the roof quiver. "It's too bad that cracked-up angel who sent him to the Underworld used him so terribly. It really is. But sometimes I wish he had been trapped in the Underworld forever, with all the horror that he brought back with him to this realm."

You mean you wish he was dead—he would need a soul for that, I almost shout back at him, remembering Calipher's cold words at Council. That is half the problem in the first place.

But suddenly it all clicks together in my mind. I gasp. I know how to save Adem.

Xamson's hands fly up to cover his mouth.

"I did not mean—I only meant—if he had not broken back through the realms, the war wouldn't have started." His hand balls into a half-hearted fist and drops to his side in forfeit. "All of this...it is making me someone I do not want to be. This is not working."

"Wh-what?" The excitement of my new idea, the possibility of saving Adem from all of this, and for good, is still whirring through my mind, and Xamson's twist to the conversation is too abrupt to understand. Something within me flickers.

"No—you are right," I say. All my anger has receded, suddenly ignited with this idea. "If Adem could die none of this would be a problem. The Forger could not do anything to him. He needs to be human."

"Jordan?" Xamson says, cautious. "Did you hear me? This is not working anymore. Us."

"You are worn down. Even if Bastus healed you, you were almost choked to death only yesterday. And then the battle, and Helda's drills—you need to rest. This will all be better with some rest."

Xamson shuts his eyes and shakes his head like a shudder. He comes close and places a hand on my arm to stop my chatter. "I mean it, Jordan." His expression is pained and serious.

My heart sinks slowly in my chest. I look down to our entwined hands.

"Tell me, Xamson." I do not want him to say it, but I need him to. Now that it has started, I need it to be done.

"You know. You feel it too."

"No. I need you to tell me." I will not make this easy for him. I need to hear him say the words. Because I can guess what he is about to say, but it makes it no easier to understand.

"Look at us," Xamson says. "This isn't working. I don't know what happened to us, but..." He rubs at his eye. "All this back and forth, the hot and cold, the fighting, it is giving me whiplash. Perhaps too much has happened. But I am not what you need right now, and you are not what I need. What you need is to figure out who you are. What you need is space. So...I am giving it to you."

"Xamson—no. I need you. That is what I need. I...I love you."

I hear the hesitation in my voice. Even I am not sure if what I am saying is true. I am not sure I know anything about what I need anymore. But I know I don't want to be without him.

He shakes his head. "No. Ever since Ir-Nearch fell and we came to Haven, this has not been good. Come on, Jordan. You know this as well as I do."

I do. But that does not mean I want it.

"No. Stay." I tighten my hold on his hand, but it only makes him pull away.

"If it were only that, maybe I would. Maybe we could fight through it and it would be okay again. But it is not. You know it is not."

"What else?" I ask. Now empty, my hands tighten into fists, and I am afraid of what else he will say.

"This war, it is changing all of us. And Jordan, it has taken something from you. I do not know why you insist on performing these extreme heroics, but it has to stop. You are slipping away, lost in some contorted idea of what you think you were supposed to be."

"What?" All I have ever done is what is needed. "Tell me what you need from me, Xamson. I can be that for you."

Xamson shakes his head. "What do you need? I do not think you know."

"But..."

I cannot lose him. Adem has left. The Council has turned against me. Xamson is the last thing I have.

But perhaps part of me knows he is right, and I am no good for him right now, because I reach for the words that have always served me so well, always won me favor with him and anyone I have come across, and there are none there.

A thought nudges at me from the back of my mind. The necklace could solve this for me. If I would only unwrap it from the folded cloth in my pocket and place it around my neck, its power would be enough to keep Xamson with me forever. My fingers itch for it, but then I shake myself free of its lure. I would have to be mad to let it bend my will and wear it.

So instead I reach my hand out, as if to keep him from going. He takes it and gives it a gentle squeeze. Then he lets go.

"Where will you go?" I ask, a final, feeble attempt.

He gives me a weak smile. "The tents at the shore have been good enough for the others. It will be fine for me, too."

"No, you stay, let me—" I start.

Xamson shakes his head. "Gods, Jordan, this is exactly what I am talking about. That is ridiculous. This hut has been yours since you were a boy. Stop trying to save me, I do not need saving. I will be fine in a tent. All my friends from Ir-Nearch are out there anyway."

Then he gathers his pack off the ground and leaves. This room, which has felt so tight and small these past weeks, suddenly feels like too much.

But I cannot dwell on this now—Adem needs me. Xamson just gave me an idea of how to save him, and I let the thrill of its potential drown my sadness.

Chapter Eleven

Word of what happened with the Forger spreads through Haven, and by nightfall the air is full of crackling embers of biting truths. We thought our defeat over Koreh would earn us more time. But war offers no reprieves.

"What are you doing out so late?" Calipher asks as I approach. His glowing figure against the dark sky made him easy to spot. He has taken over Adem's spot at the bluff for the night's watch.

I skip over the pleasantries. I have waited all day to ask him certain questions without the prying of others around us. "Let's say I were going to make a soul. How would I do it?"

The angel's dark, glossy wings bristle, catching moonlight. "Let's say you don't." He turns away toward the Wasteland.

But I will not give up so easily. This is the answer, the way to save Adem, I am sure of it.

I try again. "This is important. How would you do it?"

When Calipher turns back to me, his pale marble face is darkened with a snarl.

"How can you possibly consider dealing in such dark magic, with all the consequences we have seen come of it? Have you not learned your lesson by now? I know you have seen what an attempt to make a soul looks like. I have heard the rumors of what came out when you opened Kythiel's jar. And you have seen the fallout of dark magic. This is exactly how we got into this war."

"Dark magic? That's not what I am looking for," I say. "What if I wanted a real one? Souls are of the Gods, they are not a corruption."

"And they are for the Gods alone to create," he snaps back. "It is not something for men to deal in. Or First Creatures, even. Can't you leave well enough alone? Maybe if we had all done that from the beginning, we would not be in this mess now."

I shuffle my feet and look down at them. The imprint where Adem left the necklace, its tidy spiral of chain, still rests in the sand, and the weight of the emerald sits heavy in my pocket. It brings my mind back to Calipher's own dalliance in stolen magic. No wonder he is hesitant—he paid for his last magical sin dearly. It is not anger in his expression, but fear. As I realize this—that he is only too afraid to help—rage burns deep.

"I'm not talking about stealing someone else's soul like what Kythiel did." The image of that terrible blood-smeared jar, the twisted face squished against the glass, the way it gasped and fought to stay in this realm and helplessly faded way, still fills me with a terrible sinking feeling. It was as if it were drowning. "I mean a new soul. A true one."

Calipher raises his eyebrows. "You just might yet manage to save the realm, Jordan. But you cannot save every single creature in it. Let this one go."

He turns away.

"No."

He ignores me.

"Just tell me. Hypothetically. How would such a thing go."

The angel lunges as he twists around, moving so quickly he is a blur of light, and then his hard eyes and sharp teeth are a breath away from my own face.

"Listen to me, human. You have no business meddling in these things. There is no process. There is no hypothetical. No spell. The Gods alone create souls, and they do so at Their own whims. Not yours."

There is a pause as he waits for these words to settle within me. His chest rises and falls rapidly. But he says nothing more.

"So..." I try to think this through. "I need a prophet to beseech them for me?"

"Maybe," he concedes. He talks slowly, as if speaking to a child. "But you would need to find a prophet who can send messages to the Gods instead of only receiving them. I have never seen such a one." Calipher shrugs. Applying logic to it is calming him. "And then they would need to convince the Gods to do what they already decided not to do, and create a soul. For that specific being."

Never have I felt the loss of my connection to the Gods more than now. Before, I would not have had to go to Calipher at all. Back then, reaching the Gods and understanding their will was as easy as breathing. Could I have demanded such a thing of Them then? I do not know, but considering it fills me with an ache for what I have lost. Sometimes I forget that the connection is gone, like a phantom limb, and reach for it—only to find the blunt end of a cliff into nothingness waiting for me.

The Gods have left me, so I will have to find another way to make Them listen. If only I could think of one.

"There is another way to reach the Gods," a new voice cuts in.

I am so startled by the unexpected addition, my first instinct is to reach for my sword before I realize it is coming from within Haven, not the Wasteland, below us at the foot of the bluff. Bastus stares up at us. As he approaches, his demon's aura creeps under my skin, itching with cravings and impulses.

Calipher seems unimpressed, resentful even, and merely purses his lips. "Don't eavesdrop," he snaps. "And don't meddle."

The necklace's whispers creep back into my mind, tinging my mood with jealousy as I remember the way his hands cupped around Xamson's face as he healed him. But my eagerness to get Adem a soul wins out—after all, my troubles with Xamson existed long before Bastus joined us.

"What do you mean?" I prompt.

Bastus glances at Calipher, considering, then continues. "Well. If you need to speak to the Gods, why not go right to Them?"

Calipher lets out a hard, mocking laugh at the suggestion, bristling his wings and resettling them.

But I am not so quick to understand.

"Wait," I say, trying to catch up to the conversation. "Go to Them? Like in a temple?"

We do not have any temples here in Haven—we find the Gods in the nature that surrounds us. Ir-Nearch had temples. But those are burned down now. Epoh had temples. Old ones, rotted and unkempt and boarded up.

"You could try it, but that is not what I meant. Temples are more for men than the Gods," Bastus replies. His piercing blue eyes strike me. "I mean you need to go to Them. In person."

I frown, trying to understand. And then in a burst it comes to me. But no—he could not possibly mean that. Could he?

"Are you suggesting I go to the Host?"

Bastus shrugs in affirmation.

My chest twinges with excitement and fear. "Is it possible?"

"It is sacrilege" Calipher says.

The idea sinks in, and a laugh bursts from me. Break into the Gods' own realm? Surely not.

"What is so funny?" Bastus looks at me, head tilted

"Sorry," I say. "Only, you make it sound so easy. As if we could knock on the door and They will let us in, and we will drink together."

Bastus shakes his head. "Simple, yes. But easy? Oh no. Far from it."

"Impossible," Calipher corrects. "If I remember right, you used to have a strong inclination for the Gods' Order. What happened to all that? It would actually be useful right now."

"That was less to do with the Order," he smirks, "and more because you were just bad for her."

Calipher's nostrils flare and his eyes light with outrage. Bastus steps back, adding a concession. "A lot has happened since then. The Order the Gods set, I do not know about it so much anymore. Nothing is what it was in the Beginning, including me. Are you?"

Calipher narrows his eyes, but he lets it go.

"Besides, this is not impossible," Bastus says calmly. "Hard. Unlikely. Dangerous. But not impossible."

The more I think on it, the more Bastus' idea sweeps me up like dust in a windstorm.

"Bastus is right," I say. "It has to be possible. The rebels crossed between realms to be here in Terath. And so did Adem and Rona."

"That is the Underworld," Calipher says. "This is the Host. It is a different thing entirely."

"The details, perhaps. But not the principle." Bastus replies.

Thoughts are still swarming me. Perhaps it is Bastus' aura, but whatever it is, it is shaking ideas loose, making me hungrier, more confident. "Calipher, you had to cross over from the Host at some point, too. The Host is your home."

"That was different," Calipher argues. "The Gods banished me here Themselves, and in those days, I already spent most of my time in Terath anyway."

"And how did you cross between the two?"

"I passed between them at the will of my Goddess, as we all did. Everything was by the Gods' will in those days. It was a simpler time."

He bows his head and looks down to the sand.

"But still. Why would it work for one realm and not the other?" I push. "There has to be a way. There just has to be."

"The Texts do not agree with you, either, Calipher," Bastus adds.

The Texts? Was there something about getting into the Host in the Gods' holy book? I ravage my memory for the passages, wishing I was carrying my old weathered copy.

Calipher huffs, his wings spreading. He has had enough. "Go away, Bastus. Your meddling is not wanted here. As ever."

Bastes shrugs. "If you say so." Then he breaks into shadow and whooshes away.

But the spark of this idea has already caught in my mind, and my thoughts are alight with hope and a buzz of half-formed ideas.

Out of places to be and in need of space to think, I return to my hut. When I open the door, I almost think I have gone to the wrong one—it is hauntingly empty, with all of Xamson's things removed.

He is really gone.

I wonder how he is faring in his new tent. If I were to go to him now and plead with him to come back to our bed, our room, would he? But that is nothing but wishful thinking. I will not win Xamson back with comforts. I will need to prove myself. How, exactly, I do not understand, but I will find a way.

For now, all I can do is search the Texts for the hints I am missing. I sit on the edge of my cot and stare at the empty space opposite me that Xamson used to fill.

CHAPTER TWELVE

I MUST HAVE DRIFTED to sleep while I wrestled with my thoughts, because I wake up to light creeping into my hut. The haunting image of the Forger again looms in the aftermath of my dreams, but I sit up and fight free from drowsiness. As I do, all the pieces Calipher and Bastus gave me last night settle into place.

I bolt to my feet and grab the Texts off the floor.

Suddenly, I have a plan. Or at least, I think I do—but I still have questions. New ones.

I grab my old copy of the Texts and burst out the door, still tying my robe with the bound book tucked under my elbow. I scan the village for Calipher. He has left his post guarding against the Wasteland and its creatures, a sprite now there in his place. I find him instead at morning prayers, meditating among the others. He must hear me approach, because he cracks one eye open to peek at me.

"You again," he says, His lips press into a thin, irritated line.

"I've been thinking," I say.

"You changed your mind then?" he says.

"I have a question. Well. A favor."

"Oh good. Finally I can pay you back for all the times you helped me." He bristles.

He has a point. Through all of this he has done nothing but help. He has already saved my life once against Koreh.

"Why do you waste so much time on this chthonus?" he says, pushing up off the ground to tower over me. "We should be focused on destroying the necklace. That is the root of all this."

Of course he feels this way. The necklace, after all, is a physical manifestation of the sins that have kept Calipher out of the Host all these ages. I have not forgotten it. It nestles against my side in my pocket even now. But I have no idea where to begin to destroy it for him, though it has been at the forefront of all our minds since Koreh used it against us. But this—Adem, a soul—this I can do something about.

I think.

I need to do something about it. He is my friend, Haven's friend, and we owe him for all he has done.

Persuading people is something I am good at. Usually, I am pleasant and charismatic. Usually, people listen to me. But whatever I had that enabled me to do this, I seem to have lost it lately, along with everything else.

Calipher has already settled back onto the ground and closed his eyes again.

I clear my throat, letting him know I am still there.

His wings twitch. "What is it you want?"

I take a deep breath. "I want you to take me to the Host."

Something between a scoff and a laugh bursts from him. "The demon got in your head more than I expected."

"Bastus was right. The Texts speak of a climb to ascension," I say, pulling out the Texts and flipping through the pages for the passage. "I didn't think of it at first because I always assumed it was metaphor, but what if it isn't? The ascension goes up a mountain—Mt. Analypsi. Our greatest heroes have made this climb. They have seen the Gods with their own eyes. Face to face. If the stories of Mt. Analypsi are too, then the mountain must be real. And there must be a way to get to it."

Calipher raises his eyebrows. "So you are one of Terath's greatest heroes now?"

I was supposed to be.

I look away. "That is not the point. The point is, this has been done before. It's in the Texts. So much of the Texts has already proven to be more than story. I think this could work. I even think I can figure out where this Mt. Analypsi is."

I pull out the Texts and flip through it until I find the passage. "See? It's right here—"

"I do not need to see. I know it," he says.

Of course he does. But my heart pounds with excitement, and I cannot help but run my eyes over the familiar lines anyway, still unable to believe the new information I am seeing in them for the first time. "In the great beyond, in the nothingness between man and the unending seas, they found the mountain with no tip extending into the skies."

The gateway to the Host. It's out in the Wasteland.

Calipher is all determination, fists closed tight, eyes hard, mouth set. But my plan is simple, and I cannot leave it pent up in my head any longer.

"All magic has a trace, right? We'll track down Mt. Analypsi from its trace. We'll climb it. We'll appeal to the Gods for a soul. I'll bring it back to Adem, and I'll make him human. And then the Forger will never be able to lay claim to him again. Nor anyone else, either."

Calipher stares at me with a coldness that could shatter glass. "You should not meddle with what you could not possibly understand."

"I have no choice. Not if the rest of Haven insists on turning their backs on Adem." I level my gaze to meet his glare, until finally he blinks.

"There is always a choice. You do not like the idea of standing still instead of taking action. The idea that perhaps you are not meant to be the one to save the day this time. But you could still choose it."

I stretch my hands out at my sides, a surrender. He's wrong, I tell myself. This isn't about me being the hero. This is about my friend who needs my help, and I will not give up. "Fine, fine. I didn't mean to upset you. I only thought that we could help each other. That if there was a way you could go back to the Host—to go back to your home—that you might want to take it."

His wings ruffle and he bares his teeth in a grimace. "I know exactly what I must do to go home. I must help set this world right again. Until I have done it, there is no point in trying to force my way in, especially not as part of some campaign to break the Gods' Order even more."

"Just..." I start. His wings and the muscles of his back flinch in response to my voice. "Think about it."

"You are the one who has thinking to do," he snaps.

Then he huffs out a hard breath and walks away.

He will come around, I reassure myself. He has to—he is my only hope.

Chapter Thirteen

"Calipher says you have gotten it in your head that you are going to break into the Host."

I look up from my dinner bowl of fish and grains. Xamson is towering over where I sit, the sun blinking its last stretch of the day over the sea behind him. His hands are on his hips and his brows are pulled down, forcing a deep line in his forehead.

It has only been a day since we parted ways, but seeing him kicks up whirlwind of emotion. It is good to see him. And it hurts. It tugs at my heart, so I look away again and focus instead on my bowl.

"And Calipher would not help me. Don't worry about it. It isn't your problem."

I look back down to my food and scoop another bite. Even before Xamson and all of Ir-Nearch came to live at Haven, these ideas and adventures of mine were a sore spot between us. Surely now that he has left me, I don't have to listen to this anymore.

Part of me wants to stir up the flames from the embers, argue with him for as long as he will let me. But I know there is no point. It won't make him come back to me—if anything, it would probably make things worse between us.

His fingers tap against his leg, the way he always does when he gets irritated.

"Forget it? Don't give me that. I know you, and you are not about to forget this. And you are not going on this foolish quest alone. I'm coming with you."

"What?" It is so far from what I expect him to say, in such contrast with the sharpness of his tone, that I look up at him before I can remember I do not want to.

He rolls his eyes. "We both know you've already made up your mind to do this. And if you are going, I am going. With all that is going on in the realm these days, Gods know what could happen to someone out there on their own."

Xamson stares at me with burning heat in his eyes, and I stare back, unsure of what to do, my emotions tugging in opposing directions.

I want to shove him, tell him that if he wants to be free he is free, and he has no right to worry about me anymore. I want to leap up, wrap my arms around him and squeeze him tight. I want to tell him I am not worth it, that he should not let himself get dragged down into yet another foolish adventure with me, that he is too good for it.

I do not do any of those things.

I say the stupid thing. The petty thing. "Why? You don't think I am enough of a warrior to make it on my own?"

Xamson only laughs. "Of course you are. But the only thing worse than going off on this insane quest is doing it all alone. I'm coming."

What is the point in fighting it? Especially when I so badly want him with me. Perhaps I can figure out a way to win him back along the way. It is no wonder he left me. I don't deserve him.

"Fine," I concede.

A broad smile stretches over Xamson's face, and it lights up everything about him. My heart melts. Even if no good comes of him coming with me, this alone was worth it.

"Me, too. I'll come."

Bastus steps forward next to Xamson, cutting into our little moment.

I think back on my churning emotions—was it Bastus' aura? Has he been listening this entire time? I did not see him, but a demon could have hidden himself a thousand ways. I am starting to understand why they are so widely mistrusted.

I look to Xamson, searching his eyes for his thoughts. Xamson pulls his shoulders up and tilts his head. If Calipher does not change his mind, having another First with us could be valuable. But then, can a demon be of any use in reaching the Host? Calipher didn't think so. And while having a new, unknown, self-proclaimed ally in Haven is one thing, I do not think I know Bastus well enough yet to trust him with my life alone in the Wasteland. Even if he can be trusted, if he is with me, he is not in Haven helping to protect its people. There are too many ways for things to go wrong.

Besides, I do not like the way his eyes run up and down Xamson, the way he leans into him when he speaks. Each time he does it, my mind drifts back to the gentle way his hands cupped around Xamson's neck when he healed him yesterday.

No. Definitely no.

"I thought Calipher already settled this," I say.

"I thought Calipher was not willing to help you," he replies. "I am."

"He will come around," I say. I wish I felt the confidence my voice projects.

"But not if you are part of it. Besides, he is right. We do not know you yet. Not really."

I know the words will cut, but even so, the pained expression on Bastus' face makes guilt cloud around me like a fog.

"And what do you say?" Bastus prompts, turning to Xamson.

"I say..." Xamson glances to me, then shuts his eyes. "This is not my quest, not my choice to make."

Bastus bows his head, nodding in concession. He breaks away into shadow and whooshes off without another word.

For a pause, I stare at where he stood and the unsettled buzz of his aura fades away. Perhaps I am being unfair. Perhaps I should bring him just to keep an eye on him, keep him away from Haven's people. But it is too late now. Xamson is still standing next to me, waiting to settle this.

"What are you going to tell Calipher?" I ask.

He shrugs. "I don't know. Nothing, if I can help it."

I grin.

"Who else did he tell about this, besides you?" I ask.

Xamson looks out over the people in the distance. "No one for now, that I know of. I am sure if he hears I haven't managed to talk you out of it, he will tell more of them. Rona, maybe."

I consider, remembering the anger in Calipher's eyes as he tried to persuade me to back down.

"Then if anyone asks, I'm reconsidering."

Xamson nods. He knows it is no use trying to stop me, that as soon as I had the idea it was as good as done. No need to have a scene over it, as the others try. He knows if I had to, I would simply go, and leave him behind in the process.

I finish my food and stand up.

"I have preparations to manage. If you really want to join me, I am leaving at midnight," I say.

I try to be casual and aloof as I get up, but I cannot help it—as I walk away from him, a smile spreads across my lips.

But there is still too much unknown about this for me to start getting distracted now. The stakes are too high. Having Xamson along only increases the risk, because now it is not just my own life on the line, not just Adem's fate, but also the person I love the most in this world.

Midnight comes as fast as a blink. The night air is hot and thick with moisture, pressing against my skin. The sky is covered in a thick paste of cloud.

"Ready?" I whisper.

I shift my stuffed pack on my shoulder, giving myself an excuse to stop short of where Xamson stands. He may insist on coming along on this crazy quest, but as I gathered supplies, I spent the afternoon reminding myself that all the reasons he left me are still there. Gods, this is exactly why he left me. Heroics. All the running around trying to save everyone else.

"Let's go," he says.

We pass through the rows of huts as quietly as we can.

Clouds blot out the moon to an obscured halo, making the night dark. The promise of rain is thick in the air, along with something else. Magic. It crackles and bites against my skin like static. Something big is building.

We get past the huts and up to the bluff, but then a voice cuts the silence from behind us.

"Wait!"

My first instinct is to panic, thinking the others are trying to stop us. But it is not Rona or any of the others—it is Calipher. And he's running. I have not seen him run before, even in battle. I don't know that I have seen any First Creature run before. For the first time, the angel does not seem so intimidating.

"Wait, I'm coming with you," he calls out again.

I stop and wait for him to catch up before responding, to keep from making any more noise than necessary.

"But you wanted to stop me."

He slows as he reaches us and refolds his wings. "Not anymore."

"But—" It doesn't add up. A nagging buzz of suspicion itches under my skin. I press him. "What changed your mind?"

His head droops and he glances down, taking a deep breath.

"Thinking about the Host is...hard. I cannot tell you what it has been like, being cast out for so long. It is more than a homesickness. Like a hole that cannot heal. The idea that, when I had been cast out for so many ages, you were just going to walk in uninvited...but then it made me think. It would be nice to be back again. Even if Theia will not allow me to stay. Even if it is only for a little while. It would be better than nothing."

His anxiety draws mine out, too—an uncomfortable hunger that urges me back to focus. But this is no time for nerves.

"How do I know you won't try to sabotage us?" I challenge.

He glares at me. "You wanted me to come."

"You said you needed to stay here and figure out how to destroy the necklace."

He shakes his head. "You were right. We do need to destroy the necklace. But Adem is our only hope to protect it until we do—and Gods know how long it might take. If we can get him back, we should."

I look to Xamson. He hesitates, biting his lip, but then he nods.

"Then let's break into the Host," I say.

I take a step forward into the lead, shut my eyes tight and try to summon a trace of magic to lead us.

A faint breeze rustles the night, and my skin tingles in response, hungering for a hint of the magical flow of the realm that used to seep into me, flow through me so easily.

I turn and take another step, moving north. "This way," I call out.

Calipher releases a dismissive chuckle. "To Mount Analypsi? No, this way," he says, starting to the west, deeper into the Wasteland instead of up the coast. "Maybe I had better lead."

Heat floods my face and burns through my cheeks. I pause a moment, staring down to the sand. No matter how well I understand that my connection to the Gods and the magic of this realm is gone, every reminder of what I have lost burns just as deeply. I take a breath and will the feeling to pass.

Xamson pauses, and I feel his eyes on me.

"I guess you don't have to come now. Calipher will watch over me," I say. Releasing Xamson of his promise makes me feel hollow, but if Calipher is coming, everything is different now. I am not worth it.

"Are you kidding me?" he replies. "Every night you're gone, I'd be lying awake wondering if you two finally murdered each other out in the Wasteland."

He turns to follow Calipher.

I take a breath, relieved, and follow after them.

We march off together into the Wasteland, a failed Chosen one, a fallen angel, and a warrior who will not let two fools wander off to the edge of the realm alone.

CHAPTER
FOURTEEN

WE WALK THROUGH THE night and through all the next day, leaving Haven far behind us. By the time anyone else realizes we have left, we will not even be a speck on the horizon.

The Wasteland is as devastated as ever, all bleak destruction and haunted emptiness. The ground is hardened and crackled with thirst, no matter how much rain accosts us these days. It is a reminder of all we have still to lose in this war if we are not ready for it, if we are not strong enough to bring this war to an end.

The Wasteland has been like this longer than any man living could remember, or anyone who anyone alive now has ever known. Generations. Only the Firsts have any understanding of what this realm was like before the wars. Their stories of lush growth and peaceful coexistence are almost as grand as how the Texts describe the Beginning, feel almost as impossible. Did this realm truly ever possess such effortless harmony? If we were to win this war, if we somehow find a way, could it ever return to that again?

By the second day I have handed over the pack of food and water to Calipher. "Here," I say.

He frowns at it, as if puzzled.

"So you can charm the food supply so it won't run out," I prompt. "Like you did last time."

His frown deepens for a pause, but then he quickly brightens. "Of course! Of course."

The darkwolves are more than howls out here—their shadows lurk at the horizon at dusk, and their snarls always feel just over my shoulder. Strange shapes and sounds warn that other terrible creatures wander its desert as well. The humidity rises with a heavy anticipation of looming pressure.

Each night, my dreams are restless, tinged with a hunger I cannot define and dark shapes that both call and repel me. Beyond the dark, something calls me, something with a turbulent, throbbing power, a power I want to possess and own. The Forger's voice looms through it, murmuring and fevered as if casting spells.

On the third day, a familiar and unwelcome shape emerges on the horizon. It is one that I never thought I would have to face again: The walls that hold in the city of Epoh.

As we near, it becomes clear that something has gone wrong—even more wrong than the Epoh I knew as a boy.

The walls are crumbled and knocked to the ground in some parts. The great stones that built them have been felled and shattered into the city towers and streets, as if something from the Wasteland had forced its way in. All those years the dictator Zevach trapped us within that place in the name of protection from the outside, and in the end it was all a lie anyway.

We pass right next to the wall, and I can almost hear the tap-tap-tap of the Silencers' boots even now, as they lurked through the streets guarding us in the king's name, stirring up more trouble than they stopped. A chill shoots through me despite the beating sun.

"Ash," Xamson says, pointing.

I follow his gesture, and he's right. All through the streets and spattered against what's left of the tower walls, the city is darkened with ash.

"It's just like Ir-Nearch," I reply.

The very same scenes, another city with very different kinds of memories. I can still smell the singe of Ir-Nearch burning to the ground after Koreh's attack, the sharp tang of blood, as if it were fresh. It turns my stomach. The rebels have been here.

I have no love lost for Epoh's ruthless dictator and his army who were destroyed in this fight, but what happened to the thousands of innocents who

Zevach held under his rule here? How much more destruction have the rebels already wrought elsewhere across the realm?

People like my mother, my sister, who so stubbornly persisted under the grimmest terms that life can serve up, day after day, surviving on will and hope.

I try to push my mind to happy times, but they are too far away, and my mind will not stay there. Instead, I keep flashing to the day the ash soldiers burned Ir-Nearch to the ground. The day we knew the Third Realm War had reached Terath, and nothing could continue on like it had before. The realm had always been troubled, but looking back, I wish I had understood then how relatively simple we had it—how well we had carved out our corner of happiness within this dark realm.

Xamson stares at the wreckage too, his expression pained. I fight the urge to wrap an arm around him.

"Better times," I say.

I hardly know if I mean in general, or specifically for the two of us, a retrospect to the past or a hope for the future. It doesn't matter, really.

"Better times," he agrees.

But the words feel hollow in the midst of such destruction. Are we fools to go on this quest? Are the Gods even still out there to be found? Am I lying to myself to think our small choices in this matter at all, that we have any kind of chance against the rebels? From here among the destruction, I feel as small and insignificant as I ever have.

"We have much farther to go," Calipher urges.

His voice breaks the hold the wreckage has over us, and I discover that in my concentration, somehow Xamson's hand and mine have entwined. With a jolt, Xamson pulls away.

But as I start to turn to go, a dark figure emerges, crossing the walkway at the top of Epoh's wall, between the towers. A spindly man with a winding walking stick, the hood of his deep blue cloak pulled low over his head.

Alarm stings from my fingertips all the way into my chest. It is the Forger. What is he doing here?

"Look." I breathe out the word so quietly I can barely hear my own voice over the pounding of my heart. But Xamson and Calipher catch it.

They turn, following my gaze. Xamson breathes in a gasp. His muscles ripple as he tenses with rage. Calipher takes a step closer, eyes squinting from strain. Or maybe it is disbelief.

We watch without a word as the Forger makes his way to the tower at the far side of the wall segment. As he approaches, a rose-gold angel emerges from it, and they stop and speak together. Then the angel points in our direction, and they look right at us.

Suddenly I am overcome with a chill of dread. Yet something calls to me, a lure like I should run toward them. Tranced, like the unsettled dreams I keep having, laced with the shuddering dread I felt when he thrust his curse at me in our last encounter. What is this strange lure that keeps tugging me toward him in my dreams? What has he done to me?

With the Forger so close, the necklace strains for him, pleads for him, remembering the power he unleashed from it. I realize that my hand has reached into my pocket and wrapped around the chain. Heat rushes over my cheeks, I slowly untangle my fingers from it and set my hand at my side.

Fear extinguishes my curiosity, but there is nowhere to hide.

"Gods," Xamson exclaims.

The Forger reaches up an arm, then slashes it downward in a deliberate motion.

There is movement below between the crumbled segments of the wall. A figure emerges and stands there, staring out. I do not even have to think to know who it is. My heart seizes. Xamson's hand clenches onto my arm.

How did Adem end up here?

I suppose once he was beyond Haven's protections, it would have been easy for the Forger to sense and summon him. And without the rest of us there to bait and threaten and put on a show for, there would be no reason for the Forger to hold back.

"You want to run in and save him, don't you?" Xamson says.

I clench down my jaw to keep from speaking, because I do. Everything in me wants to shake loose of Xamson's grip, free my sword from its hilt, and do something, anything, to get Adem back, consequences be damned. And that is the worst possible thing I could say to Xamson right now.

But I do not have to say it. He knows. It is written in the knotted muscles of his neck and the twitch of his eye as he steps in front of me to catch my gaze.

Calipher can see it too. He groans and rubs his hand over his golden curls, exasperated.

"Jordan, tell me one thing and I'll charge in there with you this instant," Xamson says. "How?"

I turn to him, frowning.

He continues. "Just tell me how. What plan do you have to win against the Forger? If you can tell me how you think you could possibly win this fight, I'm behind you. Otherwise—please—let's keep going. Finish the plan we have already started. You know it is our best chance."

I wrack my brain, but even with all my years of military training and strategy, I can come up with no plan that is stronger than the sheer force of power the Forger possesses. I look past Xamson to Adem, still a statue at Epoh's edge, and something inside me splits.

Yet again, I am not enough.

"Jordan?" Xamson asks, pulling me back.

Unable to do anything else, I swing out my sword and stab it into the ground between us, then storm past Xamson toward the mountain peak on the horizon.

Behind me, I can hear Xamson tug my sword free again, the blade ringing as it vibrates.

Then the steps start behind me, and we go on.

I cannot believe I am turning away from Adem when he needs me most. But deep down, I know Xamson is right. Our best chance is finish what we have started.

We have to get to the Host. We just have to.

CHAPTER FIFTEEN

IN THE NIGHT, THE swelling clouds finally give way to rain. It drizzles in a mist, never building to a storm, and never relenting. As it continues day after day, the air builds into a thick humid pressure that swells against my skin and makes even the barrenness of the Wasteland feel crowded.

Finally the outline of the mountain on the horizon becomes a great towering thing in front of us. The whites and grays of its stone blur up into the dull sky, stretching up beyond what can be seen.

We peer up at its towering grandeur.

"So this is the mountain with no end?" Xamson says.

Calipher reaches out and squeezes his shoulder. "We are going to make it, I promise."

I fold my arms and fight back the impulse to swat Calipher's hand away from him. Instead I tighten my fists and remind myself the many reasons I have no right to jealousy, and no reason for it. I do not love that Xamson seems to be closer to everyone else than to me, even this prickly angel, but anything else I feel is merely the necklace's work on me, and I have to be stronger than its lure.

"Of course we will," I say. But I cannot help but agree with Xamson's point—the way up the mountain towers over us, rocky and steep, and true to the Text's words, there is no hint of a peak. "But perhaps, first, we should rest. At least until morning. We will start the climb then."

The others agree. Calipher casts a spell to protect us from the wind's debris and keep the smattering of raindrops off us, as he has every night in the Wasteland,. We gather a fire and eat together in quiet.

Under the fire's crackling whispers and flickers of light, my mind stirs with worry. Here we are, presumably at the foot of the Gods' door, and are we really any closer to Them than before? If we are, they are withholding their presence from me. I feel nothing but the chill of the damp night.

Are They up there? I dare not ask.

In the darkness, the restless dreams continue.

They are so vivid they could be visions, so real I could pick up chips of the hard Wasteland earth and put them in my pocket. The Forger's hooded figure is far in the distance, his staff planted into the ground. The clouds build thicker and darker, closing in on us, and lighting strikes, stretching across the sky so bright that for a moment I am blinded.

My skin goes cold in dread and I blink, fighting for my vision back.

When I do, my heart sinks like a stone dropped onto thin ice—the Forger is right in front of me now, his calculating eyes hard and focused, a cold smile spreading slowly over this face, only inches from mine.

He reaches out and grabs my forearm, and the pressure of his boney fingers jolts me awake.

I gasp as shock throws me upright.

"What's wrong?" Calipher asks, turning around to face me.

The night is still. Beyond the shimmer of Calipher's protection charms, the Wasteland is still. My heart pounds so hard I am sure it can be heard for miles.

"Nothing," I say. "Just a dream."

I steady my breaths and lay down to avoid Calipher's watchful gaze and, eventually, I drop into a dark, blank unconsciousness.

When I come to the next morning, the fire is dead and sounds of a struggle fill my ears.

Next to me, Xamson still rests. But outside Calipher's protective shields, the angel's wings are spread tense, the features pulled out of sorts.

I leap to my feet and rush to him, pulling my sword free.

But by the time I reach him, there's nothing to fend against, the only sign of a fight some rolling rocks along the mountain's edge.

"Calipher what's—"

He turns to me, and I lose my words.

He is covered in swollen welts and scratches that run deep and jagged from his face to his broad shoulders and down his arms, drawing smears of his silver blood that mar his robes and stick in his golden hair.

"What happened?" Xamson is up now, too, pushing past me to Calipher's side and studying the silvery blood dripping from the angel's wounds.

"They attacked in the night, after the moon came out," Calipher says. He frowns slowly, still stunned. "There were so many of them."

"What came in the night?" I prompt. I cannot imagine what could do so much damage to a First Creature.

He shakes his head. "It was dark—and the rain—there were so many of them," he repeats. He stares up at the mountain, a wrinkle forming between his brows. "They were dark and stony like the rocks, but they moved so fast."

"You should have woken us," Xamson says. "Why did you not retreat within the protections you cast for us?"

He shakes his head. "They came in a blur, down the mountain, in a rockslide. They swarmed, they pelted at me with stone from all sides...and then they were gone, a blur back up into the mountain."

The first hints of sunlight stretch out over the horizon. I squint against its brightness.

"That was it?" I frown. "What would attack like that and not take us down while they had the chance? Why would they retreat?"

I study the welts over his face, swelling one eye half shut and pushing his perfect nose out of place.

"Will you be all right?" I ask.

Calipher arcs his head back and stretches out his wings. A burst of shadow envelops him, and when it is gone, he is healed. "Good as new."

I turn and begin the work of packing up the campsite. Calipher joins me, but Xamson continues to stand, arms folded.

"They were warning us," he says. "It's the only explanation. Why else would they retreat when they had us at their mercy?" Xamson asks. "Is no one going to say it? I will, then. We need to turn back."

I finish rolling my equipment into my pack, and stand to face him.

"We made it all this way. We found Mount Analypsi," I say. "I am not turning back now."

Xamson's eyes widen in outrage. "Don't you see it? The Gods are telling us not to meddle in this."

"The Gods?" Rage explodes over me. "The Gods are not here. The Gods aren't telling us anything. That's how this all started."

"I thought this started with Adem disappearing." Xamson watches me, arms folded. "Or no—this started with Adem leaving you behind."

I lunge toward him, rage biting down the back of my neck.

"We cannot quit at the first sign of trouble," I say.

Xamson scoffs. "The first sign? You think this is the first sign of trouble? As if wandering the Wasteland wasn't enough, or navigating the threat of darkwolves and other monsters? Or the destruction we witnessed at Epoh? The run-in with the Forger? We have seen nothing but trouble from the start."

My blood turns to burning fire in my veins. "If this is how you feel, you should turn back now. Why did you come at all?"

Xamson holds his ground, his muscles tensing so tightly his shoulders hulk forward.

"I came because someone had to," he says.

"That is ridiculous," I spit back. "Why? Why would someone have to?"

"To protect you from yourself," he snaps.

As soon as he says it, his eyes grow wide and his hands slap over his mouth, as if he could somehow stuff the words back in.

But it is too late. My heart throbs, angry and aching, but I cannot find any words to throw back at him.

"We do not have time for this," Calipher says. "We only have seven nights until the full moon."

"Full moon?" I say.

"Yes—it is the only time we can cross over to the Host. Or we will have to wait until the moon cycle comes around again."

My shoulders tighten, the pressure upon them mounting. I narrow my eyes at him. "Why didn't you mention this before? We should have been pressing on through the nights. We should have—"

I do not know what we could have done, not really. I do not know what difference it would have made.

Calipher's wings twitch. "I thought you knew."

"I did not."

The way Xamson's brows pull together and wrinkle tells me he did not know, either. But his help is the last thing I want right now.

"See," he says. "This is impossible. We should go home."

A helpless anger simmers under my skin.

"All the more reason to get started." I pull away. "You left me, Xamson. I am no longer your problem. Do as you like, but I am going up. My friend needs help, and I will not abandon him, even if that is all everyone else wants to do anymore."

Satisfied with my final dig against him, I turn away, secure my pack over my shoulder, and start the climb. I focus on the rocks in front of me and do not turn back to them. Soon I hear their footsteps grind over the pebbles as they make their way up behind me.

The climb is cumbersome. There are no worn paths for us to follow, and every step of the journey we must forge our own way. We wind back and forth at angles, the mountain too steep and jagged to brave head on. Bouts of rain make the rocks slick. I slip and fall more than once, the pain of bone grinding into rock exploding over my knees.

Seven days.

This is taking too long. We will never make it.

But we make progress all the same, climbing until our muscles ache, our chests heave in strain against the altitude, and then climbing more, until darkness forces us to stop and take cover. Whatever attacked Calipher that first night continues to come for us in the dark. In the absolute darkness of stormy nights, the stars blotted out with clouds, the world a haze beyond Calipher's shield of charms, each night a crackling like shattering stone rises, and blurred figures throw themselves against the barrier over and over.

We do not know where they go in the day.

The realm below grows smaller, starts to seem less real, as if, should we give up and return, we might find it gone. Clouds close in around us and hide it, and I am encased in a feeling that nothing exists except the next step—Up. Up. Up.

As we gain elevation, the wind increases, with sudden bouts of harsh, cold rain. Once we climb past the clouds, we face turns of arid beating sun. The extremes leave our bodies aching and exhausted. The higher we rise, the more urgent it feels that we reach the top, and the tighter my chest becomes. This climb cannot really go on forever—all the stories say they reached the Host at some point, which means this Godsforsaken climb must, indeed, have an end.

And we are running out of time. The moon swells broader each night.

Finally, we stumble onto an opening in the rocks, a flat space with a single tree stretching out of it up into the skies, and no more rock to climb.

We did it. We really did it—we reached the top of Mount Analypsi, the peak of heroes and Gods.

The flat ground beneath my feet feels so foreign, the air so thin in my lungs that I fear my legs might continue to push me onward and right off its edge. I ease to the ground and onto my back to fight the sensation. My breaths heave, my chest expanding and dropping in quick, exaggerated cycles. Xamson collapses to his hands and knees and stretches out next to me. Calipher perches on a large rock near us.

But as my body begins to recover, relief is overtaken with dread. This is not the Host. This is a mountaintop, like any other. I shift uncomfortably, trying to force my worn out mind to make some sort of sense out of this. I am not sure what I expected, exactly—maybe a gate, or gleaming marble steps—but not this. Not more of the same.

Is this all there is?

Staring up at the tree, I almost relent. I almost give up and say we can go back home to Haven. I knew this would be hard. I was not prepared for the impossible.

Not impossible. It has been done before.

I have no choice but to have faith in what is in the Texts.

Faith.

What has happened to my faith? Somewhere in this winding, terrible war I have lost sight of it. I always thought of it as my anchor, something that strengthened me in a way other people did not possess. But in the end, was it so thin that as soon as I could not hear the Gods, I lost it?

Now is not a time for questions. Now is a time for conviction. We have paid too high a price to turn back empty-handed. Failing Adem is not an option, and I will not even think of it.

Xamson sits up. The frown that has become too common on his face sets in again, and as he looks around, I know what he is going to say before he has even finished the words.

"We have seen it now. There is nothing here. There is nothing left but to turn back and return to Haven, where we are needed."

"No." I slam down the word like a gate, firm and definite.

I steel myself and rise to my feet. If other men have done this, there is a way for us to accomplish it, too. There must be something that we cannot see, that we are not understanding yet.

"But Jordan—" Xamson presses.

I cut him off. "We are not in the Host yet," I say. "So we keep going up."

"But we are up," Xamson shouts. His hands run over his head. "This is it."

"Not all the way." I step over and place a hand on one of the tree's thick branches. I raise my eyebrows and look up at it.

"You want to, what, climb the tree? This is madness," Xamson says, teeth grinding. He turns to Calipher. "Tell him. Tell him this is over."

My stomach clenches with a burst of nerves. He did not want to come at first, either, and suddenly I fear this will push him to the edge, too. Besides, he likes Xamson, the necklace whispers. He doesn't like you. I shove its nonsensical urgings aside.

But Calipher shrugs. "The Texts say to continue to ascend. So...we go on ascending until we are in the Host."

Xamson's jaw drops, and he sputters, apparently infuriated beyond words. When he finally finds them, his shoulders tighten up and shrink his long neck. "After you."

"Not yet. Tonight. When the full moon opens the path," Calipher says.

"And when we reach the top to the tree and there is still no Host at the end, then what?" Xamson says.

I take a breath and make myself look him right in the eyes, determined not to let my own fears and doubts show through. "We will find out when we reach the top of the tree."

I sit with Calipher on another of the larger stones, facing East toward the pending moonrise, anxiety buzzing over my skin. Soon, Xamson starts pacing the tight space of the mountain peak, and the tension in the thin air mounts with his every turn.

We wait.

And we wait.

The wait feels like an age. Like a breath drawn in and never let go. Like the building pressure of holding it in will make me burst. Then, slowly but surely, the daylight begins to fade and turn rosy, and darkness tinges the horizon. Then the moon, swollen and bald, settles into its place in the darkening sky.

No one speaks, but we rise and come together at the tree's great trunk in solemn unison. I step up, securing my footing on a knot in the bark, and reach for the first branch. As my fingers wrap around it, as if on cue, the rocks all around the mountain's peak begin to quiver and split, an eerie crackling of their movement filling the air. It is as if some sort of creatures were hatching out of them.

I let go of the tree hoping it will stop whatever I have just started, but it is too late.

Xamson sighs, as if this were inevitable. As if it were expected. As if to say, of course the tree is being guarded. He pulls out his sword.

"Gods help us all," he sighs. "Here we go."

CHAPTER SIXTEEN

As the crackling and rumbling of the rocks magnifies and spreads, I pull my sword out, too.

"What's happening?" I call out over the commotion. The crackling and quivering continues to build, and my mind cannot hold back the thought that the mountain is crumbling to pieces under our feet, and we will tumble all the way back to the earth and be buried among its pieces. But the ground seems to be holding.

"I have no idea," Xamson calls to me, "But whatever it is, I told you so. I told you this was a terrible idea. If this kills us, consider those my official last words. I Godsdamned told you so, Jordan."

A laugh bursts from me in spite of the panic quaking through my limbs. I have missed this rapport we used to hold between us, a camaraderie that seems somehow easier to draw out in these moments of tumult when the world might be ending than when we are together in stillness and peace.

But then I am forced back into the moment by a rise of unsettling snarls—a sound I know too well, one that has haunted us night after night in our ascent.

Dark figures start to creep up the mountain's sides from around us, dark like the stones of the mountain.

"It's them," Calipher says with a gasp. "This is what has been attacking us each night."

I whip around toward it, blade ready to strike. But when I see what we are facing, I hardly see the point.

The rocks roll toward each other on the rumbling ground and pull together, locking into joints and faces until they create monstrous forms.

A lump builds in my throat—what can steel do against stone?

"Keep going," Calipher urges, pushing me back toward the tree. A burst of chaos charges through me at his touch—I must be really wired up for the fight. "In fact, hurry. The best thing we can do is reach the Host as quickly as possible."

Even as he turns to speak to me, a flinty grey blur rushes at him and takes a swipe at his side.

Calipher turns to fight it off. "Go," he shouts, throwing a burst of shadow from his palms toward the creature.

But I do not move—I freeze, arrested as I finally see the creatures for what they are. Thick and bulky, the creatures are short, half the size of a man. They squat down on their legs and lean on their knuckles to propel themselves forward in blurred leaps, quick, but clumsy. Their faces are more shadow than contour, framed in pointed horns, and they growl through bared teeth of jagged rock. Bulky wings of stone branch out behind them, quivering with their roars.

I know what these are: Gargoyles. Guardians of the Gods.

Of course.

Panic pulses through me, but relief warms under the burn of adrenaline, too. Gargoyles' one purpose is to watch over the Gods. If there are gargoyles here, we must be on the right track.

We did it. We really found a way into the Host.

But first we must survive the climb. Our defenses are nothing more than our blades and our determination, and we are already worn down to the last strains of our energy from the climb. Calipher is right—the only hope we have is to continue that climb and break past the gargoyles' reach in the next realm.

My sword in one hand to deflect attacks, I hook my arm over the branch and pull myself into the tree. The gargoyles shriek in rage, and one of them bounds toward us. Xamson swings his sword as it charges, again and again, then while the stone beast stumbles backward he turns and I pull him up into the branches after me.

We climb. We climb as fast as we can.

Near the base where the tree is broadest, the great branches help in our ascent and offer partial cover from the gargoyles' attacks, but as we get higher, the branches turn vine-like, leaving us vulnerable as the gargoyles soar past us, their stony wings navigating the thin air far better than I could have imagined possible.

Over and over my body bursts with pain as rock slams into bone and flesh. Clinging to the vine is our only hope to avoid falling back to the hard mountain below, but it leaves us almost defenseless against the gargoyles' attacks. Xamson's grunts fill my ears as he takes blow after blow below me, and the vine quivers and swings with each hit. We try to deflect their swooping attacks, but the gargoyles do more damage to our blades than we do to them.

Calipher has better luck, rushing through the air in bursts of shadow and casting attack spells at the gargoyles that propel them through the air and send them crashing back to the ground. Bursts of shadow? Calipher's moves nag at the back of my mind, but there is no time to listen to it.

Another gargoyle breaks free from Calipher's guard and slams into me, snaps at me with a ragged underbite of sharp stony teeth. I shove at it with sword and elbows and kicks, everything I can muster without forfeiting the vine. Calipher hits it with a spell and it drops to the open sky below.

Pull, pull, pull—I order my body to keep going, to ignore the way my muscles burn and seize, and do what must be done to make it through.

The gargoyle with the jutting bite comes back, and again and again, slamming into me and biting at my arms and legs. Their mouths are small, but their teeth are sharp, and each bite pierces with throbbing heat. I swing my sword at it but all I do is dent and chip the blade on the hard stone, until finally it breaks from the hilt completely.

I have no choice but to let the blows come and climb. The sounds of the fight swell around me in a rush: hisses and clangs and cracks, the grind of stone on stone.

Then, Xamson gasps.

It is not a gasp of pain, but horror—something has shaken him beyond words. I turn back to see what is wrong, but he is looking up, staring past me. I follow his gaze to my own hands and find my tight grip, my anchor and my lifeline amidst the fight, clings onto nothing. I have ascended past the end of the tree's vine into pure cloud.

My vision tunnels as if observing from outside, and I feel the breath seize in my chest, hear the awful wheezing as my throat tightens in panic. A topsy-turvy vertigo sets in, and suddenly I cannot tell which way is up among the clouds. Only the basest of survival instincts keeps me from losing my grasp on—I know not what.

But then a small voice of reason breaks through the madness overtaking my mind: I am still here. I am still climbing. And whatever I can or cannot see, I am holding onto something. My whole body shaking, I reach up again on nothing but faith—and when I close my fist, my grip holds. I pull myself up, testing it out, then turn back to Xamson.

I shout over the roar of the fight and the wind. "We have to keep going."

He hesitates. The anger is gone from his eyes now, emptied into a fear that makes me want to tell him I'm sorry, tell him he doesn't have to keep going, that we can go back and shut the door to our little hut in Haven, where I will hold him tight and we will never leave again. But we are far past that, in so many ways.

"You can do it, Xamson. Just reach out and hold on."

From the edges of my vision, a gargoyle rounds through the air and swoops back toward us, honing in for his next attack.

"Do it, Xamson. Right now."

He looks up, registering the panic in my voice, then shuts his eyes and reaches into the open sky. His grip finds purchase, just as mine did, and he pulls himself up. He almost has enough time. But as the gargoyle swoops past he rams into Xamson and casts him swinging. His grip loosens.

No!

I reach down and grab Xamson's wrist, hold on as tight as I can. The weight stretches me taut between my shoulders. Our eyes lock. I try not to think about the nothing in my grip that is the only thing that keeps us from tumbling back to the harsh rocks of the mountain.

Xamson groans, but then his expression hardens and he reaches out, again finding his grip in the air.

Keep going.

We do. We have no other choice.

I pull and pull and pull, Xamson on my heels, and we are swallowed in cloud. The cloud grows thick until I can see nothing at all. From the haze, tendrils reach out and brush my skin as we climb, then thicken into vines, then branches. We grab onto them, relieved to have something solid to take hold of again, and draw ourselves into their protection. The gargoyles gnash and snarl, sending splinters flying as they thrash through the branches, and the tree quivers and sways with violent lurches against their fight.

A heart-stopping crack vibrates through the tree, the trunk quivers and splits, and we are thrown from its branches. All I can do is wait as we tumble upward into the blank brightness of cloud. My stomach flips. Up becomes down. We crash into the ground amid shattering branches.

I stumble to my feet, still reeling, and thrust the jagged end of my sword out in front of me, doing my best to be ready for the next attack. No attack comes. Everything is quiet and still, other than my heart pounding in my ears, and as the stillness seeps into me, I pivot around and realize with overwhelming relief that it's over.

We made it.

We are in the Host.

Unnerved and aching, dizzy and disoriented, I collapse.

Then I twist around and peer back at the great tree's wreckage.

Xamson pulls himself through the branches and drops to the ground next to me.

But Calipher is still caught between the realms, struggling against the gargoyles, a mere outline hidden in cloud. He calls out, and darkness bursts from his palms, darting in a rush to the gargoyle. It is thrown backward through the clouds. Calipher uses the opportunity to make his way to us through the tree's branches.

As he races down, the gargoyles chase after him, battering and snapping at the great tree. But they seem unable to pass through with us, as if something at the barrier between the realms holds them back. Their efforts cause the tree—already weakened from the split that runs through its trunk—to sway and thrash, and finally the trunk snaps and crashes to the ground. Leaves and branches fly in all directions.

The pause that follows is deadening, and for a moment I am sure we have lost Calipher. But then a figure rises from the debris. As the angel nears, it becomes clear something is wrong.

Calipher is not Calipher. He is a jigsaw of himself, the pieces of Calipher—wing and feather here, gleaming marble skin there, tufts of golden curls—mixed with patches of something else—ice-blue eyes and wisps of shadow and jagged gremlin teeth.

Understanding cuts me like a blade—Calipher did not come with us on this journey at all. We have been traveling not with an angel, but with a demon.

Bastus takes another step, sways, then collapses to the ground.

CHAPTER SEVENTEEN

LITTLE DETAILS ABOUT THE journey pull together and reshape in my exhausted mind, and I begin to understand: The strange shadowed nature of Calipher's magic, the buzzing bursts of chaos rushing through me, the sudden way he changed his mind to join us. I should have known.

Rage ignites through a haze of exhaustion and too many aches to know where one starts or another ends.

"You tricked us." The words launch out of me like arrows, and I wish they could pierce just as deeply.

My body buzzes with the chaos of a demon's aura. What a fool I have been.

I advocated for Bastus when he came to us in Haven. Told them all how this demon could be trusted. And now this.

The demon does not respond, or even open his eyes, but remains a slumped heap of mismatched pieces.

Anger and shame bite down my neck. How could I have been so easily tricked? I wanted to believe that I was able to persuade Calipher too much to see the truth of it. I hold out my sword to guard against the demon, then remember as I raise it that the blade that it has been beaten away by the gargoyles, and all I have now is a jagged hilt.

I remember his hand on Xamson's shoulder, the way it irritated at me, and finally I understand why. The touch was so tender and gentle—so much like the way Bastus cupped his hands around Xamson's neck after the Forger's damage back by Haven. It was not the necklace playing with my mind after all—or at least, it wasn't only the necklace.

Who needs a sword? I throw the hilt at the jigsaw of angel and demon pieces slumped on the ground, then kick him with all my might, and he slides a few feet over the smooth marble ground. He groans, and a warm satisfaction fills me. Then he bursts into shadow and shifts into his feral demon form, and the glinting black eyes and sharp teeth remind me of his true nature. Another instant, and he shifts again, into the human shape he seems to prefer, still sprawled out over the ground.

He gets up, his sharp blue eyes pleading, his hands out in front of him defensively.

"Wait!" he begs.

"Why?" I bark.

"It is true, Calipher never wanted to come," he says. "I just wanted to help. You needed my help. But you would not listen. So...I..."

His words are gentle and slow, as if he is talking to a child.

I am no child.

"So you tricked us and came along anyway."

The rage fights for release. I settle for tightening my fist until my knuckles crack from the pressure.

"All this time I kept questioning myself and wondering what was wrong with me, why I kept feeling so restless. I blamed—" I cut myself off, unwilling to say it out loud: I blamed the necklace. I thought I was not good enough, not strong enough to fight it— "And all that time, it wasn't me, it was you. I should have known."

I would have, if I had not been so caught up in the necklace, in saving Adem, in winning back Xamson, in willing the Gods to speak to me again, in all of my own miserable mess. My shame burns deeper into the heat of my anger.

"You are the one who insisted I deserved a chance, remember? What happened to that?" he asks.

You tried to steal Xamson. The words rush my mind before I can think. But that is absurd. His attentions to Xamson could hardly be called that at all. Suddenly I become aware my hand has slipped into my pocket and gripped the necklace's emerald. I relax my fingers and pull my hand away.

Instead I say, "And this is how you chose to use that chance. You lied, and tricked, and put the entire quest at risk. And now here we are with no weapons, beaten and exhausted, in the realm of the Gods, with a demon. We destroyed the way as we passed through, too. How will we ever get back to Terath?" I realize this last as I speak it, pointing to the fallen tree, and my heart tugs with panic. "What am I supposed to think of you now?"

I can't take it all in. My head is still rushing from the attack and my body is still throbbing. I have been tricked, and I have been lied to. I am too exhausted for this. But my temper still burns.

"Put you at risk? You could not have gotten here without me, and you know it," Bastus says.

I bite my lip. At the back of my mind, a small voice of reason whispers that he is right. But my anger is too big to contain, and it is definitely too big to concede to this First who has betrayed me so egregiously.

"You shouldn't be here. You shouldn't have been able to get in at all, demon. How did you do it?"

He shrugs, his expression apologetic. "Men have no more right being in the Host than I do. You are bound to Terath. And yet here we all are. Who knows what rules are true and which are rumor. Or maybe the realm is so broken by now that the old rules no longer hold the same way. I do not know. But I am here. And I know it is hard for you to believe right now, but I came to help."

I clench my fists and take slow breaths, conscious that Xamson is here, just behind me, that even now I need to show him I can be more than a loose cannon. So I squeeze my eyes shut tight and try to think.

Why isn't Xamson as upset about this as I am? How can he remain so calm and quiet in response to this discovery? The necklace threads through my chest and tightens—does Xamson want Bastus here? Perhaps this is good news to him.

Bastus bows his head as if ashamed, but then his eyes drift and he frowns.

"You are hurt," he says.

I check myself over. I am worn down, and I am badly beaten, but I can find no injury more serious than that. "No, I am not."

But Bastus ignores my comment and moves past me. He is not talking to me at all—he is talking to Xamson, who is still lying on the ground behind us. Blood is pouring from a wound in his middle and pooling out around him.

Everything else drops away. Xamson has been behind me, injured this whole time, and I had my back to him, fussing over Bastus.

"Xamson!" I race next to him and drop to my knees. "What happened?"

Bastus bends over him and rolls him gently onto his back, then rips open Xamson's robes so that his stomach is exposed. Among the rippling muscle, there is a jagged gash where the blood is flowing out.

Under my fear for Xamson, envy twists—I hate the ease with which Bastus brushes his fingers over Xamson's skin as he studies the wound. And I hate myself for how much I hate it, the necklace's threads working their way into me. Suddenly I have an impulse to cast it away and shed myself of its burden.

Xamson groans. He is conscious, at least.

I tug on my robe's sleeve to bunch it and lean forward to press it against the wound. But instead of stepping aside, Bastus leans forward, blocking me from Xamson. A flick of his wrist, and an ashy burst of shadow wraps around me, holding me in place.

"Let me go, I have to help him!" I twist against the tug of the bind.

Bastus eyes the flimsy fabric. "And what are you going to do with that, wipe his brow? You cannot save him. But I can."

The words are sharper than any blade, and even without Bastus' magic holding me back, I would have been frozen in place. But I glance again to Xamson, who is losing consciousness and becoming alarmingly pale, the pool of red beneath him growing, and I know it is the truth.

"So then do it," I snap through gritted teeth.

But Bastus does not take action. Instead he looks me over.

Then he says, "You are a man of your word."

"Of course I am. Heal him."

Still he does not budge.

"I will. But I want your word first.

"My word? My word for what?"

Xamson groans. Save him.

"What could you possibly want? Say it," I snap.

Bastus' lips press together.

"You have earned your right to hate me," he says. "But I want your word you will let this go. I will finish this quest with you. You will not fight me like this at every turn."

Xamson moans again. My fists strain.

"Fine. How can you stand here while he is dying," I exclaim. "Do something!"

"And," Bastus presses, "You will not interfere in my pursuit of Xamson. You will let him decide for himself."

So it was not in my head after all. The necklace's threads prickle through me and hate for the demon burns deep.

"He could never fall for something like you," I scoff.

"Then he will not," he says. But he holds his ground. "I have your word?"

The pool under Xamson is growing larger with every second.

"Yes! Yes! Now save him!"

Bastus nods. He places a hand over the wound and tenses his fingers, releasing an ashy burst of magic. The shards of rock wriggle free, and Bastus casts them away. Finally, Xamson relaxes. Then, as the dark spray of magic continues to surround him, the bleeding stops, and the skin begins to pull back together.

Xamson lurches back to life and seizes his stomach. Then, he turns to Bastus.

But Bastus isn't done. He stretches out his palms and moves his hands out, toward Xamson's head and feet, and as he does it, the bruises and cuts that cover him shrink and fade away. When he is done, he rests his hand on Xamson's side over where the wound was and looks into his eyes. It feels too personal, and it makes me squirm.

I try to push back against the spell that holds me, but to no avail. "Let me go."

Bastus stands and looks me over. "Not yet."

Before I can say anything else, he stretches his hands out like he did for Xamson, and I am swallowed into a dusty darkness. When it fades, all my aches and throbs are gone.

"Okay. You are free," Bastus says.

The hold on me loosens, and I rush past him to Xamson.

"How do you feel?" I ask.

Xamson blinks. "A little lightheaded. But better."

Bastus nods. "You lost a lot of blood."

The blood is all over Xamson, caked in his robe and congealing on his arms. It is on Bastus too, splotching his robe over his knee where he knelt next to Xamson, and smudging on his side where he wiped his hands clean after.

"I will be fine. Just give me a moment." Xamson offers a faint smile. Then his eyes run over Bastus again, and his smile fades. "You are not Calipher."

Bastus' eyes flicker away and then back. "No."

Xamson's expression turns blank and I know him well enough to recognize he is processing, analyzing from a thousand angles and connecting the dots. His hand drifts to his sword. He lifts it in front of him and studies it. Like mine, it is too battered and abused to be of any use to him, half of it broken clean away by the gargoyles. He frowns, then drops it to the ground.

Then Xamson stands up and looks back to Bastus. "You saved my life. If you weren't here, I don't know what would have happened to us."

Threads of envy needle through me. How can I compete with that?

You cannot, a voice urges. It is the necklace. Not alone. Let me help you.

Yearning tugs at my heart, but no—I have seen what its power does once set free. I steel myself against it.

Bastus bows his head. He seems genuinely repentant. Maybe my first impression of him was right.

Xamson reaches out and puts a hand on Bastus' shoulder. "Is there anything else we should know? This would be the time. No more surprises."

Bastus tilts his head to peer into Xamson's eyes. "No. Nothing."

Then they go quiet, watching each other, and something fills the space between them that itches between my shoulders. I want to break it to pieces.

"You scared me," I say. I work between them to get in front of Xamson. He cups the side of my face with his hand. "I'm all right," he breathes.

His color is returning, and his hand is warm and comforting against my cheek. I could stand like this with him forever, just watching the way his lashes flutter over his deep, dark eyes. But before I can even sink into the feeling, Xamson's gaze flickers, and he pulls away. The moment is gone, almost like it never happened at all.

I let Xamson walk ahead and linger behind, turning on Bastus.

I drop my voice low to keep Xamson from hearing. "I will keep my word, but you have a lot to answer for."

Bastus rushes at me in a burst so fast it is a blur, stopping inches from my face.

His ice-blue eyes are hard and sparking with anger. "I would never really put Xamson's life at risk. I would not even do that to you. You do not know me yet. Do not forget it."

My jaw tightens, grinding my teeth together. But before I can respond, Xamson calls from up ahead.

"Gods, what happened here?"

A quiver in his voice warns at something terrible. I have been so preoccupied with Xamson and Bastus, I have not turned to take in our surroundings yet, beyond the sense of stillness that promised our safety.

I turn away from the great destroyed tree, toward Xamson's voice, and what I see makes my chest seize.

Chapter Eighteen

IT IS ONLY NOW hitting me: The home of the Gods. We are actually in it. It rushes over me in a wave of warm, pulsing power, an aura that curls up within my core and welcomes me.

In the Texts, the Host opens into a grand hall—the grandest of halls. Gleaming white marble that reaches as far as the heavens, the tallest, proudest columns ever constructed, long tables that stretch into eternity for the most celebrated of guests—the bravest of warriors and legendary heroes, the greatest souls of all the realms.

But that is not what we find.

It could have once been such a place—its aura tells me it must have been. The marble floor below us stretches far past where we stand, as far as I can see and beyond, and from it springs once-proud rows of broad columns. At the far end stand three great thrones. The Great Hall is empty except for this, all the same gleaming white marble—marble so bright and pure it strains my eyes.

It would have been stunning.

Except for what has become of it.

The marble tiles of the floor are cracked, and roots and sprouts tangle between their splits, forcing unevenness throughout the great floor. The columns are beaten and shattered and knocked to the ground. There is a shuddering menace to the quiet of this place. The reality so contrary to its aura I wish I should shake it out of me.

But it is worse than that. The pristine white of the hall is splattered in congealed silver and tufts of scattered feathers, silver and golden and dark as midnight. Sprays of ash mar the marble.

The Host's Great Hall is covered in the blood of the Gods' First Creatures. It screams of death.

No wonder I have not heard the Gods in so long. Have They fled from Their home? Are They captured? Dead? Is such a thing possible?

Fear burrows into me deep and curls up in my stomach in a cold knot. My gut screams in warning to flee to this place. Everything in me wishes to turn away, to forget I ever saw any of this. And Xamson—what have I dragged him into?

This was supposed to be the end of our quest. The hard part was supposed to be getting here. We should be before the Gods now, here in the Great Hall, and then on our way back to Haven. But now it seems we have stumbled into something much graver.

And the way we got here—the only way I know to get us back to Terath—seems to have been destroyed. I turn back and look at the fallen tree that brought us here and sparks of panic bite through me.

Snap out of it. One step at a time.

I take a slow breath in, then release it.

We have come too far to flee now, just because it has become more challenging. I take a hesitant step forward, then another, and with shaky hands, make my way between the long, shattered tables. Xamson and Bastus follow.

"What happened here?" Xamson says. His voice echoes through the hall.

I can find no good answer.

"Angels," Bastus affirms. Then he points to the silver splatter against the column. "Sprites. Demons, too," he adds, nodding to the ash, and a nearby pool of shimmer.

Rebels. They should not have been able to even break into the Gods' home.

But then, as we've already gone over, neither should we. And here we are.

Is it possible the rebel Firsts broke into the Host the way we just did, and attacked the Gods in their own home? Is it possible they won?

A hollowness swells within me that echoes with fear—I have never missed Adem more than now. His presence has always made me feel stronger.

But Adem is not here.

And right now, I have never felt more lost.

But under the terror, I feel a selfish relief. If the Gods have fled their posts, maybe that is why I have been unable to feel Their presence. Maybe it is not me that is broken.

The thought is blasphemy. But it is a comfort.

We wander through the towering pillars until we reach the thrones at the front. They are just like the thrones described in the Texts: three majestic, oversized seats of marble in a row, facing the tables of the Great Hall. To the far side, one is detailed with elaborate patterns of onyx, a throne for Shael. In the middle, a throne laced with swirls of diamond, for Theia. And just in front of me, a throne framed in delicate gold plating for Gloros.

Their elegant detailing stands in contrast to the destruction around us, and despite some cracks, their majesty is not ruined by the damage.

We stand there in silence, mesmerized by the terror and glory of it all, until finally I can't stand it anymore.

"Are the Gods dead?" Xamson asks the question I was too afraid to think.

"No," I say.

Xamson and Bastus turn to me, concern etched into the lines of their faces.

"How can you know that?" Xamson asks.

"I refuse to believe it. It isn't possible for the Gods to be gone. They are here somewhere, and we will find Them. We have to."

"You refuse? You refuse?" Xamson exclaims. He is scared, I hear it in the pitch and quiver of his voice. "Look at this place. It is already destroyed whether you accept it or not. The Gods are not here. There is nothing left to be done, Jordan. It is time for us to go home."

His betrayal burns through me in a burst.

"This again?" I say. "We have come all this way, we have broken into the Host, and you want me to give up at the first sign of trouble?"

"The first sign?" Xamson exclaims. "This is hardly the first sign we shouldn't be here. Remember the gargoyles? The Forger? Rona warned us before we even left—and Calipher. All of this, and now the Gods aren't even here. We don't even have the guide to the Host we thought we did," he says, gesturing to Bastus. Bastus stands, arms folded, shoulders tucked forward. "I almost died getting here, Jordan. How much is enough for you? Does one of us have to die for you to realize you have taken this too far? Would that have stopped you, or would you have left my body here among the ruins and continued on even then?"

"Of course not," I fire back "I would have—"

But I do not know what I would have done. I may have done exactly what he is suggesting.

"We are in the Host," Xamson hisses, cutting me off. "We have already gotten so much farther than we should ever have been able to."

My heart pounds, indignant at Xamson's words, and his accusations click together in my mind.

"You never thought we would make it," I realize.

"What?" Xamson's expression goes suddenly blank at the accusation, and I know I am right.

"What did you think was going to happen, Xamson? We would hike up a mountain, reach the top, see I was wrong, and go home? You said you believed me. You said you wanted to be part of it."

Xamson's fists clench, and he shakes them in the air. "Because you need someone looking out for you. Because I know you. You are so desperate to be the hero—everyone can see it. You soar too high, and then you crash. And someone has to be there to pick up the pieces."

A terrible pause settles between us.

"This is not the time—" Bastus tries to step in, his voice straining with a forced calm, but this is none of his business.

I cut him off, reaching a point of combustion with Xamson. "So that is how you see me then? I am nothing but a broken, messed up thing to be looked after? No wonder we didn't last. Here I was thinking I broke us, but it was you. You did this to us."

It all crashes over me, a rockslide of emotion that takes over my body, and I slam my fist down into the throne, welcoming the catharsis of the inevitable pain of flesh on marble that is sure to follow.

But it does not come.

My hand goes crashing through the panel of the throne's seat, and its shattered pieces go flying.

Shocked, I stare down at the broken throne. I really do destroy everything I touch.

CHAPTER NINETEEN

"YOU SHATTERED THE THRONE of Gloros," Bastus says.

I am stunned to dumbness. "Yes," I whisper, too horrified by my sin to speak any louder.

Bastus leans over my shoulder toward the rubble and reaches over me to pick up a slab of the shattered throne, and studies it.

"Rot," he says, holding it out for us to see. Under the marble finish, the inside of the slab is porous and chalky. "Like it has been eaten away from the inside out."

"Marble does not rot." Xamson says. But he frowns and steps close to Bastus to study the slab. As he leans into Bastus, the necklace sends a pang over me. Determined to keep its power in check, I turn back to the throne and study the shattered seat of the throne. More angels' blood oozes out from the between the pores and drips down between the shards, thick and silvery.

I open my mouth to point it out, but then something else calls to me, glistening metallic under the shattered panel. I push the rotted marble aside for a better look. Underneath, hidden within the rubble of the throne's seat, lies a great sword. I take its handle and pull it out, brandishing it in a wide swoop over my head. Its blade catches the light with a flash, and a swell of excitement sparks within me.

"What is that?" Xamson says.

Bastus is at my side in a whooshing blur of ash, frowning. "Put it back. You have meddled enough as it is."

But before I can respond, a roar rumbles over the marble, shattering through the quiet of the Hall.

I whip around. A large, bulky figure bounds toward us so fast its edges blur. More attacks? My tired muscles groan at the idea of another fight, but there is no other option.

Xamson grabs for his blade, but both our fingers stumble over the empty sheaths in our belts—we already lost those in the last fight. My heart catches in my throat, and I shift my grip on the great sword, bracing for the fight as well as I can.

The beast is approaching at a ferocious pace. Hints of its figure become apparent as it nears: three separate heads in a row across hulking shoulders, each with gnashing teeth; six legs that charge in tandem to propel it forward with horrifying speed.

Bastus breaks into shadow and rushes at the beast to meet its charge head-on. Bastus rematerializes for his attack, and they collide. The beast snarls, then swipes him away. Bastus is cast down to the ground, slumped on his side, but he left behind a jagged wound in the beast's chest. The beast thrashes and snarls in rage, but no blood pours from it. Instead, it knits back together, and the beast is good as new in a blink.

And then the beast is charging us again, and faster than I can process, it is upon us. It swipes at us with razor-like claws.

Xamson. No.

There is no time to think.

My hands thrust the great sword forward.

As I cut through the beast, the sword sings through my fingers, up my arms, into my soul, as if it were created just for me. As if this sword were my destiny, and I could never fail while it is in my hands. Victory and glory, the glory I always deserved, will be mine.

The blade lodges into the beast at the shoulder. The two sides sag as they split apart, two heads to one side, the third to the other.

The beast pauses, waiting for the healing to pull it back together.

Except, it does not.

The beast's three faces contort as it claws at the split. The heads roar at mind-numbing volume as it stumbles back. Then it tears away again into the realm.

We are all frozen for a moment, catching our breath as we watch it disappear into the distance.

"What was that?" Xamson says.

"I—I could hardly tell. It was moving too fast. But it healed like Adem." I glance back to Xamson, and then to Bastus. Their expressions mirror the confusion that stirs in me. Surely it can't be a coincidence. "Is it possible the Forger is responsible for all this?"

Xamson glances back at the destruction of the Great Hall and shakes his head. "I would believe almost anything at this point."

I shift the sword in my hand and it hums in response. Oh, how it sings.

"Thank the Gods we had this sword, or we would not have had any chance at all."

Bastus folds him arms over his chest. "I told you to put that down," he says. "You think you have saved us with that thing? You have only brought a new wrath upon us. A worse one."

He reaches to take the sword from me, but I pull away.

"It saved our lives," I say. But I am only half listening, charmed by my new blade. "We were defenseless against that beast without it. You were not able to stop it."

Bastus' nostrils flare, his eyes darken. "Don't you understand? This is the Mantle of Gloros."

His words prick me like a cold shock. The Mantles of the Gods.

"The Mantle? This is it?" I hold it out in front of me.

"What else could it be, hidden within Gloros' throne? Surely you know the story?" Bastus asks.

"Of course I do."

The memory is dusty at the back of my mind. I haven't heard tales of them since I was a boy. But I know the tales.

In the First Realm War, the Gods fought for Themselves, side by side with Their loyal creatures. And They crafted for Themselves the most powerful weapons that have ever existed. Shael fashioned Himself a battle axe that always soared true to its aim and had no mercy; Theia crafted a scythe that would tame the fields and plow down anything in Her path; and Gloros made Herself the purist of swords, one that knew only bravery and glory, and nothing else. And it was with these tools of Their own creation that the Gods defeated the rebels in the First Realm War and restored Their Order.

But when the war was done, They looked around and witnessed the destruction Their weapons had wrought upon the creation They loved, and They were overcome with mourning for it. They swore to never use the weapons again until the end of the realms, when the final curse of plagues would rain over all creation, and the last of the great heroes would finally break the wars' hold on the realms.

Bastus is still staring at me, and restless tension scrawls under my skin in response.

"What are you saying exactly?" I ask, "That because the Gods swore not to use the Mantles again until the end times, that using one of them...you think that it will cause the end times? That the plagues will begin?" I lower the sword and shake my head. "What if this is when the end times were meant to be? What if we found the Mantle because it is time?"

Bastus bites his lip. He glances to Xamson, whose face shapes into a worrisome frown. They look back to me, silent.

"We do not hold power over such things, the Gods would not allow it," I say. Indignance creeps up my neck with heat.

"Even the Forger and the rebels who dared to break into the Gods' home and attack Them here, the ones who drove Them out to Gods-only-know where, did not pick these up," Bastus says.

"Maybe they did not know they were there." My throat tightens. "Or maybe we were meant to find them."

"Or maybe even they did not dare take them," Xamson says. "Did you see the blood, Jordan? Gloros' throne is bleeding."

Bastus adds, his sternness sharpening, "Even before they were put away and hidden, only the Gods and their greatest Chosen warriors were meant to wield these."

Chosen.

That is exactly how I feel wielding this sword. For the first time in a very, very long time, I feel like myself again. I take another practice swing, lifting the sword high and swiping it down to the ground. The sweet hum of its singing drowns out all the fear and doubt, drowns the possessive cloy of the necklace, makes me feel whole again, like I am what I was meant to be.

"Listen to him, Jordan," Xamson urges.

But I am past listening. All I want to listen to is the sword's song, to be the hero it believes me to be.

"We lost our weapons to the gargoyles in the climb. If we are going to keep going—and I am, even if you are not." I glare at Xamson. "Then we are going to need weapons. What if the rebels who did all this are still out there, somewhere in the Host?" A thought occurs to me. "Do you think the other thrones are hiding the other Mantles?"

"No—" Bastus starts.

He reaches for me, but I duck, feeling light and giddy under the sword's hum, and use the hilt to smash the seat of the middle throne—Theia's. Again the marble shatters to expose a rotting middle, and within it, a scythe, oversized, with a glinting blade so sharp it looks as though it could split a single blade of grass.

"Jordan!" Xamson begs, stepping up to the thrones' pedestal and reaching out to me.

Giddy with the sword's hum, I spin around him. When I shatter Shael's throne, the seat crumbles away to expose a great battle axe.

So these are the Mantles of the Gods.

Bastus whooshes to my side in a blur of shadow and grabs my wrist.

"How can you not understand?" Bastus says. "You are taking something even the Firsts—even rebels who dared to come into the Gods' home to overthrow them—did not dare take."

"Stop worrying. I do not see any plagues coming for us. Only now we are armed against anything that might come our way," I say. "Besides, the Gods need us. Whatever happened here, They fled from it. Wherever They are now, They need someone to finish what has been started."

If what Bastus says is true, it is too late anyway. I already used the sword. We might as well be armed for whatever else lies ahead.

Bastus glares at me. "And you think that is you. The Gods need you to save Them."

The sword sings to me and fills me with certainty. Yes. Me. They Chose me. And this is the moment for action.

"Do you see anyone else here to do it?" I shrug, trying to hide the pulsing certainty I feel. "The Texts speak of fate, of Chosen ones, of heroes tasked by the Gods. And here we are, Mantles in hand, on the cusp of the Third Realm War. Is it so crazy to think that this is ours? That this was all meant to be?"

With the Mantles in my hands, it is easy to believe, clear as daylight. I pick up the scythe and weigh it in my hand—it is sturdy, but lighter than it looks, and cuts through the air with a light whistle. I hold it out for Bastus, but he draws away. I turn to Xamson and hold it out to him, but he will not meet my eyes, his arms folded and shoulders hunched.

"The first plague is blood," he says. "We are all covered in it. We are surrounded by it. Look at this place."

"That was all here already, whether we found the Mantles or not." Neither of them answers. I try another approach. "Listen. If what you say is true, then it is already too late. I have already doomed us, and we are about to face the plagues anyway—in addition to that beast and whatever else might be out there in the Host. And we are going to need these weapons to defend ourselves. And if it is not true...well, then there is no harm in taking the weapons anyway, but there is still a wrathful beast with three heads out there on the hunt for us, and these are the only thing we know it cannot heal itself from. Either way, no more harm can come to us from these weapons now, and we will need to be able to defend ourselves."

I hold it out one more time.

Xamson hesitates, starts to reach for it. He turns to Bastus, who glares at him like he has been betrayed. But then Xamson pulls back.

"He's right," Xamson says. I look to him, hardly believing what I hear. His eyes meet mine. "Everything is already dire enough across all the realm. We hardly need the Gods' wrath upon us, in addition to the rest of it."

"Suit yourself," I say. "But whatever lies ahead, I want to be ready for it."

Just as I stop speaking, as if to prove my point—or maybe Bastus'—droplets start to fall from the sky. Droplets of blood, all different kinds: Red blood of men, silvery angels' blood, glimmering sprite, and dark demon drops.

Bastus stares down at the splatters on the marble and exclaims, half-laugh, half-aghast, an unspoken I told you so.

Doubt pinches my chest, and I place the battle axe on the ground. Perhaps this was not so wise after all. But there is no arguing that, whatever lies ahead, we will need to be armed for it, and I hold onto the great sword. There is no room for failure in this, not anymore. We must find the Gods.

Chapter Twenty

Now ARMED AGAIN, I press on past the thrones and deeper into the Host, Xamson and Bastus on my tail.

As we get farther from the Great Hall, grass and weeds force their way, overgrown and unwieldy, between the great marble tiles of the ground, and up into their cracks. The further we go, the more weeds overrun everything else, spotted with clusters of wildflowers and dandelions, until the marble is nothing but crumbles and fragments, and we are no longer in a hall but on a field that stretches far beyond what I can see, possessing the same haunting unending-ness.

We go on until the Great Hall is a distant memory.

We go on until my muscles begin to ache again, despite Bastus' healing.

We go on until it becomes clear that the relentless brightness will never dim for night, and day should have passed long ago.

In time, something else takes form out ahead of us in the Host's vastness—a great tree lays out, felled to the ground. Its proud branches stretch up and out from the felled trunk, and others are strewn and splintered over the ground. Its roots are pulled up and exposed from the tension of the fall, and where it split, the trunk glistens and oozes with thick sap. Something glints in a blur around it. Then another glint chases after it. And another.

I squint to make them out. "There is something up there, around the tree," I say.

I pull out the great sword.

"Is it the beast from the Great Hall?" Xamson asks.

"No," I say. I strain my eyes to see. "I do not know what these are."

They are creatures of some sort, faster than any other I have ever seen. Though they are similar in manner and size, their appearances vary. Some are almost like children, while others are plated head to toe in hard, gleaming silver, and some in between. Small, scaled wings burst from them in odd places—an arm, a calf, a neck.

The way they dart about, so fast they all but disappear, it is hard to tell how many of them there are, but there must be about ten or so in all. Too many for us to take on in a fight.

As we near, it becomes clear they are not just darting around the felled tree's debris, but clearing it.

"Nephilim," Bastus grumbles. "Stay back, and perhaps their game will occupy them too much to bother with us."

"But nephilim are just the offspring of angels and their human loves. Back from the Beginning before they were separated," Xamson says.

"'Just?' Nothing that corrupts the Gods' power is 'just' anything," Bastus says. "The nephilim are extremely powerful and unpredictable."

"Man's will and angel's power," I add. I can hardly believe what I am seeing. "The Texts say they are...unpredictable. But I never thought they were real. The way they are referenced in the Texts, they were used as a symbol of the consequences that can happen if you do not follow the Gods' Order, nothing more."

Bastus shrugs. "And yet here they are. There used to be many more."

"They are so strange," Xamson says.

I slow to watch them. "But also...kind of beautiful."

"Beautiful?" Bastus yanks me by my elbow and pulls me along with him to keep walking. "They're dangerous. They are not meant to exist, and they know it. We need to keep going."

"Why did the Gods allow them into the Host, then?" Xamson asks.

"Because someone had to take them in, and they were created by Theia's beings," Bastus says.

"And men," Xamson says.

"Men are fools," Bastus snaps. "They did not understand what they were getting into. Nor could they have handled what they had created."

The bite in his voice makes me look to Xamson. He meets my glance with a furrowed brow. It is in that pause of hesitation that I notice the restless quiet that has taken hold in the air.

Xamson's ears prick and his frown deepens. Bastus straightens as his muscles tense. Almost in unison, we turn back toward the nephilim.

They have clustered together like a murder of crows. Every one of them watches us, still as statues. As we stare back, one near the edge—plated head to toe in silver, with large, blank eyes and tiny sets of wings over all of its body—leans forward, tilting its head. A pair of tiny wings set behind its ears flutter, then tuck back again.

A creeping caution winds up my spine. I do not dare move.

"What do we do?" I ask. "They do not look like they mean to attack. If anything, they look curious."

Xamson flexes his fists. "That doesn't mean they won't."

"We get away from here as quickly as we can," Bastus says. "Go. No sudden movements."

The nephilim watch as we inch away, then return to their game.

Everything about the Host seems to stretch on with a sense of unending-ness, as if there is no time here, no sense of passing, only a stationary stretch of eternity. Without the cycle of days and nights, it is impossible to know how long we have walked. There is no sense of hunger, no need for sleep.

After a time I could not measure, a low humming chirp rises, like cicadas. Despite all we have seen, it is almost peaceful—it takes me back to the summers of my younger years in Haven, playing along the shore in lazy summer twilight with Avi and the others, back when he and I were still brothers. The feeling is more like what I had expected the Host to be. I take it in, enjoying the soft, warm light. Then something flutters past my elbow.

"A butterfly!" I turn to take a better look, eager to finally take in a small piece of the beauty I expected to find here.

Bastus stretches out his hand and guides the fluttering thing toward him for a better look. "No, a moth," he says, tilting his hand toward me so I can see. The small gray wings flutter—he's right.

How strange, I think. A moth in the Host.

Steps later, Xamson flinches, kicking his leg up and swatting at his calf. "I think something bit me," he says. As we stare at his leg in disbelief, a small red welt forms on it.

Then, a sting flares on my bicep—a mosquito. Soon, the tiny pests are swarming in clusters in the air around us, and we must swat constantly to keep them off our arms, legs, necks. Crickets hop through the grass. Spiders' webs stretch through the air, and as we break through them their threads stick to us. Centipedes slither near our sandaled feet. Bees buzz around our heads.

"Infestation." Xamson calls back to me over the hum of the swarm. He slaps at his arm.

"What?" I hear the word, but do not grasp his meaning.

"Infestation," Xamson repeats, turning to me and waving his arms through the air for emphasis. "The second plague. It's infestation."

Now I understand—he thinks this is my fault. My hand drifts absentmindedly to the hilt of the sword at my hip, and its soothing power sings through me.

"But—"

"Beasts. That's what is coming for us next." Xamson goes on, stomping through the swampy field and swatting clusters of gnats, his hands waving at them wildly. He looks like a madman. Under different circumstances, in different times, I would have teased him for it, and we would have laughed over it together. But those times are not these times.

"And infection," he rants on. "Then—"

He stops to swipe again at the swarms gathering around us.

"Then drought," Bastus says, picking it up. "And darkness—"

"Enough," I say, cutting them off. I squeeze my hand tight around the hilt of Gloros' great sword, trying to hide the way it shakes. I do not want them to finish. We all know what the plagues are. We all know what the final one is. But still I do not want them to say it. Not here in this open field of this strange, broken realm, where I feel so vulnerable. Everything is already far too grim right now.

"Can we just get through this field—a very natural place for insects and other bugs to be, by the way—and then worry about the wrath of the Gods after?"

Neither of them push it further, focusing instead on the swarms and their steps through the high grass of the field. I do not think they want to say it, either.

The word looms over us anyway.

Death.

That is the last of the plagues.

A swarm of bees rushes around me and I swipe at them with my arms. Did I really bring this upon us? Were the Gods' pledge about the Mantles as much curse as promise? A reasoning voice in me argues that for all we know this is what the Host is always like, or at least, this is what we would have found here anyway, with all the destruction that has been wrought already by the Forger and his allies. But no matter how I rationalize, guilt rises within me like choking smoke.

"Ah!"

An abrupt exclamation startles me from my reflections, and I turn around toward it, swinging my sword out and ready to attack. But I can find no attacker. Only Xamson, clutching at his face.

"Are you all right?" I ask.

He looks at me, eyes fiery. "It stung me. That giant Godsdamned bee stung me!"

He pulls his hand away for me to see, and sure enough, a red mark is already swelling up against his eye and reshaping the contour of his perfect cheekbone.

"Watch your language!" Bastus exclaims. "This is not the place to be meddling with damnations."

Xamson shoots him a dark look, but says nothing else.

The necklace whispers to me from my pocket, reveling in the tension between them, but there are more important matters to tend to.

"Here," I say, tearing another swatch of fabric from my remaining sleeve. Xamson takes it from me and presses it against his face.

"We can do better than that," Bastus says.

He approaches until he and Xamson are face to face, and then he gently pushes Xamson's hand away and places his own across the side of Xamson's head over the swelling, a caress so intimate I glance away for a moment, but then I have to watch, I have to know.

Bastus takes his time, basking in the moment. The longer he soaks up Xamson's closeness the more resentment kicks up in my chest—he is yours, the necklace whispers to me, not the demon's. Set me free and he will come back to you. But I squeeze my fist and choke back my longing, reminding myself its lure is nothing but lies. No.

There is a pause before the magic starts—Bastus' nostrils flare, his fingers twitch with tension, and the familiar ashy magic bursts forth. The swelling of the sting subsides under Bastus' power and Xamson's face returns to normal, bright and proud.

When he is done, Bastus smiles, and runs the back of his fingers over Xamson's cheek. "There. Good as new."

Xamson stares back into his eyes. "Thank you."

I clear my throat. They both look to me.

"We need to keep going, or we will all be stung soon."

Bastus steps back, allowing more space between them. My shoulders ease. "Let's go."

We trudge on through the field, fighting off the swarms, until finally we break free of it, exhausted and irritable.

We walk for what feels like an eternity—a time that surely must be days, though it is hard to tell when nothing ever changes. Still we do not hunger, nor do we crave sleep, as if time is not passing at all. Unsure of what this might cost us, we finally agree to rest and eat anyway.

As Bastus casts a web of protective spells around us, his jaw tightens, and his pallor turns even paler than normal. How strange, I think, for a creature of darkness to turn so light from his efforts. But then I scold myself for my pettiness and focus on my own work, setting up my sack for sleep.

We settle into the rich earth and lay in quiet while Bastus stands guard. With my body finally still, my mind begins to churn.

There is so much to do, so much that could go wrong. Where could the Gods have gone? How will we ever get back to Terath? There is an unhinged chthonus on the loose, and it seems I have singlehandedly unleashed the plagues of the end times. But am I giving myself too much credit? Perhaps they had already been unleashed, and us finding the weapons was merely the next step in the prophecy. If there is any consolation to be drawn from all this, I can only think that there is surely no way anything could get worse. This is my last thought as sleep overtakes me.

My dreams are rushed and fevered, darting between flashes of images like lightning.

A boy in the woods, his large dark eyes frowning and a hand clutched tensely around the trunk of a tree.

A bouquet of flowers withering, dying, turning grey and dead.

The colors rush together and warp into darkness. The Forger's voice echoes in me—We are the same, you and me.

And then the boy comes into focus again, cheeks flushed, his large, dark eyes tense and familiar under his frown.

A glowing rose-gold hand takes his hand and shapes the fingers, spreading them and positioning them in a particular fashion. "You must pay attention to your fingers." Her voice is smooth as honey.

"You said I was special," the boy says.

"And you are. But special is only the beginning," the angel says. "Power is nothing without control and purpose."

The boy repeats the shape the angel pushed his hands into, and stones and sticks rise a few inches off the ground. The boy gasps and looks up, eyes wide.

The angel beams down to him. "Well done."

Then the crunching of leaves and twigs pulls his attention away.

The boy twists around toward the sounds, and a girl appears between the trees. A rotted bouquet dangles from her hand. A green emerald rests on a delicate chain around her neck—the necklace—and draws out the intensity of her eyes.

Something within the boy leaps to be with her in spite of himself.

"Are you lost?" the angel says, her words clipped in spite of the sweetness inherent to her voice.

"No." The girl looks to the boy.

The boy stares back. "What do you want?"

"We are alike," she says.

The boy puffs his chest out. "I am special."

The girl raises her eyebrows. Then she holds out the rotted bouquet in her hands, and the petals uncurl, regain their colors, and come back to life.

The boy's lips part. He meets her level stare. Her chin tilts up, a dare in her eyes.

"What is your name?" the girl asks.

"Maelcolm," he says.

"Koreh," the girl says.

A hunger fills Maelcolm, a challenge he cannot leave unanswered.

"Jordan? Jordan?" The voice cuts through the dream and its pieces scatter, pulling me back to myself.

I awaken with a lurch.

"Jordan? What's wrong?"

Xamson is leaning over me, frowning, and Bastus hovers behind him.

"What are you doing?"

"I couldn't sleep," Xamson says. He cracks a smile. "But you sure did. You have been tossing and murmuring. Are you all right?"

Bastus rests a hand on Xamson's shoulder, leaning in. But the necklace's aura twinges in my chest—I know better than to think he is concerned for me. What were they up to while I was sleeping? My eyes linger on his pale fingers pressed against Xamson's dark skin.

"I am fine," I say. I push myself up and start rolling my pack. "We should keep going."

We move on. After a long while, a glint catches along the horizon, a brief blur of brilliant light, like sunbeams catching on a wave. Then more of them. The flashes grow as we approach, becoming greater and more frequent. It is more nephilim.

Seeing them again now, I feel more prepared for their strangeness. They are unlike anything else I have seen in my life, possessing a sharpness that is both threatening and beautiful. In the middle of their circle is a sapling, just sprouting its first few leaves.

"Careful," Bastus warns.

I pull out Gloros' sword. Its courage pulses over me, and it gives me an idea.

"I think we should talk to them."

"Why?" Bastus' entire body stiffens. "No way. The risk is too high."

Xamson sighs, running a hand over his head.

"They could help us—maybe they know where the Gods are. We have trekked for what is surely many days, and we do not have any better sense of where to go or what we are doing than before. The only other creature we have come across is the beast that attacked us. We need help. We need to try."

"Even if they were to answer you, rather than attack, who is to say if they would tell us the truth," Bastus says.

Then he places a hand on Xamson's shoulder and guides him, so that our path takes us a wide radius from the nephilim and their little tree. A prickling pulse takes me over with a flash of resentment.

"Well, I am going," I say. I turn and start toward the nephilim.

"No," Bastus says, pulling me back. "Trust me, even if they do know something, they are not worth the risk."

At his words, all the little resentments that have been building up against Bastus explode.

"Trust you?" I snap. "After how you tricked us to get here? Besides, I thought you had not been to the Host before. Or was that a lie too?"

His jaw tightens. "I have not."

"And to your expert knowledge, the nephilim are kept in the Host?
"Yes."

"So really, you do not know anything about them, do you?"

He frowns. "But—"

"They're half human. Making connections with people is what I do best. They may look strange, but how different can they really be?" I say, talking over him. "Besides, do you have a better idea? How long can we continue to wander the realm without a plan? How long until we come across something even more treacherous than the nephilim again?"

I pause, letting the thought sink in. Then I add, "When Adem went to the Underworld, he said he encountered all sorts of strange and inexplicable things. Spirits and traps and terrible beasts...it seems more and more the Host may not be so different. Shouldn't we at least try?"

Thinking of Adem sends a pang through my chest. I've got to find the Gods. I need to get Adem his soul.

Bastus sighs.

"Fine, then. But I am staying here."

At this, Xamson straightens, inserting himself between us. "No. If we go, we all go. No more sides."

The sword's warm confidence hums over my skin. I shrug and turn my most charming smile on Bastus. "I guess we are all going, then. Because I am going."

As we inch closer to the nephilim, several stop their game and watch us instead.

Their heads tilt side to side, curious, but cautious. They watch us with large, blank silver eyes. Teeth sharp like a saw's blade peek from their mouths.

"Excuse me," I say, calling out as I approach.

Not one of them moves a muscle.

I swallow back my nerves and continue. "We are hoping you can help us."

The others turn and stare now, too. Some tilt their heads, like they are listening intently.

Still they stare. But they aren't attacking. They lean toward me, which I take as an invitation. The sword's confidence swells in my head. See? Nothing to worry about. For a demon, Bastus worries far too much. I move a step closer, emboldened.

"Jordan... " Xamson says. A warning.

I ignore it. What does he know? He has never seen nephilim before either, after all.

"My friends and I," I articulate carefully, gesturing to Bastus and Xamson. "We have come a very long way, and we need to find the Gods. Do you understand?"

One of them, a smaller nephilim, gleaming silver from head to toe, with small wings sprouting just behind its ears, leans forward and tilts it head. It responds with a soft chirp.

I take it as a yes.

"Good! Good. Thank you." A laugh escapes me in my relief. "Can you tell me where the Gods are?"

At this, more chirps rise and some of them twitch their wings. Another, with silver speckling over its shoulders and small wings at its elbows, rushes around the sapling in a burst of movement, then settles next to the first one. They chirp more, their silver eyes flashing to me, the sounds turning sharper.

Then the speckled nephilim whooshes at me in a blur, stopping inches from my face. Its silver eyes flash sharp and unfeeling.

"How did you get here, human?" it snarls.

Hearing it speak my own language takes me aback.

It does not smile, the hard corners of its mouth pointed stiffly downward. But then, they did not smile when they played either, so perhaps it is their way.

I take a breath, trying to steady myself. The sword's hum steadies me—remember why you are doing this.

"We climbed up Mount Analypsi into the Great Hall. It was deserted and destroyed. Do you know what happened there?"

The nephilim rushes back to the pack, and they chitter amongst themselves.

I wait, unsure of what to do, exactly, except that I most definitely should not interrupt. My palms turn slick with anxiety.

Finally, they turn back toward me, a hiss rising from them.

My hand tightens around my sword, and it responds with a pulse that emboldens me. I open my mouth to try to reassure them, but before I can, the largest nephilim rushes forward.

"Intruder," it says, spitting the word out between sharp teeth. "You dare break into the Gods' realm? You dare approach us, the last of the nephilim? You do not belong here."

"We want no trouble, and will soon return to our own realm." I say it slowly, trying to project a calm I no longer feel. "We just need to find the Gods. Help us, and we will be gone all the sooner."

It lets out a hard squawk akin to a laugh. The sound catches across the flock and they all begin to laugh, a hard laugh, a cold laugh, and their large silver eyes settle on us. There is just enough time for Xamson to clasp my wrist tight in alarm, then, they pounce.

They move faster than even my trained soldier's reflexes can react. By the time I pull my sword up it is already too late, they are on us, from all sides, and I cannot gain my bearings to fight back. Their sharp little claws scratch at my skin. Their teeth prick me as their tiny mouths clamp down on anything small enough to fit in them.

Beyond the angry hisses, I hear gasps and grunts. I twist and do my best to assess the scene. Xamson. They are ganging up on him, and there are more than he can fend off. Everything else drops away—the nephilims' screeches, the way they scratch at me, all of it, and my heart stops in my chest. I have to help him.

I power my way to him, swinging the sword wildly to block out the swarm of nephilim snapping around me. I did this to him. He did not want me to approach the nephilim in the first place. He did not want to even come to the Host. I cannot let anything happen to him—not anything more than already has, at least.

As I close in, I stretch out my arm and call for him. He looks to me and half-reaches, but another nephilim dives at him and he has to pull away to defend himself, swiping at them with the scythe.

I am not going to reach him. I am not enough to save him. I failed him.

Just as this realization bites into my stomach, a wave pulses through the air, and the nephilim collapse to the ground, unconscious.

Chapter Twenty-One

ALL I CAN DO is stare at the nephilims' limp forms on the ground, my heart still pounding. What just happened?

"Next time, listen to me," Bastus says. "You are welcome, by the way."

He flexes his fingers, and I realize he must have cast a spell over them to cause this.

"Do you know anything about nephilim at all?" he goes on. "Next time, at least wait for us to formulate a plan. I wasn't ready."

The sword's righteous indignation pulses over me. I try to suppress it, understanding this anger is not my own. But Bastus looks at me with such disdain, and at Xamson with such warmth, and my frustration only fuels the aura more. I need an ally, even if it is only a sword. Besides, we already established that none of us are exactly well versed in the creatures of the Host.

"I know anything there is to know. Everything in the Texts," I say.

"The Texts," Bastus scoffs. "Always the Texts with you. You are making decisions that affect all of us based on a few mentions in a single book? I know you humans like to hold the Texts up as the ultimate authority, but how long can you stick your heads in the sand?"

Xamson tenses. "What do you mean?"

Bastus sighs. Looking to Xamson, he straightens and relaxes a little. I can see the anger drain out of his eyes and he regains some of his composure.

"Think about it. What were the Texts created for?"

I frown. "To give men the history of the Gods and creation."

"No," Bastus says. "Think. They were created to give mankind the case for worshipping the Gods, after the First Realm War, after the Gods hid themselves away from the ones They want to worship Them."

Xamson frowns, too. "So you are saying the Texts are just deity propaganda?"

Bastus tilts his head back and forth, weighing Xamson's words. "Let us just say some of the passages may be sparse on details for a reason."

For a moment, as this sinks in, we are too solemn to say anything. Have the Gods been hiding things from all of mankind? What does it mean, really, to have been Chosen by such a being? The thought stuns me thoroughly. What are we really fighting for if we side with the Gods in this war?

I am pulled from my thoughts by a gentle touch—Xamson is running a finger over my arm.

"You are injured," he says.

But all I can feel are Xamson's fingers on my skin, with a warm tenderness I thought he would never offer me again. Something lights up inside me. I look to his face, then to where his eyes are focused on my arm.

He is right. On the outside of my upper arm, through a tear in my robe's sleeve, blood is trickling from a rounded set of tears in my skin. One of the Nephilim must have bitten me.

"Oh."

It is hard to care too much about it when Xamson is looking me over with so much care in his eyes.

"I have survived this far. What is one more scratch?"

"We both almost died." Xamson looks up from the wound to my face. "You saved me."

"No. I put you in danger." I take his hand in mine and stare down at them folded over each other, the dark and light fingers intertwined, too ashamed to meet his eyes. "I am a fool. I am sorry. I do not know what has been wrong with me lately."

The sword, my subconscious tries to whisper, the necklace. But no, it's not that. This started long before I started picking up enchanted objects.

"It is hard times. We are all struggling. And for you especially, none of this has been what was expected. You are doing as good as any of us are."

My heart pounds, setting my chest to aching and my arm throbbing under the rip of my skin. The wound on my arm is forgotten as he leans in, our foreheads press together. His breath is warm on my cheek, and it is like returning home.

Maybe everything between him and Bastus was just in my head. Maybe it's not too late. Maybe we can still reclaim what we lost. I lean in, hoping to steal a kiss.

It is too greedy. Xamson pulls away.

"We just...it is hard. This is better. For now."

He will not look me in the eyes.

Place me around your neck, and he will kiss you, the necklace prompts. He will have eyes for no other. A pang of desperation over comes me, but I shake my head and willfully loosen its hold on me.

I want to say more to Xam, but the distraction of the necklace lost me my chance. Before I can try again, a flurry of restlessness kicks in. Bastus has moved closer, and his aura ruins my moment, sends the pieces flying like embers kicked up in a wind.

He clears his throat, and the moment is gone.

"Right. We need to keep going." Xamson pulls away. "But aren't you going to heal him first?"

Bastus eyes the wound, hesitating. But then he clears his throat. "Of course."

He reaches out and hovers his hand over the wound on my arm, but then he hesitates. A knot tightens in his jaw, his eyes narrow, and for a moment I am sure he is going to change his mind and leave me bleeding.

But finally the dark shadow rushes from his fingertips and around my arm. The gash pulls back together.

"There," Xamson says.

I smile back at him. "Never better."

Bastus smiles too, the edge of his mouth tense. When he turns away, he runs a too-comfortable hand over Xamson's shoulders before dropping away and taking the lead.

From my pocket, where the necklace lays coiled, a burst of rage bites into me. Your history will never be enough, not while Bastus is here. But you love him more, you are the one who deserves him, it urges. Let me help you, we can win him together. He will adore you. He will never leave you again.

Before I know what I am doing, the necklace is out in my hand—it is only the glint of the green in the Host's sharp light that calls me back to myself. With a stab of remorse, I hasten to shove it away again.

CHAPTER TWENTY-TWO

WE WALK AND WALK and walk, deeper into the Host, and eventually we stop to rest again. We still do not feel hunger, or thirst, or the creeping need for sleep, but we try to fuel ourselves anyway. Then we lay down for rest. As soldiers, we know it is best to take rest where we can get it.

All the while, the necklace has strained and writhed, trying every way it can to tempt me. It pushes images into my mind, all the things Bastus and Xamson could do while I sleep, all the ways they could grow closer.

Let me help you, it urges. You deserve all his love. His adoration. Let me give it to you.

I glance over to Xamson stretched out next to me on the ground. His eyes are closed and his jaw tense. Bastus stands a few feet away, finishing the protection charms. He has turned pale again, and when he is done, he slowly drops himself to the ground and takes a heaving breath.

Good, it urges. Let him be tired.

I try to silence it and find peace, but instead the sword's aura joins in. Its hum is prideful and eager. That's when I realize; they are feeding off one another. The necklace's power alone wasn't enough to tempt me before. But it is wearing me down, and worse, now it has an ally. I should toss them both aside. I reach for the pocket where I keep the necklace tucked away.

You are a hero, the sword whispers to me. If you cannot wield control over the necklace, no one can.

My hand stills.

If the Forger can do it, so can you. You are better than he is. You have more good in you.

I shake my head, but it is not enough. I peek again at Xamson and Bastus. Xamson's breaths are slow and deep, the knot in his jaw finally dissolved. Looks like he managed to find rest this time. Bastus is feet away, curled up on the ground with his back to us, watchful over the Host's endless stretch.

There is nothing to be worried about between them, not for now. I can control the necklace and the sword. I have to. To discard them risks someone else finding them and using them against us. I imagine pushing away the urgings of the necklace and the sword as if building a fortress around my mind, and relax into sleep.

The moment I drift off, visions seize me again.

In the middle of the woods, not too far from the village, the branches of a tree turn to rot. Then they are brought back to life again. Then rot, then life, then rot.

Beneath it, Maelcolm has Koreh pressed against its trunk, and he kisses her. They are older now by a few years, Maelcolm is tall, his arms and shoulders roped with lean muscle. Koreh's dark hair reaches down past her shoulders in soft waves.

Everyone knows about them now, and the stares they once got when they walked together through the village have faded. But Maelcolm still prefers the woods. When they are in the village, the other boys and even some of the older men, even some of the women, follow Koreh wherever she goes, too eager to please her.

They do not talk about it. But he knows why they do it. And he knows how to fix it.

He draws back from her and pulls a small wooden box from his pocket and pushes it into her palm.

"What is this?" she asks. A smile curls over her lips as she holds it up to study.

"I made it," Maelcolm says. "For you. But the real gift is inside."

She opens it, and as the glint of gold catches the moonlight, her eyes widen. She takes it out and dangles it in front of her—a simple golden chain with a teardrop pendant.

"It is beautiful," Koreh says.

"It is cursed," Maelcolm replies, He reaches out and gives the pendant a playful push, sending it swaying.

Koreh frowns, a small line forming between her brows. "There is no magic in this."

"Ah, but the one I gift it to is cursed with my undying loyalty forever. Wherever you go, I will follow."

She smiles again, and runs a hand over his cheek. "Thank you." Then she draws him in and kisses him.

Maelcolm is pleased by it, but not satisfied. Not yet. There was more to his plan.

"Let me put it on for you."

He reaches around to the back of her neck, his fingers searching for the fastening of the emerald she always keeps on.

"What are you doing?" she says, pulling away.

Maelcolm forces a laugh, trying to keep the pounding tension in his head out of his expression. "Helping," he says. "So you can switch to the new one."

"No." She pulls away and runs her fingers over the emerald.

Maelcolm's blood turns icy in his veins. "You don't need it," he whispers against her neck. "Not anymore. You think I am only here because of that? I am not like the others. I am more powerful than it is. I love you. You don't need it anymore. You don't need them."

She clasps the necklace and shakes her head. Then she runs away, back toward the village.

Maelcolm is left alone under the tree, its branches still partially rotted, his heart cold and already calculating new ways to deal with this problem.

The dream releases me and I jolt awake with the sensation of freefall. The necklaces is pulsing in my pocket, hungry and eager, as if it knows I was dreaming of it and its masters. Desire for its powers throbs through me like a craving.

What has the Forger done to me with his curse? We are the same, you and me...

I press my palms into the ground at my sides and breathe in. I hold it a moment, bracing against the tension in my chest. Then I release it.

It is only then that I become aware of the movement behind me. Bastus and Xamson are packing the supplies, but they have not noticed I am awake yet.

"I'm sorry," Bastus says. His words are quiet, meant for Xamson alone. I prick my ears, determined to hear.

"What for?" Xamson replies.

"For deceiving you. I had to trick Jordan to come along, and I knew I could help, that he would need it. But I never wanted to start off with you like that. With a lie."

Start with Xamson? Start what? A knot tangles around my heart—I know exactly what. How dare he imply such a thing, with me lying so near to them, to my own partner—but then, Xamson is not my anything anymore.

I told you so, the necklaces whispers to me. He cannot be trusted.

Even so, we have hardly even broken up. If it could be called that at all. Xamson has said more than once—it is only for now. I cling to these small words, lock them away like promises even though I know they are not, cling to them so I can tell myself that it is okay.

Let me help you, I can win him back for you.

"Oh," Xamson says, and I can tell by his tone he is flustered. "Well...thank you. That is...that is..." He is fumbling now, trying to find a way to fend him off. How could a demon think someone like Xamson could be interested in him? "Flattering," he finishes.

Flattering? Does he actually like this...this demon?

Then he adds, "But you know where my heart lies."

My heart squeezes. I fight the impulse to leap up and wrap my arms around him.

"What I know is that you have only just finished things with him. And I know it was not working," Bastus says. His tone is low and intimate, the way lovers speak to each other, and it awakens bursts of rage under my skin. "I can wait, if you need me to. But I was struck by you from the first time I saw you, out in the battlefield against the Forger, and I will not give up."

I cannot help myself any longer—I roll over onto my stomach as carefully as I can and prop up on my elbow to watch them. Their backs are to me, but they face each other enough that I can read their expressions in profile.

And is Xamson actually blushing? My jaw clenches. When was the last time I made him blush like that?

"Oh—well—um," Xamson stutters. "I cannot promise anything."

"I understand," Bastus replies. He strokes a single finger over Xamson's strong jaw. "I would not ask you to."

Xamson does not pull away.

My throat tightens with fear, and suddenly all the realms narrow down to Bastus' neck, and the powerful wish to sever it with my blade.

I can end this before it begins, the necklace promises. He belongs to you. We can remind him of that.

I settle for yawning loudly and stretching my arms. As I rise to my feet, they turn to me. Bastus takes a step away from Xamson.

"Are you ready?" I fight back the rough edge in my voice. "Let's go."

We finish packing the supplies and begin walking again.

We hit a rhythm, and after a time, I realize something presses against my chest with each step, and a different kind of aura has slowly shut out the Host's—tucking under the folds of my robe, the necklace rests around my neck. I remember the burning craving for it, but I do not remember choosing to put it on. Yet here it is.

I am surprised to find that, now that it is done, I feel fine.

Xamson reaches out and squeezes my arm. He walks a little close, looks into my eyes a little too long, warm and smiling. It is so familiar, like our good times before Ir-Nearch burned, and my skin tingles with the promise of his touch.

I am stronger than the others who have tried to wield the necklace. I am stronger than the necklace. I will not allow it to get out of hand.

Yes, it is going to be just fine.

CHAPTER
TWENTY-THREE

WE TREK ON. No one says it, but I know we all feel it—this realm is endless, and our journey in it may be endless, too. I lead us on anyway, the two of them trailing a ways behind me. What other choice is there?

We walk for a very long time, an endless stretch of flat wasteland with nothing at all on the horizon, only bouts of overgrown marble tiles and overgrown fields, more of the same as when we first arrived. As we go, Xamson stays close to my side, and his hand entwines with mine, and something in me finally feels settled again, despite the sense that Bastus' eyes are on us always.

Forget him, the necklace urges. He does not matter. Not anymore.

Finally we come upon a young tree. It is rooted proudly, a spindly spread of branches reaching up, hardly taller than me. Around it, childlike figures whoosh and dart about in blurred flashes.

It can't be more nephilim.

We passed them, we left them behind long ago. They said they were the last of their kind.

But it is more nephilim. I would know those sharp features and even sharper teeth anywhere. Do they always cluster around trees like this?

"Take my advice this time. Let's go around them," Bastus says. "Maybe if we do not interfere and keep our heads down, we will get lucky, and they will not find us worth bothering with."

The great sword hungers for a fight, to take this challenge head on, but I dare not challenge Bastus again after how my plan went last time—how close Xamson came to becoming their victim. I resist its call this time. Besides, with

Xamson at my side and the necklace's warm satisfaction pulsing over me, I feel no desire to argue.

Bastus in the lead, we arc far around the nephilim and their tree. I keep my eyes on them with every step. Xamson, however, traipses at my side, relaxed and unconcerned. With his hand in mine, I am unable to wield my great sword as a precaution.

As strange as the nephilim are, some of them look familiar, too. Some have markings just like the others we saw before. But before I can wonder on this oddity, one of them looks up, and its blank silver eyes meet mine.

It chirps. The others turn to it, then to us. Soon they are all chirping.

At first it sounds like the chittering the other group used among themselves—almost like birds. Almost, except that this sound is harder. Biting. Taunting.

The rude sounds start to shape into words, and I finally manage to catch some of it. "Chosen," one chimes.

Is he calling to me? Gloros' sword bursts with eagerness at my side, lighting me up from the inside. Do they have a message for me from the Gods? I almost turn to them to ask. But then the cawing voice cuts through again. "Un-Chosen."

Anger flares through me and stings to my core.

"Here he comes," another says in a singsong crow. "The Un-Chosen."

"Least favored of the Gods," another chimes.

"The Abandoned One!"

They are laughing at me.

Heckling.

The words burn through my veins like ropes of flame.

Who are these creatures, banned by the Gods and hidden away here to contain their sacrilege, to deem me Un-Chosen? To call me anything? What could they possibly know about it? I prefer the ones who bit and scratched at us.

"Chosen," more of them crow in chorus, "Chosen, Chosen, Chosen, Chosen."

The word is mocking and cold.

I whip side to side to steal glimpses of how Xamson and Bastus are reacting, but their heads are down. Xamson loosens his hold on my hand and inches away. They are so embarrassed by me they will not even look at me. Fury and shame wrap around me in crackling sparks, stinging my skin in blotches and catching in my chest.

Because the worst thing about their taunting is that it is true.

I finally admit it to myself: I have been un-Chosen. The Gods have left me. I am nothing anymore.

What did I come to the Host for at all? What did I expect?

A soul for Adem, a determined voice in my mind answers back.

And it is not a lie. I wanted to do this for my friend, and it was the only option left. But it was more than that, if I am really honest with myself.

Deep down, there is a small part of me that thought if I could only reach the Gods, if I could find them, that somehow it would fix all of this, and I could get my Chosen-ness back. That I was still the one meant to fix all this. As if any of it was ever fixable in the first place.

This understanding aches deep down to my bones.

The only thing worse is that Xamson and Bastus are here to witness my shaming—a fitting one, yes, after all my pride and willfulness, but does it have to be in front of them?

Yes, I realize. It is just what I deserve.

I dragged them into this. I talked them into this terrible idea, and they have suffered, even put their lives on the line for it.

I duck my head down and will myself to keep putting one foot out, and then the other, and do my best not to fall into the singsong rhythm of the nephilims' chant.

My now-empty hand takes hold of the hilt of Gloros' sword and clenches down so tight my fingers ache. It fills me with a swell of heroic vengeance, indignance for the injustice of the nephilims' taunts, a surge of determination to silence them no matter the cost.

But then, a rumble rises and the ground trembles. As it charges our direction, it muffles out all else.

Chapter Twenty-Four

At first it is nothing more than a slight groan of the earth, but the trembling grows until the ground rattles, and the sound of hooves and thundering paws charging toward us is unmistakable. The nephilim's taunts die under its thundering.

It is a stampede.

Beasts. The word forces its way to the front of my mind. The next of the plagues.

I look past Bastus, disbelieving, and squint through the mass of rising dust headed toward us. It is just as the Texts describe. Birds and boars. Lynx and lions. Creatures I have never seen before, too strange to take in amidst the chaos.

Their charge has become thunderous, each stomp quaking through the ground and into my body, shaking loose a terror that vibrates into my bones.

The nephilim squawk and scatter.

I turn on my heels, and together we race to stay ahead of the charge.

The muscles of my legs and shoulders knot. My lungs heave, the air stinging as it pumps through me, never quite enough. But there is no time to give in to it—we must run.

Run, run, run.

The rumble of the stampede rises in my ears until it is pulsing through my chest, and at the edges of my vision, the beasts are catching up and closing in. I am thrust forward as something rams into me, and my thigh is pierced with a hot, cutting pain. I stumble, a gasp catching in my throat.

Run.

But I cannot.

I tumble toward the ground, sure I will be trampled under the furious rain of hooves, but a hand catches me and a voice is in my ear, "Faster."

There is no time to whimper that I cannot, that I have already given all I have, that I am not enough. The hand grips me tight and my body disappears into whooshing shadow.

In a blink I am solid again, thrust to the ground from the remaining momentum, and even as I tumble I am aware of the stillness around us. Bastus has brought us safely away.

Sprawled over uneven slabs of marble, I try to steady my breaths, try to recover from the sensation of breaking apart and pulling back together, try to get my mind around what just happened.

A stampede.

Beasts.

It is certain now, then. I have set off another round of the plagues. Gloros' sword presses against my side with new weight.

I steady myself, pushing my hands into the broken marble slabs at my sides to fight the sense that I am spinning out of control. A few feet away, Xamson is on his hands and knees, gasping.

I wish to the Gods I had never done it, that I had left that Godsdamned sword right where it was, that I had never brought us here at all, that we were all still in the relative safety of Haven.

But it is too late now.

Un-Chosen. The nephilim's taunt echoes in my head.

That is exactly what I am. As if the Gods looked down, and they saw what I had become, and they knew I was no longer worthy to be Theirs. Nothing but more bad has happened ever since I led us off on this quest. Me? Favored by the Gods? Definitely not.

A singsong swell fills me in resistance, the great sword's aura pushing back. What I did when I took up the Mantle saved us from the beast. What else could I have done? If I had not taken swift action to defend us with it, we would not be fleeing a stampede right now, sure—because we would have been finished long ago, torn apart by the beast back in the Great Hall.

But another voice, a doubting one, the voice that has haunted me ever since the Gods left me, creeps back in around it. Maybe the terrible truth is, it does not matter why I took it. Only that I did. And that Bastus was right—it was the wrong move.

Un-Chosen.

The unforgiving truth of the word stings.

"Where is that blood coming from?" Xamson rushes to my side and places a hand on my waist as he looks me over.

My skin tingles where he touches me, and under it, a tremor of satisfaction from the necklace, still tucked under my robe and pressed against my chest, to have his attention. Still, my impulse is to reject his concern.

"I'm fine, I'm fine," I say.

To prove it, I try to get up, but a white hot pain flares in my leg. I gasp and drop back to the ground, remembering the stabbing shock that tore through me as we ran.

My robe is slick with red, and when I pull it away for a closer look, I cringe. In the flesh of my thigh there is a deep hole and blood rises from it in steady surges. The flesh is torn and jagged, exposing the flinching raw muscle within.

I was pierced from behind, I think faintly. That means this wound runs all the way through my leg. And that the other side is worse.

I try to process the significance of the wound and come up numb.

As Xamson studies the wound too, his nostrils flare and his brow pulls low over his eyes. He strokes a hand through my hair, and despite everything my chest fills with light. The necklace is doing just what it promised. I try to lean into him, but the pain shoots over me with the movement.

"Easy, easy," he says, pressing his lips into my forehead. Then he turns to Bastus, who has kept his distance. "You have to heal him. Fast."

Bastus studies me with arms folded over his chest, his eyes narrowed and sharp with suspicion, and his lips press together until they are nothing but a thin line. Is it only jealousy at Xamson's attentions toward me? Or is it more? In what ways would the necklace's power influence him? Suddenly I realize I have no idea—can the necklace influence First Creatures? He moves to us slowly and cuts between us, forcing Xamson to step away.

Bastus leans in close to study the wound. He flashes me another suspicious glance, then he stretches his hands out around it, and the whirling darkness seeps out from his fingers. I wait for the healing to start.

The smoky magic disperses, but my wound remains open and throbbing. A knot twitches at Bastus' jaw and his fingers quiver.

Bastus mutters something under his breath. He stretches his hand out again, and again the shadow that disperses is halfhearted.

Un-Chosen. The nephilim's chant rushes back to me and cuts through my pain.

"I get it. It's okay. You don't have to pretend," I say. I try to pull away but only manage to shift an inch or so.

Bastus tilts his head. "What?"

I glance at Xamson, leaning over Bastus from behind him. I lift myself up to talk low into Bastus' ear. "I said, I get it. Okay? I know you only came along for Xamson. And I...I am nothing to you. All I do is make everything worse. I'm just a fool who thought I could chase down the Gods and somehow set things right all on my own. Un-Chosen. As if I were ever capable of fixing any of this."

"Un-what?" Bastus says.

"Un-Chosen. Just like the nephilim said," I say.

"The nephilim?" Bastus frowns. "They did not say anything about an Un-Chosen. They didn't say anything about you at all. They were attacking me."

My mind jams. "What? No—they were—they said—"

"No," Xamson cuts in. "That wasn't about either of you. It was me. It was all my fault."

Oh Gods, he heard me. I had not meant for him to hear me. But what he said...the confusion is too much, I cannot bear that Xamson has been thinking that this was somehow on him.

"You are both confused," I say. "They were all chanting it. Un-Chosen. Me. The boy who the Gods chose, then changed Their minds about. I was not enough. And they all knew it."

"No, it was all about me," Bastus insists. "They were not saying Un-Chosen. They were calling me demon. Traitor. Unworthy."

"I don't know how you heard that, but you are both wrong," Xamson says. "It was all about me. How ungifted I am. How I do not belong here among the Gods, among the Firsts and heroes of Terath."

We frown, staring at each other.

How could we all have heard such different things? How could they so easily believe such lies about themselves? I may not like Bastus' attempts to get close to Xamson, but with the necklace pushing against me, even I have to admit Bastus has proven himself to be anything but a traitor. He has done all he could to fight with us for the Gods. And Xamson has proven time and again he is among the bravest and best of warriors, even including our supernatural allies.

The answer slams over me like a hammer—they believed these things for the same reason I did: Because they already thought them.

"How could they know?" I exclaim. "They knew. All of our deepest insecurities. They targeted us with what they knew would hit us hardest."

We fall silent, stunned by the revelation.

But then I realize, it does not matter. The same truths plague us as before.

"Just because they playing with us, though, that does not mean they were not right, at least about some of it. They were right about me. This is all my fault. You should leave me. One decision after another, all I have done is make things worse for all of us. You would be better off without me."

It sounds flimsy now, my plan for all this. As if we were ever going to simply march into the Host and make demands of the Gods. How did I ever think this could work? Now, stuck on the ground and bleeding out, I cannot think of anything more foolish. It is all over. I have pushed them both past the breaking point, I am sure of it.

But then Bastus turns, and kneels next to me.

"I am not holding back my power from you because I do not find you worthy," he says. "There is something wrong. Every time I use my magic since we got to the Host, it is harder, like the realm is rejecting me. I did not want to tell you. I have been slowly losing my power."

He stares down at his hands as if they have betrayed him. A twist of guilt for judging him is chased with a fear that burns at the edges. If he is losing his abilities, we are more vulnerable than we can afford to be.

"Which means we all have a much bigger problem than being lost, or this little love triangle," he continues. "I tricked my way into this quest with you because I thought I could help. But at this rate, I will soon be completely worthless. You were right. The Gods do not welcome my kind here."

Speechless, Xamson's mouth drops open and he runs his hands over his head. "But—you just saved us from the beasts," he says.

"Yes," Bastus replies. "And now I seem to be...out."

He shakes his arms, as if he could loosen the magic free from them, as if it is hiding in his crevices. "I will try again."

I sigh. "Bastus really—"

"No," he says. His brow creases and his eyes flash like lightning. "I can do this."

I am not so sure, but I do not dare tell him so. I let him place his hands over my leg a third time, try to hold as still as possible as his hands quiver, an unstable heat emanating from them.

What if he cannot?

His jaw clenches. His eyes glaze over. The quiver in his fingers turns into a shake.

Then, slowly, a thread of shadow wraps around my leg in a wobbly spiral. Against all odds, it seems to do its work. Something tugs and knits deep within the wound. The bleeding slows. Then, the shadow dissolves away again.

"I am sorry. That is all I can do." Bastus' head bows forward, and a tuft of black hair falls over his face. His complexion is tinged and clammy.

I look at my leg. There is still a wound, but the bleeding has stopped, and with the blood gone, it is clear that it no longer runs all the way through my flesh.

"This is a lot better," I say, forcing myself to my feet. The pain is at least manageable now. "Thank you."

It is not just the wound that feels better. With everything out in the open now—the nephilims' taunting chants, the terrible doubts that have haunted me, the guilt I have carried ever since we started this quest—it is as if clouds have cleared away. I cannot cleanse myself of the responsibility for any of this, but it would do no good for me to give in to the guilt and turn away from Xamson and Bastus now that I have led them here.

"Great," Xamson says. He does not sound great, and when I turn to him, he does not look great either. He looks furious. "Then maybe one of you can explain what you mean by this love triangle."

His anger takes me off guard. I thought he was coming back to me. I thought the necklace was doing its work. But then it hits me—ever since we retreated from the stampede, he has stayed back, letting Bastus work on my leg.

I have to get close to him again.

I glance to Bastus just as he looks to me, and as soon as our eyes meet I realize it was the worst thing I could have done—now it looks like we were scheming together. Xamson scoffs.

"There is nothing calculated going on here," I start. The necklace doesn't count, I tell myself. He was mine first. We belong together. He will remember that soon. "You know, you have to know, I still love you. Is that so bad?" There is a pleading tone clinging to my words, thick like fog.

"No, this is my fault," Bastus says, stepping out in front to face Xamson. "All I asked Jordan for was a chance. For him to let you make up your mind about me for yourself. And he has been more than honorable in this. And if you tell me now you think he is better for you, that he is the one who can make you better, and this is done, I will be just as honorable."

"I only did it for you," I move toward Xamson. "You have to understand, you were injured—unconscious—and I needed him to—"

"I don't have to anything. Here is what I understand," he snaps. "I understand that the two of you are making deals behind my back over who gets a shot at me. I understand that we are in the Host, and everything possible has gone wrong. We are suffering a series of plagues. The Gods are gone. Our magic is running out. And you two are bartering for romantic advantages like children vying for the last sweet. Am I missing anything?"

I glance to Bastus, who meets my eyes then drops his gaze to the ground, his cheeks flushing. My face grows hot with shame. Xamson is right.

I do not know what to say, and for once, I do not try.

When no one else has anything to say, either, I get up. "Nothing to do but keep going."

What other option do we have at this point? What other chance?

Xamson drops his head and kicks at the ground. "Keep going where?" he mutters.

"Forward," I say, pointing to the horizon.

"Like there is anywhere worth going in this Godsforsaken realm," Xamson grumbles. But then he storms forward, fists clenched at his sides.

And he's right. We have no idea where we are going at all. But what else can we do? There is no going back. Giving up, turning back, does nothing for us.

I start after Xamson, but Bastus takes my arm and holds me back.

"I may be losing my own magic, but I can still sense when it is in use around me," he says through gritted teeth. "I can still see plain as day what you are up to."

The necklace throbs against my chest.

"I don't know what you are talking about," I say, tugging my arm back.

"No more lies," Bastus says. "In fact, don't say anything. Just hear me. I know you have the necklace, and I know you are using it. He will keep getting more irritable, you know, when he is away from it. And when he is near it, his affections will get more and more...intoxicated. You forget, I have seen for myself what the necklace is capable of before. It is not a toy to keep a loved one close. It is a curse, and it will hit both of you with its wrath. It will destroy you, if you let it. Stop it now before this gets out of hand. Before it gets all three of us killed."

Then he thrusts me away and storms off behind Xamson.

Guilt bites at me, then is swallowed in anger.

He is jealous, the necklace whispers. Forget about him.

It is enough for me to start following after them.

Besides, we have bigger problems. If Bastus is losing his magic, we are far more vulnerable now.

CHAPTER TWENTY-FIVE

IT IS NOT LONG before the next plague is upon us.

Illness.

With Bastus' powers to heal becoming so limited, we trudge through the Host in a feverish haze, aches in our bones, boils and rashes on our skin. I cannot be sure, but at times it seems like the haze becomes literal, as if we are being wrapped in a blank white nothingness that wraps around and through us. Is it a hallucination? Is it part of the Host? There have certainly been tales of prophets whose visions manifest in strife and sickness. All I know is what I see.

A figure looms on the horizon.

At first it appears to be Adem, walking away from me into the wasteland. He will not turn back no matter how I shout and cry and plead with him.

Then a twist in the light, and it is the Forger. He is coming toward me, that crooked walking staff swaying overhead. We are alike, you and me.

The visions continue to change as we walk.

Sometimes it is nothing but a tree, broad and tall, its branches reaching out like it is calling me home.

Silence hangs in the haze like death, punctuated with nephilim chirps, cruel and taunting.

Visions loom and twist through my mind, and I weave in and out of them like a restless sleep.

Churning. Spinning. Hands in wet clay, molding it into shapes.

Maelcolm is determined—maybe Koreh does not yet trust that their love stronger than the magic in the necklace, but he can be strong for both of them. He has been training all year, and now he has the power.

To overcome her resistance.

To prove himself to her.

The others may only be drawn to her because of the jewel she bears, but he is different. Better. Real.

"Careful," his angel companion warns. She hovers over his shoulder behind him. "Your abilities have come a long way, but bringing a chthonus to life is precarious and unpredictable."

"Enough, Syliel. I have heard your warnings," he says.

He is no fool. His power has grown so great not even Syliel can keep up. She may have tapped the well and shown him the key to drawing his power forth, but now it flows with a force that cannot be slowed.

He will not be held back.

Night after night, he waits for Koreh to fall asleep at his side, then slips away to the woods. One chthonus after another springs to life, each a shadow of what is possible, a promise, but not strong enough. He can do better. He casts them aside, putting them to sleep with a charm, and moves on to the next. The chthonus to hold and protect the necklace must be perfect, and perfect he will reach.

The Forger's memory flashes me through each creation, each chthonus roaring to life, then failing to be enough. Moons swell to full, then ebb to nothing, and return again. The Forger works through pressing heat and crashing storms and shrouded fogs.

Finally, a chthonus thrashes to life with a rasping shriek. The Forger cackles with delight. The creature roars and struggles to its feet, its chest heaving as it tests its limbs and takes in the woods around it.

It is Adem.

The Forger's work is done.

Almost.

Adem lurks after the Forger all the way back to the small home he shares with Koreh. When he goes in, he orders the chthonus to stop next to the door and wait. A moment later, he slips back outside, the necklace coiled in his fist.

Next, he carefully tucks the necklace into a small box—one he crafted moons ago for this very purpose, layered in the most powerful of charms. A green light bursts from his hand as he uses one final spell to seal it shut, then places it in Adem's hands. He gives him another command, just a few words of spelling. Adem marches for the woods, with no sign of stopping any time soon.

We stop for rest often. I drop to the ground and spread out my limbs, not bothering to lay out my sleep sack or even let go of my blade. Xamson lays at my side, our arms pressed against each other.

Sometimes I hear Bastus and Xamson's voices threading through the air around me, though I do not know if they are real or part of the visions.

"I could be good for you," Bastus would say. "If you would let me."

This again. Even in my fever haze I roll my eyes at his persistence.

"Are you not already in a battle over another love with Calipher? How has that worked out for you?" Xamson would reply. "Do you really want to wedge yourself into a second couple?"

"I loved Nia, and I mourned for how it ended for her," Bastus says. "But she has been gone for many ages. Angels may have immovable loyalties in their hearts, but demons are more flexible, if we want to be. I am able to let her go. I am able to be whatever you want me to be."

There is a rustling sound, like leaves in a forest. Then again. And again.

"Stop!" Xamson says, his tone suddenly taking a turn.

I bolt up, my head swaying from the fever and sudden momentum, and force my eyes open to see what is wrong. When I find Xamson, he is standing face to face with—me. I tilt my head, the ground spinning, and then collapse back into my haze.

Another rustle. A long pause. When the voices return, they are softer than before.

"I could have loved Nia forever, if she had let me. But she did not. With time, I adapted. I have loved others since—Demons. Women. Men."

"Just keep moving on until you find some easy affection, do you?" Xamson replies. "I'm afraid I am not so flexible as that, and find it nothing to brag about."

"It is not like that," Bastus says. "And do not be so sure. Humans are change. You will get over that boy. Maybe sooner than you think. All I am saying is that, when you do, I will be waiting."

Xamson says nothing else.

Will he get past me so easily? Has he already started to?

Real or delusion, I search myself for the festering resentment and jealousy to rise, but I cannot find it, not with the stinging heat I had before. The necklace's power throbs with comfort around my neck—there is nothing he can do to take Xamson from me now.

As if to reaffirm this, Xamson sidles up to me and entwines his hand with mine, and in the haze an overwhelming sense of connection and intimacy swells through me.

We keep walking. My mind dips and spins with the fever, between worlds, between realities.

"Where is it, Maelcolm? Where did you hide it?"

Sparks fly from Koreh's fingertips in her tantrum as she tosses items out of drawers and sends them crashing into walls.

The Forger stands in the corner, waiting for her to tire herself out. He does not expect it to take her long.

"It was my mother's, you fool. It is full of power you cannot begin to understand."

"I understand enough," the Forger replies. "Enough to know that we do not need it, you and I."

Koreh shrieks and throws a candlestick at him, which he catches mid-air with his power and lets it drop to the floor.

Days pass. Weeks. A month. Koreh still does not forgive him.

And the Forger finds that his patience wears thin.

And his passions, too. He deserves more.

He deserves gratitude. Praise. She has no idea what he has accomplished, does not even care. She cares only for the Godsdamned necklace, even still.

Only one has ever truly recognized him for what he is.

"She does not deserve you," Syliel urges to him, stroking his neck and leaning into him close. He can smell the warmth of her glowing skin, an un-sweet florality like roses, the unforgiving judgment in her voice sharp as thorns. "Forget her. She will come back and find it is too late, and she will regret it all her life. But you will not. You and I, we will do great things."

The Forger considers. What he finds in his heart is that the lure of great things entices him more than this girl and her tantrums now. He turns away from the village, and together they disappear past the trees and onto whatever lies beyond. The Forger folds his bitterness into his heart, keeping it close so that he never forgets and makes the mistake of giving away so much of himself ever again.

The fever continues to rise until I would be willing to rip off my own skin for relief from the heat. The ache in my muscles coils in on itself and multiplies. The ground dips and sways. I put one foot in front of the other, but I cannot make sense of the movement.

Xamson's hand clutches mine, hot and slick even through the fever. While my mind has been lost to visions and haze, the necklace is doing its work to bring him back to me. The pressure of his hold is like a tether, holding me to reality, the reality I want. I grip his hand tighter.

When a tree comes into view on the horizon, with the familiar flashes of nephilim silver catching on its branches, at first I am sure it is another hallucination. But the vision does not disperse into haze as we approach. My confusion turns to irritated bursts of rage. More nephilim? More trees? It does not make any sense, and I cannot bear one more thing that defies reason.

"No," I exclaim. "That is it."

Instead of turning to avert our path around them like before, I let go of Xamson's hand and pull Gloros' great sword from its hilt. It sings, assuring me that I have nothing to fear from the nephilim. I stomp toward the tree.

"Wait—" Xamson reaches for me, and I dodge around him, too focused to stop to explain. He calls after me, "What are you doing?"

I have no patience left to explain myself. But as I storm away, I hear rushed steps as Xamson follows. It feels good to finally have him on my side again, for him to be fighting to help me rather than to stop me. The necklace's power pulses through me.

Bastus whooshes to my side. "What exactly are you doing?" he asks.

"Don't you feel we have been going in circles?" I say. "I do not know how, but we have to be. And I am going to prove it."

My head dips and sways, and I cannot tell whether it is from rage, or illness, or the sword, or the necklace. I am pulled in too many directions to balance. Too many to bother distinguishing them all anymore. This is what I want to do, and I will do it. Demons, nephilim, Gods be damned.

"No," Bastus says.

"Yes," I reply.

"What if they attack again? I do not have the power to heal you again, not now." Bastus may be a First Creature, but he has fallen prey to the plague of illness as much as any of us, and now his steps are wobbly, his pallor clammy and tinged.

"They will not." I reply. I do not bother explaining why I am so sure of it. I hardly understand it myself. But sure as I hold Gloros' own sword, the nephilim are done attacking us.

Even if I am wrong, it would be worth another attack, just to know. My leg still twinges with every step from where the beast pierced me in the stampede, the wound still fighting to heal and no better for the bouts of illness. But I cannot stand the oppressing strangeness and confusion and unanswered questions any longer. At least in this, I can gain some clarity.

"But—" Bastus starts again.

No more. My anger hums around me in waves and twitches so tense they could combust. The tree is getting closer. I cut him off.

"If you cannot do anything to help, then stay out of the way," I say. "You are only jealous that Xamson is returning to me."

"Jealousy? You think that is what this is about? We both know better than to think you have won him back in earnest," he says. A large finger pokes me in the chest, right over the emerald, and sends a shock of chaos through me, and a nagging guilt kicks to the surface. He continues, "You do not want to be meddling with such forces, mortal. And I will not let you drag Xamson into danger with you just because you choose pride over reason."

Then he storms away, leaving me with my blade and my resolve and the whispers of the necklace. He takes Xamson with him, despite his protests.

Fine. I will do this on my own then.

The tree has grown even more since the last time we saw it—if it is indeed the same one as the others we have passed, and now I am convinced it is. The trunk is as broad as Xamson's shoulders, its branches stretching out proud and strong, its leaves full and rich green. As I approach, the nephilim leer at me from their branches, but I brandish the great sword, and they scatter like birds. Though I did not believe they would attack again, it is still a relief to have their strange watching eyes off me.

Now it is time to get to work. I square off with the tree and swing the great sword into the trunk as hard as I can. Despite its legendary power, the blade barely sticks into the wood. Has the plague's illness made me even weaker than I thought? I should be able to do this. I will do this.

I hack at the trunk again, and again, frustration clouding my chest with the futile effort. Finally I stop, worn out from the exertion, but unwilling to let this go. I change tactics and stab at the tree with the blade point-first, wedging it in as deeply as I can at an angle, chipping away at it over and over and over. The chips gradually fall away, creating a gaping wound in the side of its trunk. Still, I keep at it, unable to stop the cathartic, repetitive motion, until a hand squeezes my shoulder.

"Jordan?" Xamson pleads. Bastus must have given up on holding him back any longer.

He reaches for me and runs a gentle hand down my back, reestablishing the connection between us. My arm relaxes to my side in response to his touch. My chest heaves from the effort, reminding me how far from well I still am. I step back and wipe a film of cold sweat from my brow with the back of my arm, my muscles quivering, the ache of illness so deep I cannot determine where it starts and ends.

I turn to Xamson. His eyes are seeking and hungry—an expression that looks foreign and ill-fitting on his face. They bore into me as if they are searching for something they cannot find, something the necklace promises, but that I cannot deliver. Guilt settles in me like a layer of ash.

I turn back to the tree. Its side bears a raw, open wound, already oozing with a glaze of sap. Guilt nags at me for attacking something so defenseless, so beautiful, but it is flooded out by triumph. The next time we come across the tree, we will know if we are going in circles or not.

I nod and rest my sword. Xamson continues to cling to me. The necklace's power warms my chest and dances through my veins. He is mine again, finally, and all is as it should be—as I wanted it to be.

He is yours. Like he should be. Take him.

I lean in abruptly, intending to kiss him, but something holds me back. Xamson waits, head tilted, lips poised, and tension builds like electricity in the small gap between us. Finally I drop my head and pull away from him, afraid of the truth he might find in my eyes. Why can't I push off this nagging guilt and enjoy his touch? I don't want the answer that lies beneath the necklace's aura. So I block it out.

"Let's go," I say. Then I push past Xamson, head bowed to avoid Bastus' studying eyes, and keep going.

We slowly recover to full strength as we continue to walk, and for a stretch the way is quiet. I am grateful for it.

All the while, Xamson stays close, lingering around me and touching me frequently—stroking my arm, taking my hand, running a finger down my back. And with each touch, tension knots in my chest. Bastus trails somewhat behind, occasionally letting fly a disapproving scoff. Is it me, or is the sweet perfume of the air turning sour?

Finally we stop for rest. Xamson lays his sleep sack right next to mine, and as we settle in, his arm wraps around me like it used to. My cheeks flood with satisfied heat, and the necklace's aura curls up in my chest, warm and satisfied.

Underneath it all, a tinge of guilt keeps me awake.

"Xamson?" I can tell by the rhythm of his breathes against my shoulder he is awake, too. "I'm sorry."

It rings hollow, even to me.

But Xamson squeezes me. "What in the realms for? You have nothing to apologize for. I am just glad to be here, with you."

I roll over so we are face to face, and finally I make myself look him in the eyes. They are clouded, unfocused. Nothing like the warm, brave Xamson I love.

And I finally admit it to myself: This is not Xamson, not really.

I should take the necklace off.

The necklace pierces me with a punishing clench. And then what? Are you prepared to lose him forever?

The thought fills me with despair like a well, too deep to see the bottom, and I cannot do it. I glance to Bastus, his back to us as he looks out to the Host, standing guard. His spine slouches forward and his shoulders hunch. He is still sulking.

Maybe the Host was not the most dangerous thing, or any creature within it. Maybe it was the thing I carried on me into this realm, all along.

Or maybe it was me—my own pride. My own weakness.

Whispers rustle through me, pushing back against my doubts.

It is what you wanted, the necklace says.

You are a hero, the sword insists. You deserve this, and all good things.

A sickening twist rolls through me, though I know the plague has passed. For the first time, I am afraid that may be all too true—that this may all be exactly what I deserve.

I wake up still entwined with Xamson, his arms so tight around me it constricts my breath, and Bastus towering over me, his icy eyes sharp and accusing.

"This is what you choose for the person you claim to love most? I thank the gods you have decided I am your enemy."

The necklace's aura surges in resentment, but I push it down before it can start to feed its lines to me.

It is over.

And if I'm honest with myself, I am relieved.

I wriggle free of Xam's hold and push myself to my knees. I don't dare look up to meet Bastus' eyes. I have never been so ashamed of anything in all my life. I chose this, eyes wide open. I knew to expect the necklace's lies, and I let my ego convince me I was stronger than it was—this magical thing that has started wars. I knew better.

It was the height of hubris.

And now I've caught myself in my own trap. I did not have the strength to resist it, and I most certainly do not have the strength to forfeit it, even if what it has given me is a mere echo of what I crave.

"Help me," I whisper.

Bastus' feet stumble back, and his voice catches. Then he finds his footing again. "What happened to the warrior who was so great, he did not need help from a demon like me?"

I flinch at the hard truth in his words, but it is no more than I deserve.

"I was wrong. I know that now. If I am honest, I knew it all along, somewhere deep down. I don't know what's happened to me, I have lost sight of everything...I..." I hardly know what words will spill out of me next, I only know I can't keep trying to carry everything alone, or it will ruin us all. "Please, help. I need to get it off. But I do not know if I am strong enough."

I pull on the chain to draw the emerald out from under my robes and expose it to him.

Bastus hesitates. But then he sighs, and kneels down next to me.

"I cannot remove it for you, it will not let me. But I can help you do it." His eyes are steady, pulling me back from the ledge of my desperation. "Come, we will do it together. Ready?"

"Now?" My voice breaks. I am not ready. Maybe one more night with Xamson, just to say goodbye, and then—

I shake my head free. Bastus is right. Now. It will never get easier, no matter what I try to tell myself, no matter what lies or bargains the necklace throws at me. I will never be ready. Not to let Xamson go. But it's past time for me to do it.

"Okay. Let's do it."

The necklace threads through my chest in resistance, tugging at my heart. I run my fingers over the emerald and then up the chain, gripping my hands around it. It calls and pleads, whispers promises to me I know it cannot keep. I shut my eyes hard, my chest heaves.

"Don't listen to it, Jordan, listen to me. Do you hear me?"

His large hands take hold around mine, reinforcing my grip.

"Yes."

My fingers squeeze tight around the chain on both sides. The aura courses through me like a current, trying to drown out everything else. My head rolls back and a gasp parts my lips.

A large hand grabs mine, tight and strong. "Jordan? Do not let it win. You are stronger than it is. Are you ready? With me now, one, two, three."

On three, he nudges my hands, and we lift up and over my head. I follow his lead and bow my head forward. As we lift the chain away, the necklace fights one more time, filling me with a full-body ache, a loneliness, a promise that this is all my future holds without its power. More isolation, more fear, more anguish.

I freeze, trembling at the thought.

"Jordan." Bastus' hand presses into my shoulder. "Don't stop now. You are winning. Keep going. Let's finish this."

I forfeit to the emptiness. Maybe I will feel this way the rest of my life. There is no other partner for me than Xamson. I know this much. But I cannot keep him, not like this. My love for Xamson runs deeper than my need for him. This is what I tell myself. I do not know if it is true, but I want it to be true enough that it gives me the resolve I need.

I lean forward and drop the necklace to the ground.

The sense of loss, of emptiness, swells until it is bigger than me, and I collapse to the ground under its pressure.

Bastus' pale hand sweeps the necklace away.

"You did good," he says. Another hand presses into my back and runs back and forth between my shoulders. Under the current of chaos, I feel release. "I'll put new charms on it. I'll carry it now."

"Won't it tempt you, just the same?" I ask.

"It is different for Firsts. Its pull is not as strong. My magic against it is stronger. Even here, in my weakened state. It's over, Jordan. You won."

But it is not over. Not yet.

It can't really be over until we find a way to destroy the necklace for good.

And in the meantime, I have Xamson to face. Does he know what I did to him? What will he remember from being under the necklace's influence? What could I possibly say to him to explain?

Despite the ache still quaking through me, I force myself to my feet and go to his side.

When I reach him, I can't help but laugh—he slept through all of this.

I drop beside him, and as I do, he shifts toward me. When he opens his eyes, they're clear and focused again.

"Xamson? Are you okay?"

My heart pounds like a drum.

He sits up, that slight crease I've always loved forming between his brows. "Sure. Other than being woken up for no apparent reason."

I can't help it. My relief spills out of me in a laugh, and I squeeze Xamson and kiss him hard on the cheek. "Sorry."

Am I really so lucky to have been spared this final shame? It is more than I deserve.

We gather our things, and soon we are walking yet again. As we set off, I catch Bastus watching me as he settles into his stride next to Xamson, and in his eyes, I think I catch a glimmer of newfound respect—and a promise that what has passed will remain between us, that it will not become a weapon for him to use against me to win Xamson over. Gratitude flares in me, and I nod to him in response.

Perhaps we've managed to earn a fresh start. For all three of us.

CHAPTER TWENTY-SIX

EVENTUALLY, SURE ENOUGH, A tree takes shape in the distance again. My heart throbs in my chest—finally. We will get to the truth of all this. We will see if we have been walking in circles from the start.

I dodge around Bastus and Xamson, and run toward it, my weariness suddenly gone. I am too eager to see the proof of what I am already convinced is the truth.

As I approach, I look around for flashes of silver, but the nephilim are nowhere to be found.

My muscles tense—did they never come back after they scattered? Why not? Or maybe I'm wrong. Maybe there were never nephilim around this tree. Maybe they really have each been different. The stillness of their absence is haunting. Like a void.

The tree has grown again, now with a trunk stout and broad, and thick branches that bear nuts and cast a shadow over me as I approach it. It is remarkable how quickly it has grown. Unless it's not the same tree at all. The very thought makes my pulse race. If I am wrong, then I will have only succeeded in making myself seem mad to Bastus and Xamson. Maybe, with all this time in the Host and the whispers of these enchanted objects, I am going mad. I circle around the trunk, searching, searching, searching, my anxiety tangling in my throat. But I cannot find the raw cuts I left in it.

No. I cannot believe it. I circle the tree a second time, slower, studying the patterns of the bark more carefully.

This time, I find a great knot that disrupts the pattern of the bark, where it seems to have grown over something. If it is indeed the same tree, the great hole

I hacked into it has healed over as it grew. It feels too much to be a coincidence. But it is not enough for me to be sure.

I trace my fingers over the raised, swollen knot, and flames of anger burst within me. I want to shout to the skies until my voice cracks under its weight, but I swallow the rage back down. Xamson and Bastus close in behind me. Xamson puts a hand on my shoulder.

Am I going mad? Have I lost myself in this strange realm after all?

I shake my head and run my fingers over the knot. "I did it—I would have sworn my life on it. Was it all a fever dream?" I squint, trying to sort the delusions of the plague from the true memories.

"I saw you do it," Xamson says. "I thought you had lost your mind. But this..." He frowns as he stares at the scar. "Could a tree grow so much since we were at the last one? How long have we been walking?"

Our bewilderment gives way to silence. I shake my head. Who knows. With no sun or moon we cannot even witness a passing of the days here, let alone track the hours or weeks.

"No time. There is none. Not here, not here."

The words drop from overhead. A panic quivers over me, but then I realize the voice is a familiar singsong lilt.

I look up and meet the gilded gaze of a nephilim, now perched over us in the tree's branches. It is the solid silver one with the small odd wings all over its lithe body. Has it been here the whole time? Could I have missed it before? It stares down at me, the pair of wings behind its ears fluttering eagerly. Its mouth hinges open, almost like a smile.

My heart hardens and cracks. I do not know how, or why, or what any of this might mean, but there is one thing of which I am now beyond certain: this is the same tree we passed the last time, and the time before that, and before that, and all six rounds of our trek through the realm.

Anger wells up and overtakes my fear, spreading through my body like wildfire, biting at my fingers and all the way down to my toes.

If the Gods had not fled in our time of greatest need, in a time where we are fighting for Them, I would not have needed to come here at all. I could have closed my eyes and reached out and felt the answers I needed in my heart, easy as breathing. They always told me what I needed, what to do. I always had what I needed to feel what was right, like there was a compass planted in my heart. Their absence has been like a hole torn through me.

"What do you want?" I cry—not at the nephilim, but at the sky. "What do you want from me?" The last word cuts into a quiver as tears threaten to come forth.

The nephilim cackles with hard laughter.

Out of words, I kick at the tree, as if I could shake the nephilim out of it and to the ground, relishing the throb in my leg's wound.

It stares down at me and tilts its head.

"Chos-en?" it lilts.

It is the final straw of what my soul can bear. I set my anger loose.

"Enough!" My hands tighten into fists.

Bastus steps next to me, glaring up at the nephilim. "It's time we settle this once and for all."

"Gods, yes," I exclaim.

We lock eyes, an in an instant we're in sync.

Bastus whooshes into the tree. The nephilim bolts to fly away, and his fingers just barely seize onto its clawed foot. It leaps and flails, but Bastus tugs and drops back to the ground, bringing it with him.

Between us, Bastus and I manage to wrangle the nephilim and pin it to the ground, despite its many flapping wings and thrashing limbs. Bastus holds it in place with his knees on its largest wings, and his hands pressing its shoulders down, panting from the effort of using his magic.

Finally, we will get some answers.

CHAPTER TWENTY-SEVEN

ON MY KNEES ALREADY from the struggle, I shift to lean over the nephilim and peer into those eerie blank eyes. Xamson remains standing, leaning away from us with his hands in tense fists at his sides.

"This seems like an awful idea," he says, stepping a little further back. "Are we sure we want to do something that might make the nephilim even more antagonistic toward us? What if the rest of them come back? What if it escapes and tells the others?"

I glance to Bastus. He shrugs. "It is too late now," he says.

I nod. "We might as well get what we can from it. Try not to let it escape."

Xamson runs his hands over his head, groaning. "When did the two of you start conspiring together?"

A long pause stretches out. The tingling pressure at the back of my neck tells me Xamson's eyes are on me. The nephilim flinches again with a loud screech.

Xamson sighs. "Fine, fine. But don't hurt it."

Bastus looks to me and nods. I lean forward over the strange creature.

"Where are the Gods?" I ask it. I try to keep the desperate edge out of my voice, knowing Xamson is assessing every syllable.

The nephilim cackles, as if I have told a great joke. "It is going to be angry at you. It is going to get you, if you stay here"

"Who is? The Gods?" I demand. But that does not make sense. I remember the strange thing that came after us in the Great Hall and haunted my fever dreams. "Do you mean the beast? What is it? Is it what destroyed the Great Hall?"

The nephilim only cackles more—a grating sound that makes my head throb.

"The tree," I say, pointing to it. "Why is it growing so fast?"

The nephilim shakes its head, laughing even harder.

"It is the same tree, right?"

The nephilim keeps laughing, breaking into hysterics. I stare at it. I am so lost and exhausted and desperate for answers, I feel I am a breath away from letting go of my sanity and joining it.

I look to Bastus and shake my head. I am out of even my worst ideas. He frowns back and twitches as the nephilim writhes against his hold.

My anger boils under my skin. What will it take to understand what has happened to this realm? What has happened to us while in it?

I lunge down close enough for it to bite. "Listen, you," I hiss. I grip its jaw in my hand between trembling fingers. "Tell us. Tell us." Something. Anything.

The nephilim squawks and writhes.

"Stop, stop, stop!" Xamson snaps, shoving me back. "This isn't getting you anywhere, can't you see that?

Now that he has forced me away, Xamson takes my place over the nephilim and smiles down at it.

"What is your name?" he asks.

Its name? Do nephilim have names?

The creature looks as stunned as I am. The hardness flickers out of its expression, and it tilts its face toward Xamson, questioning. Xamson waits.

"Phedre," it finally says.

Xamson's smile broadens. "Phedre," he repeats. "I hope you can help us."

Phedre's muscles relax, and its scaly wings pull into its sides. It blinks.

"I—I do not know," the nephilim says. Its head lifts with eagerness and it seems to relax. "What is it you want?"

I can't believe it. Did Xamson really unlock its willingness so easily? He does have a way with difficult creatures. The thought almost makes me grin.

"Do you know what happened in the Great Hall?" Xamson asks. His voice is slow and gentle. More like he is talking to a scared child than to a monster.

Somehow Phedre's eyes grow even wider. "They came for Them," it says. "They came."

My heart's beating thuds quicker at its answer. "For the Gods? Who came?" I demand, leaning over Xamson.

Xamson stretches a hand out to quiet me.

"Do you know who they were, Phedre? What did they look like?"

Phedre shakes its—her?—head. "Destroyers. Made of ash, made of mud. Big angries with big magics." She throws her arms out swinging, making soft shpew, shpew sounds as if she were casting spells.

Bastus looks to us. "Soldiers of mud— chthonuses."

"The Forger," Xamson agress.

It fits—the beast healed like a chthonus. It must have come with them for the attack.

"But how?" I am too stunned to worry that Xamson and Bastus are now finishing each other's sentences. "It simply cannot be possible."

Only the most righteous were supposed to be able to break through to the Host. But then understanding strikes me like a rod over the head. Only those Chosen by the Gods for such a gift were supposed to be able to create chthonuses, too. Whatever the realms and the Order once were, everything has gone terribly awry a long time ago.

"The Order broke—snap!" Phedre says. "Snap-snap!" She giggles, as if it were a joke, in love with the sound. "Snap!

"What did they do to the Gods?" Xamson presses. I bite my lip, anxious for answers but afraid to break whatever hold Xamson has over Phedre that has managed to get her talking.

"The Gods?" Phedre tilts her head. "They are gone."

I flinch in desperate eagerness. Xamson's hand grips my wrist faster than I can react, reminding me to stay calm.

"Where did they go?" I prompt.

Phedre curls in on herself against Bastus' slackening grip on her shoulders, but then her head tilts again and she considers. "Go? Nowhere. They have gone and They are here. Here, here! Safe, they went to the safe place. Seven times around, seven circles," she says.

Seven times? Seven times around what? What do we need to do? Tell us! I clench my fist until I can feel tiny beads of blood give away under the pressure of my nails.

"How do we get there?" Xamson asks.

I hold my breath.

"Oh," Phedre nods. "You are close! So close! All you need is—"

Whatever Phedre says next I do not hear, because thundering steps rumble toward us, chased with a sky-shaking roar.

In my gut I know before I even look up. It is the beast—the thing that attacked us in the Great Hall, the thing that leered over my fever dreams, the thing Phedre warned of.

It strides toward us with heavy steps, and this time I can see it clearly for what it is. Its three heads are crowned in eyes that circle all around it from every side, one sagging to the side from the wound I cut through it the last time we faced it. Its six arms reach out to swing from every direction from broad shoulders. Six legs tear toward us in heavy steps that shake the ground.

It roars again, and then its legs propel it forward with terrible speed, blurring its form at the edges. And it is coming right at us, a wall of force barreling forward like a bolt of lightning.

I am so transfixed by its strangeness that I almost forget to draw Gloros' great sword. But I will not make the mistake of failing to protecting Xamson again.

I swing the weapon in front of me, stepping forward to shield Xamson, Bastus, and Phedre. I hope I can hold it off at least long enough for us to get this final answer from her.

Beyond the rumble of its steps, shouting voices try to reach me, but I hold my focus on the creature charging at us. Its eyes are vacuous dots pushed deep into its heads, and twitches of thick muscle rope over its necks and shoulders. It is so close now I can almost feel the wind shift in its roar. I take a final steadying breath as I swing my blade—

But then something grabs me from behind and I watch as my sword and arms break apart into shadow. The beast tears past unobstructed as we fade away.

We reappear in an open field I am sure we have passed through again and again.

As soon as I am pulled back together I turn on Bastus.

"What in all the realms are you thinking?" My hand tightens around the sword's blade in anger. "That was our chance."

"He would never forgive me," he says. He does not look me in the eyes, instead turning away.

"What—"

But then Xamson runs up, throws his arms around me and holds me tight, tight enough that I feel his heart pounding against mine through our rib cages.

"Gods, I thought it was going to end you. What were you thinking?"

I see now. Bastus did not do it out of a sense that he needed to save me. He did it for him.

I put a hand on Xamson's arm, still clinging around my neck, and pull back slightly so I can look into his eyes. For a moment I am lost in them, stunned by the way they still feel like home, even full of anger and fear as they are now. It becomes too much, and I look away.

"Sorry," I say.

Xamson studies me, then lets me go, turning to Bastus.

"We have to go back," he says. "We have to help Phedre."

"I tried to bring her, but I did not have enough magic left," Bastus said. "Transporting her was different. Harder. Like she did not want to come. Or maybe she could not."

He stares down at his hands as if they have betrayed him.

"It's not your fault," I say, reaching out to give his arm a squeeze. "But Xamson is right, we have to go back for her. Do you have enough power left to get us back to the tree?"

He nods. "I do not know if I will be able to get us away again once we are there, but I can get us to the tree."

Bastus reaches out to hold us both, and we break apart into darkness again.

We materialize back at the tree. Everything is too still. The beast is nowhere to be found. Phedre is nowhere to be found.

"Phedre!" I shout. We spread out, looking for her across the Host's barren stretch and among the tree's branches. "Phedre!"

But all is silent.

In the ground around the tree, twigs and leaves from the branches are scattered as if torn away. The earth beneath is a mad cluster of marks from digging claws and frantic swipes. A few silvery scales are scattered over the ground.

Did the beast get her? Did she flee and escape? There is no way to tell.

I look back to the tree, its trunk now gouged with claw marks from the beast. I stroke what is left of the tree's inverted knot one more time. "I guess we have to keep going."

We all agree.

CHAPTER
TWENTY-EIGHT

AS WE LEAVE THE tree, I now notice the Host's power has been building within me since I freed myself of the necklace. As we depart from it again, it swells in my chest with an energizing high and pulses through my veins, sweeps through my head like a river's current.

Bastus, however, is a different story. After the escape from the beast, his complexion never returns to normal, instead maintaining an ill-omened greenish tinge. He keeps up, but I do not know how much longer he can do it.

All the same, we keep going, doubly vigilant now after the run-in with the beast. Phedre's wide eyes haunt my memory. Where did she go? Does she need our help? I keep watch for signs of her as we walk, but see none.

Bastus is wheezing now, a slight, audible strain with each expansion and release of his breath.

I slow my gait to walk beside him, letting Xamson take the lead.

"Are you all right?" I ask.

Bastus nods in response, clutching at his side.

"It must take a lot of effort to remain in human form like this. Why not go back to your true form?"

"This is my true form," he says. He spreads his arms as if to display himself.

I hadn't realized he felt so strongly about being among us, about being human. But still, the effort has to be wearing on him.

"I—sorry—I didn't mean it that way. Just that, doesn't it take a lot of work—a lot of magic—to hold yourself in this form? You're a demon. There is nothing wrong with that. Let yourself look like one for a while. It's only us here."

A soft chuckle escapes him, and then he winces.

"Sure. Magic." He smiles, but his eyes do not hold the icy fire they used to. "It is usually so simple I do not even have to think about it. But here...this realm...it frightens me, the way it is draining away my power. Even if we find our way back to Terath, I am not sure how long it will take to return to me. If it ever will."

He stares down at his hands as if they have betrayed him.

"I am afraid that if I go back to my demon form, I might not be able to turn back again."

"You need to allow yourself to rest. How long can you keep this up?" I say.

He nods. "I am not a monster, Jordan. I am not a traitor. But when I am in that form, that is all anyone can see."

The wheezing is growing worse from the exertion of speaking. His chest rattles.

"Look, you—we all—could use a break. We need to stop. We need to think. If during that time you want to take, well, a different form for a moment, Xamson and I will be looking ahead, thinking about how to keep moving forward. You have guarded over us enough times on this journey. It is our turn to take watch while you rest," I say.

Bastus tilts his head as if considering. I've almost convinced him.

I press more. "And if you cannot turn back again...well. I think we have already seen the worst of you by now anyway."

Bastus cracks a half-smile, too tired to fire back at me. But he nods, and then he goes ahead and sits on the grassy ground.

I call Xamson, and we sit facing out into the endless fields, our backs to Bastus. Shoulder to shoulder, we stare out into the Host.

"You were incredible, by the way, with Phedre. I do not know how you thought to handle her that way," I tell him.

Xamson tilts his head and looks to me. "Well, I learned from the best."

"Who?"

Xamson frowns. "You, of course."

"Me?"

He rolls his eyes. "You have always been incredible with people. Have you forgotten the way they followed you? How they loved you? You led an entire army. You built cities. You set the entire framework that allowed us to fight back when the rebels came. Without you, we would have been lost before the war ever began."

I look down and let my head droop. "That was all a different time. An easier time. When things got hard, all of that fell apart. What kind of leader lets that happen?"

Xamson shifts to leans back, and his fingers brush up over my own. "I wish you could see what the rest of us saw."

My chest seizes. "And what was that?"

"A man great enough to put his people's needs ahead of his own. One willing to admit what he did not know, to take responsibility."

I still can't bring myself to look back up to him. "It wasn't enough. I wasn't enough."

"No one person can be, in times like these," Xamson says. "The only thing you were ever steered wrong by was trying to be everything all on your own."

A weight releases from around my heart, a weight that had become so entrenched within me I did not realize it was there. In the sudden relief it grants me, tears blur my vision. I try to blink them away, then give in and let two lone drops run down my cheeks.

A quiet settles over me. Xamson and I sit, shoulder to shoulder, staring out at the Host's gleaming sky, stretching endlessly over the field.

After a time, Xamson breaks the silence.

"It really is beautiful, you know?" he says. "Even now in the destruction and battling against the plagues, and all of that. When we are not fighting or trudging along for what feels like ages. It really is. Just think how few people ever get to see this? But here we are."

Only Xamson could look out at all this wreckage, all my mistakes and foolishness that led us here, and still find the beauty in it.

"Yeah," I echo. "Beautiful."

He has a point. I try to look out at the stretch ahead of us through his eyes. The Host is not perfect like I always dreamed it would be, but there is a certain peace within it. With Bastus and his aura farther from us right now, it settles in me—in the stillness of the moment, in the heat between my skin and Xamson's—and I just enjoy it for a moment.

"I might like it better this way, actually. A little imperfect." I say. "I think it makes it more beautiful, not less."

Xamson nudges me with his shoulder. "That is easy to say when you have never seen it any other way. Maybe you would like the perfection if you were lucky enough to encounter it."

I consider it.

"I used to think that. But perfection is too much. Too much to look at, too much to ask for, too much to uphold. To be surrounded by that much perfection, it could flatten you. Look at this. What could possibly be any better?"

Staring out at it like this in such quiet, coming to terms finally with what it really is, versus what I expected from the tales of the Text—the fantasy and lies—it is like seeing it all for the first time. The crystal clear sky is tinged with a halo of pink along the horizon, the field's green is vibrant, and the gentle light catches across the long rustling blades of grass as they sway in a gentle breeze. I tilt my head back and take in its warmth.

"You two planning to sit here until eternity?" Bastus' voice reaches into my relaxed mind and pulls me back to reality.

"What if we are?" I ask. But even as I speak I am pushing myself to my feet and allowing the fears and questions of our quest back into my mind.

Bastus is in the same human form as before, his eyes the same shocking ice-blue, and his skin just as pale, though without the sickened tinge he held before.

"All good?" I ask him.

"Good enough," he says. "At least for now."

Relief floods through me, and not just because he might be able to help us now that he is stronger. True concern had wormed its way into me. Despite our impossible situation, I am surprised to find my dislike for this demon fading.

CHAPTER TWENTY-NINE

THIS TIME WHEN THE tree takes shape on the horizon, I am not surprised.

It is even larger, even grander than the last time we passed it. Its branches stretch so high they seem to scratch the sky, and its trunk is too thick to hug my arms around. The knot remains in its side, and over it, stripes of pulled-together bark have healed over the beast's clawing. Its branches are covered in great blooms of white flowers.

And against all odds, Phedre is back, perched on the tree's lowest branches. I am surprised by how relieved I am to see her there again, and break into a run to reach her. She looks up as we approach. With all her wings flapping excitedly, she gestures for us to come, come, come as if she has something urgent to tell us.

But as we approach, it becomes clear the tree has transformed. It is not just that it has grown more, becoming broad and stout. Bursting from its new, bright blossoms emanates a shimmering film. As it cascades down the tree, the flowers' bursts weave into each other, so that the entire tree is cocooned within its sheer wrapping.

"What is this?" Xamson asks. As he catches up to me, he leans forward to study the film.

"For the realms are fraught with layers of troubles, but the way of the righteous cuts through the veil." Bastus is quoting the passage from the Texts before I can fully remember the words.

From the other side of the veil, Phedre gestures again.

Come.

It is not just Phedre that wants me to cross over.

The Gods are calling for me.

Their presence is strong and pulsing through every particle of my being. It is not only through the great sword that can I feel them now, but through the tree, from inside the film. Their presence curls into me and plants within my chest.

Come.

A sense of a homecoming comes over me, sweet, eager, so powerful it strains my breathing.

At my side, Gloros' sword sings, a hum so intense it vibrates to the hilt. I place a soothing hand over its hilt and step toward the veil.

The Gods.

They are calling for me.

I have to go to Them.

I reach for the film.

"What do you think you are doing?" Xamson exclaims. He pulls me back.

"Can't you feel it?" I say, reaching toward the tree. "They are here."

Xamson's brow slowly crumples into a frown as he understands.

I place a hand on his arm and squeeze, pulling away to turn back to the tree.

"But are you sure you want to go in?" Bastus says. "What if it is a trick? What if we cannot come back out? The magic wrapped within this is powerful. It might not be the tree on the other side at all."

Xamson glances to it again, then looks me over. "No. Don't do it."

But Xamson is not mine. I have let him go. And though my heart has a split through it from this truth, in this moment, it is freeing.

I take another step toward the veil. "Phedre wants us to come. I thought we trusted her now. I trust her."

"Jordan—" Xamson's grip on me tightens, holding me back.

I hang my head, unable to look back to him.

"Jordan," Xamson pleads. "Jordan. This is not yours to take on. The world is not yours to save all alone. This is enough. You have done enough. You are enough. We can find another way back, I am sure of it. Just go home. Reclaim our lives."

How much would I give to do this, with him? Almost anything.

Almost.

The great sword's aura swells through me, eager and proud. But I let go of its hilt and shut my eyes, and I dig deep within myself to find another voice. A voice I have not listened to in far too long. A voice that is mine.

I find it. I listen to it. And I know.

This is something I must do, not to seize glory and prove myself a hero, not for the glory of proving how special I am, but because this time, the realm needs someone to go through, anyone, and I am here. I can feel enough of what lies beyond the veil to understand this. I feel it in the way the Gods call to me from beyond the tree, something Xamson cannot feel, but I can. And I know this is the right thing.

"I do not expect you to understand. I do not expect you to give me your blessing, or even to forgive me. Really, Xamson, it's all right. But I must go now." I reach out and squeeze his shoulder, and the split in my heart twinges. "I know you feel responsible for me. But you aren't. You never were."

Xamson's hands drift down to mine and stroke over my fingers. "You promised."

My heart reaches for him, and my body yearns to curl into him and let his arms wrap around me, lead me back to the life he sees for us.

But whatever lies beyond the veil calls to me. Everything is too broken, and that life feels more like a child's tale than the Texts' strange myths. Adem needs me to do this. The realm needs me to do this.

"I'm sorry." It is all I can say to him. "I have to."

He lets go. "I know."

My heart throbs, swelling out when it should pull back in.

Bastus steps up behind him. "I—" he starts.

"No," I say. "Stay with Xamson."

Then I turn to the veil. My skin grows heated as the fear flushes over me, chased with prickles of steely determination.

I draw the great sword, and with a few large quick steps, I am through. The veil pierces me with a torrent of vibrations, like it is welcoming me. Like it is hungry for me.

But as I step through, Phedre looks away, leaning forward on her branch, and screeches with a chilling pitch. Everything reels. The sense of rightness that propelled me through the veil yanks away, and my stomach drops out.

I look back just in time to see the beast charging toward Xamson and Bastus, its six legs propelling it forward in a blur, its three heads roaring.

But it is too late—momentum carries me through the film, and that is all I see before the veil drops behind me.

CHAPTER THIRTY

THE VEIL SWALLOWS ME up and spits me out the other side. Phedre's screech cuts off abruptly, leaving me in chilling silence. My ears ring, still reaching for her cry, and then flood with a heavy, pounding pulse.

Xamson. Bastus.

I push back and brace against the veil, trying to cut back through to help, but I only stumble forward into shadowed darkness. The veil to the other side is lost. I shout their names and race back and forth, sword drawn and hands quivering.

Nothing.

Bastus was right. There is no returning from this one.

I freeze, trying to force my mind to come up with an answer, but then suddenly something bursts through. I brace myself, sword raised, ready for the beast's attack—but it is Xamson. I am so relieved to see he is fine that my legs turn wobbly.

He stumbles forward, then steadies himself, and assesses me. "I thought we were past all this fighting," he says.

A laugh stutters free from my throat. But there is no time for games right now. "Where is B—"

Bastus bursts through even as I speak. A second wave of relief comes over me, but at the same time, I tighten my hold on the great sword. Will the beast follow next? I turn in the direction of the veil, but nothing else comes.

"What happened? Where is the beast?"

Bastus shakes his head. "It does not seem able to break through," he says. "It was the first thing it tried, when it saw you go through."

"We thought you were done for," Xamson adds. "He wanted nothing to do with us; he wanted you. Charged right for the veil. But it could not pass through. The veil propelled it away. Phedre knew. She cackled and taunted it."

All the same, we keep our eyes in the direction of the veil, still waiting for something to go wrong. But the silence is all that answers back.

As the quiet settles and my body begins to trust it, I become aware of a deeper feeling, something so wholly overwhelming I could not process it at first.

The Gods.

Their power fills the air here, packed so tightly I slow my movements. The others must sense it too, because they pause, their shoulders settling.

The Gods are near.

We assess the darkness, as if They might by hiding among the shadows. Across from us, where on the other side of the veil the tree had stood, three altars now stand. As if they have been waiting for us.

In the middle is an altar made of diamond.

To the left is one of onyx.

And to the other side, one of gold.

For a moment we all stare, the wonder and power of being in the true presence of the Gods seeping into us.

We found Them. Finally. We really made it here.

This is the only thing this feeling can possibly mean. Whatever we broke through when we crossed the veil, it brought us to the place the Gods have retreated to. They are so close I hardly dare breathe for fear of desecrating the sacredness of this space.

We stare at the altars, unsure of what to do now that we have made it here. Then Xamson sets his shoulders and steps forward. Standing his tallest, he places the sack with our food and water onto the diamond altar.

"What are you doing?" I say. This one sack contains all of our provisions. Even if we do not seem to need them here in the Host, we will need them once we are back in Terath for the trek home, however we finally make it back there.

But my panic is chased by a stillness that comes over me like a breeze, and I know this is the same feeling that led Xamson to do it. It is a compulsion, a need—to forfeit. To make a sacrifice.

We have to make an offering to the Gods.

One for each passenger. One for each altar. One for each of the Gods. Diamond for Theia. Onyx for Shael. Gold for Gloros.

"The fruits of your realm, returned to you," Xamson whispers, as if in prayer. Then his hand drops from the pack, and he steps back to us.

Bastus then takes his turn, stepping up to the onyx altar. He bows his head and rests our pack with the sleep sacks and other supplies onto it.

"We submit to the chaos of your creation, let it lead us where it will," he says.

There is only one sacrifice left to be made. But what could I have that Gloros would find worthy? The Goddess of Passions and Victory?

Does She even deserve my sacrifice, when She has hidden Herself away like this? Do any of Them? The question comes to me unbidden, a hard, angry seed of resentment for all we have struggled on Their behalf during this war. While they were...what? Hiding here? Why haven't They made Their presence known?

But I must do something. Can I find my way to faith again, after all that has happened?

I must, or all of this, the weary trek, the plagues, the seven times around the tree, the fights with the beast, it was all for nothing, and Adem will never have a soul. I must make this sacrifice in blind faith and hope the Gods know what They are doing.

I must choose to act in faith that They have not abandoned us, even if I cannot feel it.

I approach and kneel in front of the gold altar, still unsure of what I am doing. Xamson and Bastus already offered everything we brought with us. The only thing I have carried on this journey is the necklace—a corruption to the Gods' Order, already forfeited to Bastus—and Gloros' own sword. Only this, and my own determination.

As if in reply to a call, the blade quivers against my side.

I know what it wants, what the Gods want. The only thing I have worth giving.

No, my mind pushes back. I cannot give that. It is too much. Sparks of anger burst from within me and bite through my limbs. After everything, how could the Gods dare ask it?

Why would they want it?

But Their presence seeps deeper into me, wrapping all the sores and aches of my soul in salves, and for once I remember there is something bigger, something more important than my own understanding. It has been so long since I chose anything but fear and anger that the movements feel rusty and unpracticed in my soul, as if borrowed from another lifetime. But I do it. I choose to trust.

I pull the great sword out and lay it upon the mantle.

As I let go of it, a short burst of wind rushes through me.

You give me my own sword back and call it a sacrifice?

The voice is bigger than its sound. It fills the air, rattles my mind, quakes through my body with ethereal power.

"No," I say. "With it, I forfeit the illusion of power it offers. I forfeit myself."

Even as I say it, the words hurt.

Behind me, Xamson's gasp pierces the air.

But I surrender all the same. I kneel forward, tilting my head to bare my neck. I brace myself for the blow.

The Goddess does not take me.

As I wait for sword's cut to come, every particle of my being cries out against my will. I cannot. I have more to do, more to give. I have not finished with this world yet. I let the thoughts come, and then I release them.

Who ever said I deserved anything complete? Who said this life was ever mine to begin with? If not to the Gods, I should have forfeited my life to Xamson long ago, dedicated myself to his happiness, rather than my own glory. If I had only done that, so much might have been different.

I kneel and I wait, but the blow does not come.

"Very well."

I rise in response, and beyond the altars, something new catches my eye—an energy, a shimmering curtain that was not there before. Another veil.

I have to go through it.

As I give in to its call and move toward it, I am aware of voices—Bastus and Xamson—calling for me to keep back. But I do not stop to listen to them. I already know what must be done.

I let the veil take me, leaving Bastus and Xamson behind yet again, knowing this time, they cannot follow.

Chapter Thirty-One

I pass through the veil and am transported back into the Great Hall. But it is not the destroyed hall we found when we first came to the Host. It is the Great Hall as it was meant to be, in all its perfection and glory.

The columns stand proud, the tables are long and straight. At its helm, three thrones stand glowing and restored—no, not restored. New. Whole. It is as if they had never been shattered at all.

A burst of feeling overcomes me, and the Gods' presence courses through and around me, and all through the Great Hall.

It is more than relief, it is release.

And yet the release is tainted with a bitterness, because it comes with understanding: My gift did not fade away. The Gods went away from me. They have been right here this whole time, cocooned in their veils.

Hiding.

In Their own realm, while Their people put their lives on the line, defending Them against the most terrible of enemies.

"We thought You were gone," I say. My voice bears a gruffness I cannot hold back.

"We have not abandoned you."

I gasp. Theia—She is speaking to me. Not in the quiet, secret way She used to, planting Her words within me. She speaks to me here, out in the open, Her own true voice echoing off the marble columns.

Each syllable disperses into the air like magic, like pure light. I shut my eyes and tense my hands into fists—no. It does not change what They have done.

"You mean you have been here the whole time. Hiding," I say.

"We do not hide. We are Gods."

The anger turns and lurches in my chest, heating until it burns.

"What do you want to call it then?" I say. "Because we can call it whatever you want to, but look at Yourselves. You are not even fully present within Your own realm. You have locked Yourselves away in this...this inner sanctum."

If I have learned anything from all that has happened, from my time leading Haven, from Adem, from Rona, from Avi and Helda, it is that a leader must step out in front, be a living example of what they want of their people.

And all I see here is cowardice, retreat.

I wait. Nothing.

"Do You have anything to say at all? For Yourselves? For Your creation? You cannot create the three realms and all the creatures to populate them, and then turn away when they begin to collide."

It feels good to finally hold Them to account for what They have done, to finally let loose the embers of this raging fire that has built within me.

"Your creatures are caught in a war, they are dying over You—for You—and You have pulled so far back that we cannot even feel You in Your own creation anymore. The rebels, the beasts coming out of the helmuths, the necklace. We are not enough without You. Help us. Why aren't You doing anything?"

Suddenly I wish I'd thought to take the necklace back from Bastus before crossing this final veil, so I could throw it before Them and demand They take it on Themselves.

Still no response comes.

"Don't You see us struggling? Problems that should be Yours to resolve, created by Your creatures and magic You gifted, then failed to reign in. We're...we're failing without You."

The anger pounds through me and I keep pushing, determined to make Them give me answers. Now that the fire is set loose, it is consuming me, and everything else is set free, too.

Why won't They take it? Why won't They help?

"I have done nothing, nothing in this life but try to figure out what You gifted me with these abilities for, and to be ready for it when the moment came. All my life I was told I am special, that I was Chosen, that I had some kind of great destiny ahead of me. But You never told me what it was. And I found it, or I thought I had, leading Haven and preparing them for Your damned war, just as my mother prepared me. But it was all wrong. And then You left me altogether, just when it mattered most."

As if I were never anything special at all, I want to add. But I cannot make myself say the words, because I can see it now. What all of this has come down to, what Xamson has been on my case about this whole time, is this. The struggle to prove I am special.

What was it for?

My chest heaves with a choked sob.

"All things have purpose. Your destiny will still come for you," Theia says. "Everything changed when the rift opened up between the realms."

I shut my eyes, trying to clear my head. Finally, something They will respond to.

"You mean when Adem broke into the Underworld."

Silence.

"But we knew there would be a rift. It is in the Texts."

The Texts do not talk about how it happens, but it was inevitable. We all knew the Third Realm War would come eventually.

"Many paths to the Third War were foreseen. This was not one of them. The chthonus was not seen."

"Adem?" I take another step forward. "This is all because of him? You are going to tell me that in all the three realms three Gods came together to create—all-powerful beings—and You could not account for a chthonus?"

"He is not Ours."

The hardness in Her voice reveals resentment, and perhaps even deeper, shame at the failing.

They will never give me a soul for him now. Not when he is the root of all of Their failing. But they must.

"If all things have a purpose, so does he."

"All of Our beings have purpose. He is not Ours."

"It doesn't have to be that way. He can be so much more. He already is. He is a piece in all of this now. And if he is a piece, then there must be somewhere that he fits. He must have a place."

Silence fills the hall.

I press again. "Did You not claim him when he took down the fallen angel You had set loose in our realm? You gave him Your word."

"He was not seen in this."

"Damnit, it is too late for that," I shout. I am so fed up with this line I could burst. How many times have we been told this excuse as the Third War crumbled the realm around us? "Seen or not, Adem is in it. He is changing everything. Can't You see that? Are You able to see any of the war from in here?"

He may not be Theirs, since he was not made by them. But the Forger is a man, and that makes him a creature of the Gods. And Adem was made with angel magic. That makes it the Gods' magic.

If anyone was Chosen, if there is anyone who this whole war hinges on, it is Adem. Not me. That should have been obvious from the start, if only I had not been so set in my own significance. It is clear now, here in the Gods' light.

I could not admit it to myself before. I thought I needed to be special, or I had no reason to be at all. Now that I can step away from all of that, it is clear as day—this was all about Adem from the start.

And yet still they seem unable to see it for Themselves.

"Can't you? You do. You must."

A supernatural tension buzzes in the air, tightening and humming, a stretch of increasing pressure. Have I made Them uncomfortable? The Gods?

I wait, sensing their struggle, and allow Them the quiet.

Finally the answer comes. "He is not ours."

Anger burns through me.

"So make him Yours," I shout, throwing my words at the stoic figures on the thrones. Even if I cannot manage to hold Them to account for the rest of it, I am determined to resolve at least one thing, the thing I came here to do in the first place. "You are Gods."

"A soul," They prompt.

"Yes. Give him a soul. Make him human. Will that not claim him as Yours?"

The tension tightens and shifts, growing until the hairs on my arms rise under its pressure.

"A soul cannot be held on its own. It must be kept in a body."

I step forward so quickly it is almost a leap. "Give it to me. I will carry it back to him."

The Gods hesitate, and I get the sense that they are assessing me, determining if I am capable of what I ask.

"You do not know what you offer."

"No." How could I? "But I mean it all the same. I want to do this for him, for the realm. I do not matter in all this, but he does, and he needs a soul. Please, let me bring it to him."

There is another unreadable pause. I wait.

"Come to Us," They say.

I walk the rest of the way down the Great Hall, past the rows of columns, past the tables, to the foot of the thrones, my heart thudding with the echoes of my steps on the marble. The closer I get, the harder it becomes to distinguish where one of Them ends and the next begins, the intensity of Their light blurring them into one.

As I reach the front of the hall, the Gods rise. They are all light, dancing in all its shades and colors, pillars of energy and brilliance.

They huddle in a circle, Their backs to me. From within, I can see flashes of magic as They work, great magical bursts of light and color and promise. It the most wondrous, most beautiful thing I have ever witnessed.

When the sparks of Their work die down, the Gods step back, and Theia comes forward, the new bursting, flashing thing They have created in Her hands. She glides forward and brings it to me. She puts a hand on my arm, and Her power surges through in a blinding burst, a torrent, a force.

I fall to my knees.

But Theia continues her work. In my blindness, I feel the thing they have created—powerful, naked, volatile—pour into me. It comes in a hot burst, then curls up near my heart, as if it recognizes me. My ribs push out to make room, my chest too tight and my breath strained. Its pulsing energy burns with each throb.

Theia lifts away, and I fall forward, clinging to the marble tile as the thing she has placed in me settles, something new and alive and not mine, writhes through me.

A soul. Adem's soul.

I can feel him in it as easily as I would know Haven's sea breeze—his restless yearning, his quiet steadiness, his bold earnestness—and remember all over again just how much I have missed him.

I attempt to rise, but my legs are unsteady. I stumble with a gasp, and topple back to the ground. I am overfull and wobbly, almost to bursting. There is not enough space within me for both of us.

"Jordan!"

Xamson's voice pierces me, and I try to will myself to my feet. They let him through.

I turn my head toward the tap of footsteps, but my vision is altered by a halo of light.

He is still perfect and familiar in his Xamson-ness, but I see him now in a completely different way. What I see is not his face, his body, his smile—but his potential, his destiny, his purpose.

And Xamson is a wondrous prism of splayed lights, majestic in his beauty, noble in his strength, clear in his calling as an arrow in flight. He is whole, and looking upon him makes me more whole, too.

I fall in love with him all over again, fully and completely.

And I think I am beginning to understand.

All this time, I did not think anyone was special, not like I was, not with the purpose I had been Chosen for. I thought this was something for me to carry all on my own. An honor. I could not see the burden of this, the way it had weighed on me and broke me down.

But this was never mine to carry. Not alone.

And in hoarding it to my chest, I made my burden precious, and I blocked everyone out, the Gods, Rona and Adem, even Xamson. And I did not see the walls I built around myself with my pride. Because none of this is about me at all. Every one of us has been chosen, each of us has a purpose, and each important and special. I am surprised to find this understanding comes not with the sting of shame or disappointment, but with a freeing lightness.

It is all of us, humanity, Firsts, creation. It all fits together. This is when we are strongest.

And this is how we have to fight if we are going to win this war.

No wonder the Gods have kept away. They need for us to find how we fit together amongst ourselves. When all we do is look to Them, we do not see what They have already placed in us.

Then Bastus bursts through, and again I am taken aback. For just like Xamson, he is a prism of bursting shades and lights, a rushing blend of light and power, with his own patterns and hues, his own beauty, his own purpose. And even through my love for Xamson, I see how they could fit together, make each other stronger. And there is joy in that strength.

Bastus, too, belongs here, among the Gods. And suddenly I understand in a new way what it means for him to be a First Creature—he is a child of the Gods, shaped by their hands in love. Sacred. Just as Xamson is sacred, and I am sacred.

All of it is. Everything.

Strong hands take each of my arms. They lift me to my feet.

A voice in my ear. "Jordan? What happened? Are you okay?" It is near, but also far, too distant to reach. And I am too overwhelmed by the soul I carry to answer. Instead, I reach out to take the strong arm and squeeze.

Then the Gods' voices swell like a rumble from the earth, and the thick hilt of the great sword is pressed back into my palm.

You will need this to fulfill our Will, an inner voice urges. Now go.

And everything is swallowed in obliterating light.

CHAPTER THIRTY-TWO

EVEN AS I OPEN my eyes I know I am in another dream.

The rush of the waves is too loud. The glare of sunlight on the sand is too bright. The sky too blue. Each sensation of the shore comes through to me like a shout.

Even here, the pressure of Adem's soul within me writhes and pushes against my edges.

I turn—slowly, struggling to keep my balance—taking it all in. It is as endless as the Host. As I turn back to where I started, the Forger is there.

Like the others, I see him now as his true self, stripped and unfiltered, brilliant and vivid.

But he is not like Xamson or Bastus. The Forger's light is fractured and distorted, cutting in and out, and twisting at odd angles, broken by harsh punctures of darkness. It is as if his struggle to become more has cut away at his soul, left it punctured and torn.

But there is no time to read into what has become of him, because the Forger is staring right at me.

He comes at me in impossible rushes of movement, and before I can understand, he has grabbed my arm, a disorienting rush of his power surging through me.

He says my name.

And I know.

He is done waiting.

The final battle of the Third Realm War is here.

CHAPTER THIRTY-THREE

I WAKEN WITH A shudder, and this time the harsh dry pressure of the air tells me that it is real.

From extreme brightness, I have been dropped into extreme dark, like being hurled into the middle of the night. I fumble to gain my bearings, reaching out my hand. When I pull it back, tiny grains of hard sand stick to it.

"Xamson? Bastus?" I whisper. I dare not speak any louder into the void.

Wherever we are, I can feel...everything. All at once. I feel the stars, the sky's endless stretch, the moon. I feel the rustling breeze—is that a hint of sea salt it holds? I feel the Gods. Everything I used to. Only so, so, so much more. It is too much to take in, an assault, blinding me to the real world that surrounds me. I can feel Xamson and Bastus within the clamor, but only in flashes, in pieces.

A hand fumbles out in the dark and covers mine. "Jordan?"

"Xamson!" I take it and hold it tight in mine. "Are you all right?"

"What happened?" he says. My eyes begin to adjust, and I make out the shape of his head in front of me. "You disappeared, and we weren't able to follow. When we finally got to you, you were on the cusp of a blackout."

I try to push onto my hands and knees, but within the chaos of the sensory overload, I stumble back onto the ground.

"They called to me. I had to follow," I say.

Something tugs and twists from deep within me. Something that is not mine, and aches for its home.

"I did it. I got Adem's soul."

Xamson crawls near so that we are face to face. His eyes widen. He opens his mouth to speak, his lips quivering.

But before he can, Bastus cuts in, "Later. We have company."

My body sways—has the Forger made good on his threat so soon?

Xamson and I look up, following Bastus' voice to where he stands just feet away, and then following his gaze out. A glowing silhouette is making its way toward us, fighting back the darkness. It is an angel.

I steady myself against Xamson to stand and find my footing as Adem's soul settles and particles of air sing through me. I pull the great sword from its sheath, remembering the Gods' words to me as they sent us here. It glistens in the dark as it reflects back flashes of the angel's light. Xamson readies his blade too, and ahead of us, Bastus flexes his fingers, though it seems unlikely he has any magic to wield.

The angel calls out. "Identify yourselves. This is your only warning."

I almost fall back to the ground with relief. "Calipher?"

The glowing figure leans forward. "Jordan?"

"It is us. Xamson and Bastus are with me, too. It's just us," I say, my words rushed with relief.

Calipher turns and calls back. "Stand down! It is Jordan and the others."

"Where did you go?" he says.

He assesses us, a frown clouding his marble face as he nears. "You wreak of the Host," he grumbles. "I do not know how you did it, but Gods, I warned you. I told you not to do it."

A voice breaks out from behind him. "Jordan? Xamson?"

It is a voice I know all too well, one of intensity and anger and strength. The second soul I carry leaps in response to it, almost carrying me forward with its force, craving to be near her.

I knew something unusual was between them, but I had no idea it was like that for him, with her.

"Rona?" I call out. I squint into the darkness and step forward.

Her expression pulls into a puzzled frown as she takes us in. But then she turns and calls for the soldiers following behind her to stand down. Helda and Avi trail her, peering around her to catch a look at us.

We are back. The Gods sent us back to Terath, to the Wasteland, to Haven. My every particle quivers with the relief of the familiar.

Rona comes toward us in earnest now, relaxing her blades to her sides. But her face is still pulled into a frown.

Adem's soul lurches with an ache to run to her and pull her in, and it takes focused effort to fight back against the foreign impulse. His tears well at my eyes—Gods, he really thought he would never get to see her again.

"We thought you were gone," she says.

"We have returned," I reply. "I am sorry for how we left. But of course we came back. We always meant to. I thought you would know that."

"You...you changed your mind?"

"What? No, we—" Confusion takes my words away. "What do you mean?"

"Everything has turned strange, but you have only been gone a matter of hours. You could not have gotten far before turning back."

"But," I stutter. My mind launches back through the long stretches of time lost wondering the Host. "It was ages. It had to have been."

I look to Xamson and Bastus. They frown back at me.

"Oh, they left all right," Calipher says.

"Time in the realms works differently," Bastus says. "It appears."

"But it took days to even trek to the mountain," Xamson adds, shaking his head. "It is not possible."

"The Gods," I realize. "They sent us back. Not just to Terath. Back to our time."

The crease in Rona's brow deepens. "All I know is, Adem left, and when you found out, you lost it." Her nostrils flare with anger that is still fresh. "Then this morning all three of you fools were gone, and the sun never rose. We waited and waited and it never happened, and all the while we searched for you in the darkness, and you were nowhere."

As she speaks, the others circle around us.

"The...the sun never rose?" Bastus cuts in. "Do you mean to say it is the middle of the day right now?"

Rona's lips purse together. Helda and Avi glance to each other, their expressions somewhere between smugness at our ignorance and a genuine concern. Calipher's wings rustle. Nissa shifts anxiously.

"The realm's Order is breaking," Nissa says, joining us. "The war is here,"

We stare up at the sky. I should have known something was wrong by the feel. If I were not so overwhelmed by all of it coming at me at once, like the realm's top had blown off, if Adem's soul were not stuffing me to overfull, if I had taken a breath and really felt, really listened for just a moment, I would have. There is no moon in the sky. No stars. Just a brooding void.

"The fifth of the plagues," Xamson says. "Darkness."

At this, even in the darkness, Rona's eyes flash with heated lightning. "Plagues?"

Xamson, Bastus and I look to each other. I take a breath, and try to find a way to explain.

When I am done, the frown has melted from Rona's expression into blank bewilderment. Her lips press together into a thin, troubled line and her knuckles go white as they tense on the hilts of her blades. For once, Avi appears speechless, and Helda does nothing but brood even heavier. Nissa's wings flutter idly. Calipher shifts his stands and folds his arms over his chest, a crease deepening in his pale brow.

We wait.

When Rona finally speaks, all she says is, "What other plagues are still coming?"

We look to each other.

"The next one is drought," Xamson says. "And then—"

"Not drought," Helda cuts in.

"Not drought?" Bastus questions.

"Look around," Avi says. "Does it look like when you left? All that rain. Just gone. Overnight."

"There was no water left in the well when we woke this morning," Nissa adds. "I did not understand before, but this all adds up. Drought is here."

I squat down—slowly—and feel the ground. She is right. The earth is packed-down dust, so thirsty it steals the moisture from my fingertips.

The air, my skin, the back of my throat, all are parched and itching for moisture.

But it rained for days. Where did all the water go?

"The sea is low, too," Calipher adds. "Suddenly. Overnight."

Bastus nods, his head drooping. There is no mistaking it. Drought is here.

"Which means there is only plague left," Helda says.

Death.

"Gods," Xamson says. His arms stretch up and he runs his hands over his head. "Could we be any more cursed?"

Rona's jaw tightens. "This is a Realm War," she says. "The curse was already upon us, no matter what we have done to each other since."

A tension ripples over all of us.

Xamson peers past the others into the darkness behind them. "Did you bring Haven's entire army with you?"

Rona's mouth twitches at the corner. "I am done waiting for them to come find us."

"We are going to find them," Helda adds. She nods to Rona.

"How did you figure out where they are?" The words rush out of me in confusion.

"We did not," Nissa says. She holds out her hands. "But that is the thing about having so much undisciplined power. It is not so hard to trace, if you know what to look for."

"We know where he is," Xamson says. "We saw him."

"And he has Adem," I add.

Rona's eyes flash like lightning. "Where?"

I nudge her. "So, I was not so crazy to want to attack them after all," I say.

"You are. But maybe I am, too. Maybe we all are, after all we have been through." Her mouth sets into a slight hint of a smile. "Where?"

"Epoh."

"We better get started then," she replies. "That will take us days to reach."

I sigh. I feel I have trekked enough ground for three lifetimes, with all we walked in the Host.

"Actually," Nissa says. "Remember how I said there were advantages to having all three First Creatures?"

She looks to Calipher and Bastus.

Calipher turns to assess the soldiers, then nods. "We can be there in a flash. All of us."

"But Bastus—" Xamson turns to him and places a hand on his shoulder. Even in the darkness the contrast between his gleaming dark skin and Bastus' paleness is stark. "Your powers—"

"Actually," Bastus cuts in. He holds his hands out and flexes his fingers. Dark sparks burst from them like ashy embers. "I think I am all right. I think the Gods healed me. I feel—new. More than new. Overfull with power."

Around the circle of our unusual crew, we all straighten and tense.

"Then let's go." Rona's eyes turn steely with determination. "It's time to end this."

CHAPTER THIRTY-FOUR

BASTUS, CALIPHER, AND NISSA triangulate us and the army, gathering us all in the center. Then they stretch their arms out toward each other.

Even before they start, the depths of their combined power is palpable in the air like the energy before a storm. A brilliant current rushes out from their palms and cuts through the darkness, connecting them. Then they begin to murmur—ava metafora, ava metafora, ava metafora—and the darkness breaks under the vastness of their combined power. We collapse into light like being shoved off a cliff.

We lurch back into being as quickly as we fell. My stomach knots and tugs like an anchor. Adem's soul whirls within me at the sudden stagger and knocks me to my knees. Our souls are a cacophony of resistance and clamoring eagerness. It knows its rightful body is near. Next to me, Rona doubles over, clutching her arms around her waist and gagging. When the cocoon of light dissolves and I can see beyond it again, Epoh is in the distance behind Nissa's petite shoulders, its crumbling walls a line of dim light catching the slim waning moon.

It is no more than an hour's walk from where we stand. Just out of attacking distance.

Once more my path leads me back to this terrible city. Standing before it is one more twist to my stomach like a knife's blade. I cannot believe I am willingly entering beyond its walls once more.

I push myself up to my feet.

Rona sets her shoulders, and steps out front with Helda as the army shifts into formation in a shuffle of armor and shields. Calipher, Nissa, Bastus, Avi, Xamson, and I settle in behind them.

Rona looks back at us and nods. "Let's go," she calls out.

As we march, I move up and settle in at Rona's side.

"So, what's the plan from here?"

Her arms rest over her double blades, nestled in their sheaths on her hips. "Find the Forger and tear him and his chthonuses to pieces."

Helda grunts in agreement.

"Right," I say. Adem's soul enflames with another flare of need at the steely determination of her voice. "But how exactly do you plan to defeat them? I have to warn you, when we went out into the Wasteland to Mount Analypsi, we came across him, and he had even more chthonuses than I could have imagined. They outnumber us three to one at least. And he has an angel with him. Gods know what else he might have on his side. Maybe the entire rebel army."

Rona pulls out a roll of paper and stylus out of her pack. She holds them out and drops them into my hands.

I look down to them, bewildered, and unroll the slip of paper. It bears a symbol I have never seen before. With Gloros' power running through me, I can sense the shimmer of power contained within their rolls. I open one of them to find letters inscribed.

"What is this?" I ask.

"It is a charm," Rona says. "Or—a command, to be exact. All the soldiers have them. They're for the chthonuses. If we can get this mark on their bodies, it will make them inanimate—they will crumble away into mud again."

I almost drop the script, my fingers suddenly hot. "You mean it will kill them."

"They cannot die," she replies, squaring her gaze on the city walls ahead. Her words lack heart. "They are not alive. Not really."

"It will kill Adem."

Adem's soul writhes in response to his name, and my ribs almost crack from the pressure. I do not think he understands what is happening, but he understands the turmoil spilling from my heart.

To Rona's other side, Helda scoffs and spits on the ground. Sparks of anger burst through me in response. But it is not her opinion that matters here, so I let it go and keep my attention fixed on Rona.

"Do not get righteous with me," Rona snaps. "This is war. A lot creatures will die—a lot of humans. A lot of our own. We already went over this." She twists away, her hair rushing over her shoulders to hide her face from me. "He left." The pain in her voice is palpable.

"No. He cannot die. Not now." I grab her by the arm. "Rona. I did it. I brought a soul back for him."

The soul lurches within me, as if it knows I speak of it.

Rona looks back to me, a storm creeping into the edges of her eyes. "I will not bother to tell you that is not possible."

"It is in me right now. I have to get to him and give it to him. Tell the soldiers not to do this to him, they cannot kill him before I reach him. I can save him, I can stop this. But they cannot use one of these scrolls on him before I get the chance."

Rona shuts her eyes tight, and I cannot tell if it is to think or to fight back tears. When she opens them, she glances back to the soldiers marching behind us.

"I cannot—I will not—ask our people to put their lives at even greater risk by putting a chthonus over themselves. And certainly not a chthonus fighting for the enemy, a chthonus who abandoned us. If someone has to use this symbol against him to save themselves, that is just how it is. That is war." She seems to struggle with the words, reminding herself as much as me. But her voice, reverberating with steely resolve, does not waver.

"But—" I want to argue, I want to remind her of all Adem has done, all he has meant to her, and to me.

She turns her back on me and strides ahead.

"He loves you, Rona." I say it low, so only she might hear.

As soon as the words are out of my mouth, I regret them. It is as if I have stolen something from Adem, plucked it right out of his heart, as if I have stabbed Rona in the back, using his tie to her to hold her hostage.

The muscles of her back ripple with a shiver. She stops.

Is it working? It is too late to take it back now, so I double down, desperate to make her understand.

"He loves you. I can feel it in the way his soul tugs for you, even this very moment. He loves you more than anything, with a force I have never felt before. And you are going to turn your back on him now?"

"Enough," Rona says, whipping around so we are eye to eye, forcing me to stop in my tracks. Soldiers march on around us. The syllables are rough and cutting like a serrated blade. "It does not matter what he feels. He left. He did that on his own. So did you. You both thought you were doing what was best. So fine. But don't you dare put the consequences of those choices on me."

She shoves me. Her lips turn pale and her nostrils flare. It is only then that it occurs to me that maybe she loves him too, that maybe all this time the tightening of the air when they were near each other was a resistance against feelings bigger and more complicated than either of them were equipped to deal with.

I stagger back, speechless. She gives me a final glare and releases me with a shove. Then she resettles next to Helda at the lead.

As we approach the wall along Epoh's border, all remains quiet. Whatever lies for us within its winding streets, we know we have not gotten lucky and escaped their notice. It is bound to be part of a plan. But we forge on all the same, knowing all we can do is be ready for it, to trust in our training, our weapons, the magic of the Firsts, and the Gods on our side.

And so it is that I find myself toe-to-toe with the crumbled walls of Epoh once more, walls that once kept so many of us in but were not enough to keep the Rebels out. I arch back to look up to its top in the sections that still stand. Kick at its crumbled pieces at my feet.

This is where my mother died.

This is where my sister died.

Where I almost died, had Adem not come out of nowhere to save me.

As I step over the rubble and into the city, my shoulders pull in like I can hide myself. My breaths turn thin and fast. I am a child all over again.

Adem's soul must feel my fear, because it swells up and sends a warm pulse through me like a comforting blanket. It reminds me that I am not alone. Despite the hate and pain and tears of this place, I have always had a protector within its walls. Now it is my turn. For Adem. For Haven. For Terath.

The city is collapsed towers and fallen spires, broken splinters of wooden beams below our feet. Loose pages rustle through the empty streets, and I wonder how many hidden Texts were destroyed in the struggle. How many innocent souls mowed down in the path of this proud dictator and hungry rebels? Far too many.

But despite the destruction, too much of the city still looks like the Epoh of my childhood. Memories flash back like flickers in a storm. We pass the residential district where Miriam and I slept in corners on dark, hard floors. We pass the Hush where my mother used to scrounge for the Gods' promises for our future, promises that now fall hollow. We pass the market, where the hard tap of Silencers' boots were an ever-present threat. Part of me can still hear them.

Adem remembers, too. His soul flinches and flares in response to my memories, and his protective urges make me grateful to have this strange, strong, gentle monster on our side. It reminds me why I started all of this.

Rona makes her way next to me, her hands in fists around her blades. But when she speaks, it is in a whisper. "I cannot tell our soldiers not to attack the chthonuses. I cannot. It is their lives on the line, and I am responsible for them."

"I know." Even if I hate it, I can understand this. Despite her hardness, Rona may be the strongest among us.

She bites her lip, glances to Helda and Avi, regrouping not far from us, and then back again. "Let the rest of them fight the battle. Your job is to get to him before anything else can happen to him. Save him." Her fingers dig into my arm, a sharp pinch that smarts to the bone.

Adem's soul swells within me at her touch. I put my own hand over hers.

"Whatever it takes. I swear to it."

She glares at me a moment more, as if making sure I mean my pledge. I look back at her, unblinking, determined to make myself clear. I will get to Adem. I will free him. If it is the last thing I do.

I owe him. I owe her. I have so much to make up for.

She nods, and her grip on my arm relaxes. Then she casts me away and disappears into the marching soldiers. But there is no time to think on my new mission.

Helda turns from Avi, gives Rona a nod, then turns to the army. She calls out to the army and all around me blades are drawn, shields raised, arrows set into bows, facing out toward the darkness of the dead city. Calipher's wings are lifted and tense, Nissa's body glows with surging power, Bastus holds orbs of shadow in his hands.

"What's wrong?" I ask.

Rona turns to answer, but she doesn't get the chance. A flash of magic cuts through the dark streets and twitches over the sky. Figures burst toward us, leaping from roofs, swelling from the alleys, rising from behind overturned carts, everywhere. Bastus rushes to my side in a blur of shadow and grabs my shoulder—they are swelling behind us, too, and my muscles tighten.

First they are far off, then closer with each glimpse, as if charging forth in blinks, a cascading sea of Firsts and chthonuses, ash soldiers, demons, angels, even men. Their numbers continue to swell as they close in. They outnumber us by threefold at least, and that's only judging by what I can see so far. They're mostly Firsts at that, not to mention the chthonuses among their numbers.

One figure from among the rebels' swarm rises over the rest, a large figure with a dim glow that crackles like embers, and dark wings that cast a predatory glare of shadow over him.

"Azazel." Bastus points to the figure I was watching. "King of the Underworld."

The King of the Underworld is here himself?

This is worse than I could have imagined. This is really it. This is the battle to decide the war. Maybe the battle to end all of us. I shift my feet and brace for the attack.

"A lot of demons, too," I say.

Bastus nods. "I know many of them."

"Are you ready to fight them?" I can only imagine what it would be like to be fighting against those I had lived alongside for ages.

"As ready as I'll ever be," he says. A knot tightens in his jaw.

"I'm glad you're here," I say. And despite everything that has passed, I really am.

Before Bastus can respond, Azazel throws his arms out, and the rebel army halts.

He comes forward in front of the army and calls out to us from across the market square. "Before we fight, I offer a gift to any of you willing to take it. A chance to surrender and join us. Why are you fighting for Them? What have They done for you? Where are They now, while you are laying down your lives for Them? You do not have to die for such Gods as this. But if you do not join us now, you will."

I believe him. Judging by the grumbles and shuffling that rise from the soldiers, they do too.

But Helda steps out in front for all to see and spits in Azazel's direction. Then she turns her back on him and faces the soldiers of Haven. She is alive with power and energy. Her wiry muscles flex and twitch, ready, itching for the fight.

"This realm is dark," she shouts. Her words bring a stillness over the troops and their rumblings die down, leaving only the grumbles of the rolling thunder over the sky. "It has been for a long, long time. It is dark, and it is broken. We have all felt the weight of it. It has split rifts into the universe, a brokenness so deep even the bravest and best of us cannot step in to help without breaking things even more."

In the glimmer of flashing light over the sky, I think I catch Helda glancing my way. For once, I do not feel a need to step out with her, to add to the words being said. I am content with my mission. This is her right as the army's leader, and finally, I relinquish it to her. It is enough that I carry the soul to pass on to Adem. And it is a relief to let go of this old need to be at the center, to be special. Letting it go is like shedding a weight.

"It is an impossible way to live," she continues. "But we are strong—far stronger than the horrors these traitors have created in our realm. We here because we say, 'No more.' We are done with their terrors. It is time to bring it all to an end. This day we become sparks of flame to consume the darkness."

Helda's voice raises with each word, until she is shouting so loudly her voice crackles and her expression contorts. "It is dark. And these are the ones responsible—finally, they have been forced to show their faces to us. These are the ones who broke our home and destroyed what the Gods saw fit to give to us. What are we going to do about it?"

The army roars, a united, single being, fearsome, and monstrous, and hungry for blood, against the darkness, the rebels, the terrible brokenness that has taken so much from us. At my side, Bastus' voice rises over the others. It is time to take something back. They are starved for it like darkwolves, and their hunger has made them dangerous. The sword hums in my hand. Adem's soul swells through my chest and presses in my shoulders.

But even so, what hope do we have against an army so much larger than ours, so much stronger? We cannot give in to them, but I do not see how we could come out of this alive.

There are too many of them. They are too powerful.

My despair threatens to swallow me whole. What was it all for? Did any of it matter at all?

But then a horn sounds. Bold and loud and cutting through the darkness, pouring in from somewhere beyond Epoh's walls.

Hooves thunder, echoing off the remaining walls of towers and alleys, and both armies become surrounded by a swarm of dark red hoods atop black horses. They stretch farther than I can see, flanking the rebels from each side and trapping them within Epoh's center.

The tension closing in around my chest and stealing my breath releases: The Brotherhood of Shael. They came back, just like Thane promised.

I glance to Bastus, still ready for the fight with shadowy orbs flaring from each hand. They must have traced the necklace to us, as they have done so many times before—and they made it just in the nick of time. Even Adem would have to agree that for once, the Hunters' timing is perfect.

Maybe all is not lost after all. Not quite yet.

The thundering of their horses' hooves pulses through me and quickens my heartbeat until it is in sync with the sound. Come what may, I am ready for the fight of my lifetime.

Helda pauses a moment, letting the presence of our new ally sink in, both for our own army and the rebels. Then she turns, waving her blade high over her head and catching a glint of lightning off it.

She releases a great cry, and the cry swells as Rona catches it and joins her, and then I catch it, and all the soldiers around us catch it.

She turns, looking to me, and then Rona, and her eyes are full of the fire of the fight. She nods—as if conceding that, with the Brotherhood's arrival, I have done something right.

Together, we cry out the command that starts the end, "Charge!"

Haven's soldiers rise like a tide at her words and rush toward the rebels. The cry turns to a raging stampede, and we close in.

The sting of the air pumping through my lungs, the rush of pounding steps in the charge, is a sweet release. Gloros' great sword sings in my hands. Rona reaches back and grabs Calipher's arm, siphoning what power she still can for the fight.

This is it. The war is here. The final plague.

CHAPTER
THIRTY-FIVE

A RUMBLING EVEN GREATER than thunder swells in my ears as we charge, swallowing Epoh's ruins in our stampede. Rain drops over us in a burst, as if the sky has been sliced open. Both of the souls within me vibrate with the thrill of the hunt, the rebel army races toward us, the ground quakes, and the magical vibrations of the first attacks of battle overcome my senses.

We come together as if the realm itself has slowed, as if each moment is its own flash of action, frozen forever in blinks of lightning. The armies crash into each other. The opposing magical forces break like waves splattering against rock. We meet in a rush of striking blades and wrathful cries and clanging armor.

Everything is a blur of clashing metal and frenzied motion. The coppery smell of blood rises in the air, mingling with the flinty tension of the coming storm. I am swallowed into the chaos. In the blur of the charge, an overwhelming sense of a presence comes over me. At the edges of my vision, I catch a hint of three majestic glowing figures. When I twist to get a better look, I cannot find them among the fighting, but something deep inside me knows: The Gods are here, among us now, taking part in the fight, giving us strength. With everything else I can feel again now, I can sense Them among us, and the power they radiate over the battle gives me renewed strength.

Rona's command reverberates through me: Find Adem. This is the only thing that matters now, amidst the flying spells and clanging swords. I reach deep within myself and try to feel for Adem, let his soul to reach for him and tell me where his is. It pulls and throbs and urges—he is close.

But he is not here, among the battle.

A chthonus lurches at me with a snarl, throwing me to the ground. It claws at me with shriveled arms and jagged nails. I hardly feel it rips open the skin over my arm, too overfull with souls to pull back in time. But years of training kick in, and I throw it off me, slicing through its neck. The chthonus stumbles back, its misshapen arms flailing and its head tilting back too far, hinged from the wound. Through the renewed vision Theia placed in me, I can see the chthonus's magic fighting to knit itself back together, but the power of Gloros' own sword is too much for it. It roars and staggers backward into Bastus. Bastus turns and throws it to the ground.

In the free moment it gives me, I catch my breath and remember the symbol Rona gave me.

The chthonus staggers toward me, readying to charge again. I steady my muscles, relax into the power of Gloros' sword, let it sing to me. This time, I go for the chthonus's blade arm, hacking into it with force. A swell of relief floods my chest as it drops away. It grumbles and stumbles off course. Bastus charges it again and pins it to the ground. I rush behind him and scrawl the symbol into its flesh as it thrashes and wails.

In an instant, its writhing ceases and it dissolves into dirt under Bastus' hands. I pause, chest heaving, blinking down as if it might still attack me again any moment. But the chthonus is no more.

Laughter releases the tension in my throat, then I look back to Bastus. It works. Maybe we have a chance after all.

But then a sickening twist turns my stomach—it works. If another soldier gets to Adem before I do...

His soul claws at me, crying for its chance to live.

Before I can even push up to my feet, Bastus' eyes fix on something behind me and he rushes over me, beating away a snarling darkwolf lunging right for me.

I use the free moment to leap onto the remains of a building's wall for a higher vantage point. I survey the battlefield and beyond. Windblown sand nips at my face, narrowing my vision. There is not time to take down every chthonus out here. I have to focus. Find Adem.

My eye catches the fight in flashes—Rona's face contorts from strain, clasping at an injured demon while spouting its siphoned powers from her other palm, attacking an angel who writhes as the magic bursts against its chest. A team from the Brotherhood casts a spell at a demon, and it writhes and twists as a bubble envelops it and swallows it up.

But no Adem. No Forger. No sign of his angel companion's rose-gold glow.

They have to be here somewhere, near to the fight.

I turn—my heart throbbing in my throat and twitching in my fingers—surveying beyond the battle to the tattered remains of Epoh's once-grand towers toward its center, and to the other side, the demolished temples of the holy district.

As I do, a feeling shudders over me so powerfully I almost drop the great sword.

The temple—Adem's favorite hiding place when Epoh was at its prime.

Somewhere to my right, a feral whimper pierces the air as bone snaps. A moment later Bastus stands at my side.

"Come with me," I shout over the chaos. "I know where Adem is. And the Forger."

His jaw tightens, and he nods.

I start to force my way toward the temple through the fighting, but Bastus grabs my wrist, and before I am ready, I am dissolving into ash. We rematerialize outside of the fighting. I stumble just once from the sudden movement, then clench my stomach to steady myself and run, letting Adem's soul propel me forward faster than I have ever run before, bolting straight to the old temple's remains.

Its walls are torn down, leaving only the first few winding steps up toward the tower that used to crown it. Only a few pews remain toward the front of the old sanctuary. A rainbow of shattered stained glass is layered over the floor and crunches under my rushed steps. I skid on the fragments as I take a sharp turn toward the opposite doorframe, now empty, that used to hide the way to the cellar.

I drop down its stairs, Adem's soul clamoring. Bastus is just behind me.

"Forger!" I call for him before I have rounded the corner of the stairs. "Set him free."

They are on the far side of the vast cellar, the Forger cloaked and clutching his staff, Syliel just over his shoulder. To his other side, Adem hovers in the shadows. The only light is the soft glow coming off Syliel, engulfing the cellar in a sea of shadows.

The Forger drops a single, hard laugh, then glances to Syliel, who smiles back smugly. "And why would I do that?"

With the Forger's memories in my mind, I can see now the defensiveness in his stance, the pain of losing Koreh at the corners of his eyes, the hunger for power in the way his fingers clutch his staff. All these ages, and he is still the same cravings and weaknesses, the same aches. It was a mistake for him to cast his past onto me. I recognize his anger for the Gods in my own, but we are not alike. Not at our core. Not in the least.

"Let him go."

Adem's soul lurches within me again, desperate for release now that we are so close. The pang is so forceful it is almost blinding. I shift my stance to steady myself and hide its force.

Adem lifts his head and looks to me, his eyes anxious. Can he feel his soul fighting to reach him from within me?

The Forger looks me up and down, takes his time, then something grim settles over him.

"Are you still fixated on this?" he sighs. "So your chthonus was taken. It was never really yours in the first place. I left it here, and it was fine for you to play with it for a while, but now I am taking it back. Make your own, if you must."

The words are full of biting pride, reminding me of his incredible power—no man should be capable of such a thing, and certainly not me.

"Adem is not a toy, or a weapon."

"That is exactly what it is. Anything else you see in it is an overactive imagination."

With that I lunge toward him. This is the moment the Gods sent me back for. Finally, the moment is here. To free Adem once and for all. To take down this man whose power has turned him rotten. To end the final Realm War and start a new era for Terath.

I swing the great sword over my head toward him and set it free—and with it, all of Gloros' power.

The Forger sees it coming and chuckles, doesn't even bother to flinch. Syliel stretches out a single hand and the sword stops in mid-air, then lets it clatter to the ground.

No. Panic hums up my arms like wildfire. What good is a Goddess' sword if Their own First Creatures can stop it?

I lunge forward to take the sword back, and the Forger raises a hand, and with a slight twitch of his fingers, a bright bolt flashes out from them. It strikes me just as I reach it, the pain stabbing and seizing and immediate. I double over with an involuntary cry. My mind goes blank, and for a pause the background noise of the battle swells: cries of pain, clashing of blades, panting breaths. But I hold onto the sword.

Adem cries out and rushes forward as if he means to help, but Syliel throws a beam of silver light at him. He thrashes against it, his own magic glowing around him, but it is not enough—Syliel's spell pulls him back and binds him.

I recoil, stumbling back into a fall until Bastus catches me.

As I regain my footing, I shift the sword's grip in my hands, and we nod, the magic already clouding into shadow at Bastus' fingertips. I charge again, the curse rushing past me to reinforce my attack.

But again, Syliel deflects our charge with the flick of a hand. The Forger drops us to the floor with another bolt of power.

They are too strong.

I am going to need much more power than this. But what can we do against beings so incredibly powerful? Then I realize that we have at least one source of the Forger's own power, right in Bastus' pocket.

All things have purpose, Theia said.

Is this why the Gods refused to take it? Did They know all along?

I pull myself next to Bastus on the compacted dirt floor.

"The necklace," I urge. "Give it to me."

Bastus frowns at me, as if he isn't sure he heard me right.

I don't know how to use its power against the Forger yet, but there has to be a way. It's our only hope.

"Trust me," I urge, stretching out my hand. I have no choice but to have faith my instincts that I can figure this out, and fast.

Confusion deepens the lines of Bastus' face, but he digs it out of his robe and places it in my hands.

"Now, go get Calipher and Nissa. We'll need all three of you to have any chance against them. I'll keep them busy."

Bastus nods, and is gone in a whoosh of shadow.

I just have to keep them distracted long enough to figure out how to unleash the magic of the necklace and use the Forger's own power against him.

The distraction part should be simple enough to do, even if the prospect of the pain that awaits me makes my body cringe with anticipation. I thrust the necklace over my neck and tuck it under my robes, then push myself up, trying to hide my dread for what's next in a bold stance. Before I can think any more, I charge at them.

There is no way to be ready for the piercing pain that comes over me as the Forger twitches his fingers again.

Again, the sounds of the battle above flood into me as I collapse in pain, followed by Adem's rageful roar. The fight is getting nearer, spilling over from the market into the holy district.

We have to end this.

When I pull my awareness back to the cellar the Forger is talking again. "You could be so powerful, if you would only set yourself free. And yet here you are, in the middle of my greatest battle, in my greatest war, begging for it." He frowns, a bemused smirk passing over his lips. "Some great leader you are. Leaving your people to fight for the realm while you save your friend."

His hand twitches. Another bolt darts toward me. I fall back to the ground, helpless against his power.

How do I set free the power in the necklace?

If we had known how to do this, we probably could have destroyed it by now. But time is up. It is our only hope.

"Did you do what you set out to do?" The Forger's smile is terrible and mocking. "Did you break into the Host and find the Gods?"

Something lights his eyes with his question, an eagerness—some kind of twisted curiosity.

Syliel's eyes run over me, and her eyebrow twitches. "He did. Look at the way the Host's magic clings to him."

The Forger chuckles. He already knew. He's toying with me, the same way he is toying with Adem.

That is all I need, though—for him to keep drawing this out until Bastus can bring Nissa and Calipher back. So, I stumble, letting the pain of his last strike show.

"Did you like what we did with the place?" the Forger taunts. "It seemed overdue to shake things up in that old hall."

My limbs throb with the afterburn of pain from his magic, and Adem's soul writhes within me, overfull and dizzying. But under it, a spark of potential catches. Here is something I can distract him with. I just have to keep his attention long enough for help to arrive. How long will they take?

"It something to behold, to be sure," I say. "But any child can knock something down. And that's all you were able to do, isn't it? You never found Them. You went all the way to the Host, and still the Gods eluded you."

A flash of magic illuminates the full cellar and shoots into my body, the pain dropping me to the ground.

Where are they? Surely the others will be here to help any second. They have to be.

"They did not dare face me and my chthonuses," the Forger declares, indignant. "Did you find what we left for Them? One of my greatest creations, that magnificent beast."

"You mean you were not able to force Them to your will and make Them show Themselves? Not even you, the most powerful sorcerer of all the ages?"

I knew what would come next before I even said it. A burst of light, and I am on the ground again, my body humming with echoes of pain, my vision coming in and out in blotches. Adem's soul thrashes with alarm.

His voice fills my ears like an echo of his soul's turmoil, howling with rage.

Hang on, I tell it. Just a little longer.

"I found Them. The Gods welcomed us."

The Forger's expression darkens into a hideous snarl, his fingers quivering. Dread churns through my veins and fills every particle of me. Did I push him too far?

But then the Forger's rage drains away into a presentation of disinterest. He shakes his head and tut-tuts at me.

"Why all this resistance, Jordan? The Gods abandoned you, you have every reason to give up on Them. Where are they now? Why worry over Them so much? You do not need to submit to Them. You follow your own path. You are like us."

He shoots a bolt at me again, his eyes electric with wrath. The pain is greater this time, traveling through my chest and down my spine, paralyzing me. When the bolts stop twitching through me, my hands quiver. Adem's soul clambers to escape, slams into my walls and edges. I take a deep breath and force myself back up.

Not for me, not for Adem, but for Haven. For Terath.

What is taking Bastus so long?

If it were up to me I would let the pain overtake me and curl up in a ball on the ground. But I will not. I cannot. It is not my choice to make.

"You are wrong." I groan.

"The Gods are not worth it. Surely, if you were in the Host, if you saw what They have been reduced to."

The Great Hall—the destroyed columns, the splattered blood, the loose feathers—signs of violence past. It all comes back to me in flashes.

Just as I am questioning if I have the will to pick myself off the ground one more time, a flurry of rushed steps pound down the stairs behind me.

I do not have to look to know that Bastus made good on his word—I can feel the power of the three Firsts reverberating off each other. As Bastus, Calipher and Nissa come together and start their chant, the light of their power banishing shadow from every corner of the cellar, the Forger shouts with rage.

They cast their spell at him.

The Forger and Syliel counter. The lights of their power and my companions clash in a burst. Each of us are thrown back from the power of the explosion, casters and all. The sheer force of the magic's power bites through me to the bone, squeezes my ribs, seizes through my legs. I scramble back to my feet as soon as I hit the ground, blinking against the blinding brightness to find the Forger.

Dust catches in the light as it starts to fade, rising from quivering pillars along the walls' edges. What is left of the building threatens to collapse with a great moan.

But as the light dies, Syliel's glow brings the Forger into focus. His eyes are so enraged they almost glow, and he staggers as he tries to steady himself. But he is still alive. Even the power of all three Firsts was not enough to overcome him.

Then I realize there is another glow still persisting within the darkened cellar, and it's coming from me. I look down, searching—it's the necklace. The rough emerald pendant has been damaged, a crack stretching around its sides in thin fingers. And from them, light is pouring out.

This is it. This is how I set its magic free. Our combined powers were almost enough.

I know what I need to do now. I know how to end all of this and set the realm right again. The only answer, as ever, is forfeit.

Because the Forger and Syliel trust in their power. They know that no one would be able to attack them and get away alive. They have taken comfort and security in this. They have trusted that others will only give as much as they would.

And they are wrong to think this.

My soul cries out against my decision, and Adem's cries in tandem as it feels my turmoil. But finally I understand—the Gods were not heartless when they refused to take the necklace. They knew it was our only hope to overcome the forces we would face in the war to come. And there is only one way to make sure its power is put to its proper use.

I'm sorry, Adem. He deserves more, but there is no time. And I know that he would tell me the same as all the others have been trying to—that this is so much more important.

The ceiling quakes, the battle rumbling immediately overhead from within the temple, and smoke drifts down from the stairwell. The whole building could crumble at any moment, and our chance would be gone.

I take a breath. With my decision made, suddenly all I can think of is Xamson, and all the pain, all the fear, all the chaos is swallowed into an all-consuming swell of love.

I shut my eyes and steady myself.

There is no time for what ifs, or should bes, or mourning the life that could have been. There is only what must be done. It is a price I am willing to pay. It settles within me, and I am no longer afraid.

I wish I could go and find Xamson, kiss him one more time, wrap my arms around him and promise everything is going to be all right. Because I know for sure now. It will. And I wish I could be here to see it with him, what comes next.

Even in the midst of the pain, the destruction, the battle, his wry humor rings in my head, and despite everything the edge of a smile crosses my lips. He will never forgive me for this. And he won't have to.

A surge of warmth overtakes me. It is worth the cost. More than worth it.

I tug on the necklace and shift my grip on Gloros' great sword. Then I call out to Bastus and the others. "Do it again."

They gear up another swell of churning power between them, illuminating everything. The Forger and Syliel start building their own surge to throw back at them.

This is it.

I run at the Forger with everything I've got.

"Now!"

The Firsts and the Forger hurl their magic toward each other.

And then I charge at him.

I take in the events that follow in a series of impressions: The Forger's shocked expression; a blinding flash of light as the necklace shatters; a burning sensation over my skin; the sword sliding fast and sure into the Forger's flesh, then bursting free as it cuts through the other side.

The necklace ignites, the split in the emerald quivering with the force of power. Adem releases one final roar, and with a great burst of light, breaks free of the angel's hold. His power ignites over everything, and it is exactly what was needed. The emerald bursts open.

As the burning takes over, I am left with only a single thought: pass on the soul to Adem. I reach. and reach, and reach deep inside myself, doing my best to set it free to its rightful master.

And then all goes dark.

CHAPTER THIRTY-SIX

SLOWLY I BECOME AWARE of being enveloped in a glowing nothingness.

It is a reprieve, an emptiness different from anything I have ever felt. I will stay here, I think. There is not anything to be done in this place, nothing to be worried over. There is only being.

"Jordan." A voice calls to me, followed by pressure on my shoulder, as if to hold me in place. Which is good, because the ground seems to be shifting and bobbing...a sense of floating, of being unanchored and somehow too light.

"Jordan. Jordan."

The voice is familiar. It calls me back to myself. And I begin to remember.

There was destruction. There was a struggle. There was something I was trying to do.

I blink hard and shake my head, trying to free the memory. In front of me stands a dark, hulking figure.

Another voice cuts in from behind me, croaking and tense. "Are you mad? Leave him alone. You should not be here again. Especially not now, when the new balance is resetting. Did you not learn your lesson the first time?"

I squint, trying to force the shapes into sense. The face in front of me is frowning, worried, familiar. It is a face layered with great troubles and burdens. Despite his anxious expression, a warmth fills me to see him, and my breath draws in a raspy gasp.

"Adem."

It is as if I have not seen him in ages, and finally he has come home. Or, maybe, as if I have come home.

The rest comes back to me in a burst—the rebels, the Host, Adem's soul, my final moment, charging toward the Forger's bolt of power.

"What happened?" I ask.

Panic seizes my chest—*where is the Forger now? Where will the attack come from next?* My hand reaches for Gloros' great sword but I cannot find it. I twist around to assess my surroundings and find only flat cavernous sky and dim shadows over currents of river. We are not in Epoh, and there is no sign of the Forger or the war.

I give in to the trickle of the water and my heart calms.

We are in a rowboat on a river, pushing with the current. Along the shoreline, stony pillars stagger like trees.

"There is still an order to things, you know," the second voice breaks in. "Just because you got away with it once does not mean you can keep coming back for whomever, whenever you wish. Was the price not high enough the last time? Do you not see all you have wrought?"

Rona, they are talking about Rona and all that has happened since, the barrier between the realms, the rebels Adem set free.

"Just this one," Adem says. "He died because of me. It was not his time."

"What makes you think that?" The other voice comes from a hooded, shriveled man at the boat's helm, hunched over a staff that stretches off the side of the boat and pushes us forward. He is pale as a ghost, his skin wrinkled as aged paper. "Because he is young? Because you do not like it? I have seen younger ones than him make this journey, I have seen more tragic circumstances. Is he here? Then it was his time."

I try to pull it all together. "Where am I?"

Adem opens his mouth to answer, but the old man cuts in before him.

"No need to start asking questions. Drink this, it will put you at peace again." He leans over the side of the boat then offers me his cupped hands. They drip with water from the river.

I look back to Adem.

His head drops and he mutters into his chest. "You died, Jordan. Saving me—saving all of us. But it's going to be okay. I'm here to bring you back."

I turn over his words. I feel I ought to be shocked, or maybe afraid, but I cannot muster it.

Adem urges again. "It's over. We won. Your self-sacrifice ended the Forger. It destroyed the necklace. And it freed me. After that, we were able to banish the rest back into the helmuth."

A stillness settles over me. I am left in utter amazement. It worked.

The Third Realm War was a shadow that cast over all the realms for as far back as any memory could hold—my entire life, and far beyond it. Knowing we are past the burden of its horrors...it feels like an ending.

The boat lurches as we strike ground.

"Out," the Keeper orders.

"No," Adem says, his voice a hard snarl I have never heard from him before. He grabs my arm. "Jordan, come back. I came to take you back."

"Yes, back," I echo. Everything still feels hazy and fleeting, like catching hints of images in a fire's flames.

The Keeper presses a hand into my back, and I allow him to guide me out of the boat onto the pebbled shore. A light catches my eye from down the path, and it calls to me like the first sign of home on the horizon after a long journey. It starts to draw nearer, and I realize I am walking toward it.

As I get closer, it takes shape into two figures. They are so alike they seem to be a double image at first, both pale and tall and eager, with brilliant red hair coursing over their shoulders. But one's hair is darker than the others, her eyes blue, not the dark brown of the other. But both are familiar. Both take me back to what feels like a lifetime ago.

It is my mother. It is Miriam.

They beckon to me, and I find myself at the foot of a bridge. All I have do to get to them is cross it. My heart leaps, and I take a step.

"Wait!" Adem cries.

I hardly know what to say. I chose this, after all. I accepted this from Gloros when I placed Her sword on the altar, fully understanding what would have to come next. It's what was necessary, and it was a price I was willing to pay.

"Come with me," Adem says.

The Keeper interjects, "Do you still not understand? There is so much else out there worse than death. A hero's rest waits for this one. Do not steal that from him."

Adem frowns. Half-heartedly, conflicted, he stretches a hesitant hand out for me to take, the way he did when he saved me as a child. And I ache to take it.

But.

I cannot help looking back, over the bridge, to my family. They look so happy on the other side. And they see me. For once they are not half-starved, they are not weighed down with fear. They are whole. The same peace pulses through me, a feeling of rest that I have never had before.

They smile and beckon for me to join them. They are so close. It has been so long.

But Adem is still holding onto me.

"Please," he says. "Everything is just beginning again. We need you. What about Xamson?"

Sadness clouds over me.

"Tell him I am sorry. And—" Tell him I love him—but no, that is not fair. That is not what he needs. "Tell him to be happy."

"What about Haven? Or Rona? Or...or me?"

My soul aches to go to the figures on the bridge.

"I'm sorry for that, too."

Adem blinks. "We are starting a new beginning now. We have more adventures to take on."

Adventures. I have had more than my share. And I find that they do not call to me like they once did. I have fought my battles. I have played my part. And when the time came, I was ready for this.

I consider all the things that I will not do: Helping to rebuild Haven, and the other cities, and the realm; Xamson and me sorting through our differences and growing old together in the new world.

But I am weary, and the weariness runs so much deeper than skin, or muscle, or bone, into my soul, a fatigue I did not realize I had been carrying. Each battle fought, each strike of the blade weighs on me, and that weight has become too heavy.

I made my deal with Gloros. I gave my life to Her. This was the cost. The reward. Both.

And now it is over.

Miriam beckons to me. My heart tugs to obey.

"I cannot go with you."

I squeeze Adem's hand, and after a moment, he lets me go. I take a breath, and take another step onto the bridge—but something else holds me back.

"You cannot carry anything with you to the other side!" the Keeper scolds.

"I have nothing—" But I cut myself off, because it is only then I realize: Adem's soul. If I had successfully delivered it to him before I took down the Forger, he could not be here now. Which means I must still be carrying it.

How do I give it to him?

At a loss of what else to do, I try to emulate what Theia did to pass it to me. I raise my hand and press my thumb into Adem's forehead.

He flinches at my sudden touch.

"Shhh," I say.

I shut my eyes and breathe out, imagining a great release. A force surges forth from me, filling the air with glowing light, then settling around Adem and into him.

Adem gasps, his eyes go wide. He drops to his knees.

A final burden, freed. A final promise, fulfilled. Finally, everything feels right.

I place my hand on Adem's head, and take in the quakes of his body as he sobs with relief. After a moment of this, I step onto the bridge again, and this time nothing holds me back.

I turn around one last time, looking to Adem. "Are you going to be okay?"

He brings himself to his feet. His mouth twitches, but he steadies himself and wipes his eyes dry.

"Yes."

I move my focus now to beyond the bridge, and the promise of peace that waits for me there. Finally it feels like something I can reach. There has been so much forced effort in life to attain this, so much struggle, to the point where I was willing to break into the Host itself and demand it from the Gods.

And here it is. What happened before does not matter anymore. All is setting right, and I know that my part is done. The feeling settles into my deepest crevices. I can take this peace and know it is right.

I step forward to my family's waiting arms and let the light take me.

Afterword
Adem

When I reach the surface of the tossing sea, a desperate gasp welcomes air into my lungs. My arms and legs already ache from the struggle of staying afloat, the salt of the waves stinging my eyes. Every breathe is a brackish battle as I fight against the sea's tug.

But it is a reminder: I'm alive.

I feel it with a steady pulse. The power of it. The fragility of it.

Finally I reach the shore where Haven used to stand. No one is left here now. How long has it been since I raced off the battlefield in Epoh, all the way to the sea, and beyond into the Underworld to bring Jordan back?

And now, I have come back alone.

Perhaps it is better they have all left.

But then a figure passes between the village's little huts. It disappears behind the next one, but then comes back and freezes, staring out at me. It drops the kindling it carries and races toward me.

It is a lean figure, all sharp movement and long, dark hair that splays out behind her as she runs, tangling with the breeze.

It is Rona.

My heart pounds so hard I think it will leap right into her arms.

She is different now. The defensiveness has left her shoulders, the flinty hardness of her eyes is a little softer. But her lips set in a tense line—she is still just as stubborn.

And just as beautiful.

I am not ready for the feeling that overcomes me at seeing her now. The feeling of craving that fills not just my soul, but my body, too. A feeling that is joy, that is ache, that is longing, rolled up over itself. It comes effortlessly now, like a reflex. But it is also too powerful, too much, more than I have ever felt before. It is strange, this human body, this human soul, and I cannot tell where one begins and the other ends.

I run to meet her, unable to wait for her to make it all the way to the shore. The air rustles over my wet skin, and small bumps rise in response to the chill that follows. I feel vulnerable, strangely fragile.

She lurches to a halt just in front of me, and I am suddenly aware of the murky seawater dripping off me. My fingertips itch to reach for her.

Her chest heaves. Her breaths pant. Her eyes run over me frantically.

My entire being is overcome with the relief of being near her again.

And I know.

I am going to have to tell her now. I could not keep it in any longer if I tried, the feeling is too powerful for this new human body to hold.

But then she catches me off guard. She jumps at me and flings her arms around me tight.

Tension hits my shoulders where she squeezes me. A crushing surge of warmth fills my chest.

"You left for Jordan so quickly after the battle I didn't get to see you."

"You're here...waiting for me?"

I don't know why she would do it. But I cannot find any other reason for her to be here still. Everyone else seems to have moved on. "How long has it been?"

She pulls away, my wetness now spread over the front of her robe.

"Almost a year."

"Something is different. What happened?" She frowns. "Where is Jordan?"

I hardly know where to start. I shake my head, trying to find the words.

"He would not return with me."

Creases take shape at the edges of her mouth as she considers it. "He deserves rest," she says, finally. "He found it?"

No one knows like Rona just how troubled the Underworld can be.

"Yes," I reply. "And—"

But I shake my head and look down to my hands, turn them over. Where to start? How to say it? What Jordan gave me is too much to explain. Too much to believe.

I do not have to.

Rona looks down to my hands too, then takes them in hers and pulls them close, studies them. Then she looks back up to me, puts a hand on my cheek and squints into my eyes.

"You're warm. You're—" She gasps and pulls away. "He did it. He really did it. You're human."

Again I try to find words, but they catch in my throat, and all I get out is a rough, raspy grumble.

It seems to be enough for her. She rushes into me so quickly she bounces back off my chest, and I have to catch her and pull her in. Her arms wrap so tight around my soaking robe it pinches my skin and crowds my lungs, a sensation of mixed pain and relief so deep I do not know what to do.

Is this what being human is? Feeling everything at once?

My eyes well and a tear escapes down my cheek. My arms are wrapped over Rona's shoulders and I am not willing to move them to wipe the tear away.

It comes out then, slips right out of me before I can catch it.

"I love you."

A tension released from around my spine. The words are their own healing.

Rona does not say anything back, but she does not need to. She reaches up onto her tiptoes to nestle her face into the cradle of my neck, her arms tighten around me and we press together so closely nothing could ever get between us.

There is more to be done.

Rona leads me through what's left of Haven. The rest of them really have left. All of them. It is a new world out there, and they are rebuilding it. There are beasts to banish and helmuths to close, walls to tear down and cities to build back up. Many of the Firsts have returned to their true homes, including Calipher. There is more work to do in the other realms as well. Bastus left hand-in-hand with Xamson, Rona says.

They were not able to recover Jordan's body and bring it back to Haven. Rona offers to go back with me to Epoh to say goodbye to him, but I have said the goodbyes I need to, and Epoh holds too many memories.

I do not need to bring him back from Epoh. I only need to bring a small piece of him to Haven. It feels better for him to be here. I still remember the smile that sprang across his face the day we found this place, the way he settled into this new, safe home so effortlessly. Like he was destined for it. Who could have known then what was to pass?

I plant a tree for him up on the bluff, where it can look out over Haven and the sea, where anyone coming our way from the Wasteland beyond can see it and follow it to us.

We are going to rename Haven. This new world leaves nothing to hide from.

We might need to find a new name for the Wasteland soon, too. Already buds of potential have started to sprout from the softening earth.

It is not like the Beginning, Rona says. But it is a new start.

When I am done rounding out the earth over the seed, I stand. Rona is climbing up the bluff to join me. We sit together at its edge and look out to the sea.

It is a clear, sunny day and beams of light sparkle off the waves. The sky is bright. Birds sing. There were never birds this far out into the Wasteland before.

Everything is so much better now, but she still carries troubles between her shoulder blades. I rub her back, the muscles ease, and the fear spills out of her.

"What if we have been through too much? What if we can't fit into this new world we helped create?" Her hands fidget in front of her. "Can people like us really just leave it all behind and find happiness after all that has happened?"

I digest the words and consider them. I know what she means, feel the persistent twinges of all that has happened in my bones every day. I had not thought far ahead enough yet to worry about this.

But she is right.

The shadows and whispers of all she has been through, the weight of all her years and tortures, still flock around her. And I am no better. Night after night I bolt awake from dreams in which the eyes of Hunters who have passed still blink out at me from the darkness.

As I sit in quiet, the sheer human-ness of my existence overcomes me. Everything is still so intense. The breeze on my skin. The smell of the sea. The pounding of my heart and the warmth of Rona pressed up next to me.

I still remember the way everything used to build and weigh on me and compounded over the years. I never would have thought then that any of this was possible.

But humanity, it seems, is change.

I cannot promise Rona that the hauntings of our pasts will ever leave us. I am not sure they should—we need these memories so we can never let such terrible things happen again.

But already those old burdens have ceased their compounding. They have, in fact, started to fade by degrees.

Humanity is resilience.

And this is the real gift of what Jordan did for me. A hope for the ability to let go, start over.

I take Rona's hand—a gesture that is beginning to feel comfortable, like home—and squeeze it. I look out the sea, splattered in brilliant golds and pinks as the sun begins to rise on a new day.

I can't believe I am saying it, but even more, I can't believe how quickly I believe it.

"Yes."

THE END

Keep reading now with RAIN, the Third Realm War series prequel

READ NOWon Kindle Unlimited
All formats at EJWenstrom.com

Keep Reading with the Third Realm War series prequel

One girl. One angel. Three gods determined to keep them apart.

Nia grew up in isolation amid fear and suspicion from her village after a mysterious illness even the most powerful magic cannot heal took her father. So when an impulsive moment led to a passionate romance with the demigod Calipher, Nia falls hard.

The lovers quickly discover their auras offer each other something they cannot get enough of: For Nia, it's the comfort of the demigod's calming warmth; for Calipher, it's the free will of Nia's humanity. It's a feeling either would stop at nothing to hold onto.

Even defy direct orders from the gods themselves.

But as the star-crossed lovers continue to pursue their love and ignore all else, the middle realm of Terath slips into chaos. The land is wrought by drought, then floods, and is rocked by torrential storms. Demigods and men alike grow edgy. The gods intervene to force things back to order.

This includes forcing Calipher back to the realm of the gods. Before he leaves, he steals magic from the gods to enchant Nia's parting gift.

But Nia soon finds that breaking the rules of magic and the gods comes with a terrible cost.

Reading now on Kindle Unlimited
Free download at EJWenstrom.com

Also by E. J. Wenstrom
Departures

Tonight, seventeen-year-old Evalee is scheduled to die.

She's planned her celebration for weeks, and other than leaving her sister Grace-lyn behind, Evalee is ready. She shouldn't be nervous; the Directorate says this is how it should be, and it is never wrong. So she wears her best dress and dances the night away with all of her appointed friends and family. Then she goes to sleep for the last time...

Except, the next morning, Evalee wakes up.

Gracelyn is a model Directorate citizen with a prodigious future ahead. If she could only stop thinking about the shuffling from Evalee's room on her departure morning. Even wondering if something went wrong is treason—the

Directorate doesn't make mistakes. If she pulls at the thread, the entire privileged life the Directorate set for her will unravel into chaos. Or worse.

Before the Directorate can correct its mistake and get rid of Evelee for good, she is swept away by rebels to a world she grew up believing couldn't exist—one filled with unpredictability and messy choices. As the Directorate's lies are stripped away, Evelee becomes determined to break Gracelyn free from its grasp—before Gracelyn's search for the truth draws the Directorate's attention and makes her more valuable to them dead than alive.

A young adult dystopian adventure perfect for fans of Uglies, Divergent, and The Hunger Games.

"Departures ... delights and disturbs and allows us to see our own world with brand new eyes."

— Lance Rubin, New York Times Bestselling Author

"An absorbing, taut coming-of-age tale that grapples intelligently with mortality and liberty."

—Kirkus Reviews

"Wenstrom's masterful storytelling is on full display with rising stakes, tense twists, and emotional resonance."

—Megan Lynch, Award-Winning Author

Start reading now on Kindle Unlimited

EJWenstrom.com

Acknowledgements

Pam Grossman wrote in an article for TIME that "magic is made in the margins." So too, are novels.

Most of us are squeezing in our writing time in the spare moments of our lives, or forcing that time into being by getting up early, staying up late, sneaking away from the office for lunch, squeezing in a few minutes in the carpool line. It's not easy, and it's almost impossible to accomplish without the support of the people around you. In this way, I have been incredibly blessed.

First and foremost, I must thank my husband Chris, who has put up with an absurdly early alarm going off next to him for years, as I rise before the sun to get my writing in, rustling about our room, bumping into things, causing the dog to bark, and so much more. And also, all the lost time on weekends when I try to eke out an extra scene or scurry off for a day, or days, to partake in book events. And, for all he times you've tagged along, eagerly holding down a vending booth, taking notes during panels, and otherwise contributing to this endless hustle. It makes my heart swell three sizes when I think about all ways you not only tolerate my writing, but actively help me to build this crazy, impossible thing.

Thank you also to my family—Rebecca, Sam, Mom and Dad—who have never so much as blinked at the idea that I could be an author. Thank you for reading my stories, for cheering me on, telling your friends, and acting like this is a totally normal and reasonable thing for me to do.

Thank you also to my incredible publishing team. To Heather, the first person to believe in Adem and his weird epic to the Underworld, thank you for all you have done to patiently ensure each book in the Chronicles of the Third Realm War series is it every best.

Writing may be an act of solitude, but publishing takes a village, and I am so grateful for mine.

About the author

E. J. Wenstrom believes in complicated heroes, horrifying monsters, purple hair dye and standing to the right on escalators so the left side can walk. She writes dark speculative fiction for adults and teens. When she isn't writing fiction, she co-hosts the Troped Out and Fantasy+Girl podcasts.

Sign up for bookish news updates, E J.'s latest releases and a free ebook of the Chronicles of the Third Realm Wars prequel.

EJWenstrom.com

www.ingramcontent.com/pod-product-compliance
Lightning Source LLC
Chambersburg PA
CBHW020635260626
47157CB00008B/2757